'A totally absorbing novel on fa[...]
on the end of our worlds, grea[...]
and we fail time, with superb workings of comedy and political
insight. As odd as life and as compassionate and engaging as a
reader could hope for'
David Hayden

'A brilliant novel. Aidan Cottrell-Boyce writes with a sharp
eye for humour and emotional resonance. This is a time-
tumbling, unexpected and arresting novel of apocalypse,
upheaval and familial love'
Seán Hewitt

The End of Nightwork

The End of Nightwork

Aidan Cottrell-Boyce

GRANTA

Granta Publications, 12 Addison Avenue, London W11 4QR
First published in Great Britain by Granta Books, 2023

A CIP catalogue record for this book is available from the British Library.

1 3 5 7 9 10 8 6 4 2

ISBN 978 1 78378 952 8
eISBN 978 1 78378 953 5

Typeset in Adobe Garamond by Avon DataSet Ltd, Alcester,
Warwickshire
Printed and bound by CPI Group (UK) Ltd, Croydon, CR0 4YY

www.granta.com

Prologue

In the beginning there is endless black water. The endless God Raniga weaves the endless black material into a fine adobe with his infinitely large hands. Like a potter at his wheel, Raniga then moulds the material into a conical tower with tapering walkways. The tower is made of space and time. A new invention. Space and time wind around the outside of the tower. Raniga builds the tower to allow his sons to escape from the endless black. When the tower is completed, He Ra Ra, He Hakari Nēke and the other sons of Raniga walk out of the endless black sea and begin to walk around the walkways which are made of space and time towards the summit of the tower. From the tower, they can look down and see all of the other creatures – beastly and human – crawling out of the sea. The entirety of history wends its way along the spiral pathway which winds up the sides of the eternal tower. At the top of the tower, after an infinitely long journey, He Hakari Nēke is given a palace. But He Hakari Nēke is a prankster. He is bored in his palace. He looks out of the window of his palace. From his vantage point, the infinite spiralling walkway looks like a single, linear staircase. He decides to walk down the staircase, back down towards the endless black sea. With every step he finds that he is a different age, since with every step he seems to bisect the process of history. One evening he is an old man, and the next morning he is an athletic, aerobicized youth. With every step he encounters a different generation of Moromo people. And in each generation he apprehends one individual, and whispers in their ear and tells them what lies in store for them around the next bend in the walkway of time and space. Those he speaks to – those who understand that time is not only a tapering walkway but also a staircase – are called prophets.

The first case of what would come to be known as He Hakari Nēke syndrome was discovered, by accident, by two New Zealander medical anthropologists – Woolworth and Dobson – who were working with the Moromo islanders. They found a girl called Hakari Neke Mota. Named after the great god himself, Hakari Neke had been alive for ten years, but she had the body of a forty-year-old woman. She was venerated by her community: a living embodiment, a sign, sent to the Moromo by the god He Hakari Nēke.

Woolworth and Dobson, the two medical anthropologists, decided to name the condition they had discovered after the great god and the little girl.

Years later, the human heterochrony expert Dr Andrew McCaul travelled to Moromati to interview Hakari Neke Mota. She had experienced a second heterochronous shock in her fortieth year, which had left her with the body of a ninety-year-old woman and close to death. She could no longer move, and she spent her days sitting in a throne made of lychee wood. The other villagers called her An Tonendō – the Augury. McCaul relayed his conversations with her in his book A Worshipful Malady.

'When speaking with the Augury,' McCaul wrote, 'I have the curious sensation that I am speaking to Ebenezer Scrooge. Her

childhood and her adulthood are not lifetimes. They are, rather, prophetic episodes, episodes in a sad and sadly limited sequence.'

I remember reading that passage when I was twenty-eight: fifteen years after my first heterochronous shock, six years before my second, three weeks after you were born. But it didn't make me think of me straight away. It made me think of my father, your grandfather. And then it made me think of you. And then it made me think of me.

I

I Am the Word for God and Boy

The night before the wedding we're in a café on the corner of Elgin Avenue for dinner. Caroline takes out a piece of folded-up paper and smooths it out on the table top. She isn't going to make a speech at the wedding, but she has written one anyway. In a parallel universe, she tells me, this is what she would say.

'I'm just going to read it for you instead,' she says.

Outside the sky is black, and clear, and you can see the actual universe in the sky, and the lighting in the café is warm, like a bead of amber. We are sitting in a café, on planet Earth, on the night before our wedding day.

'Thank you especially to Pol,' Caroline says, 'for allowing me to dote on him.'

She folds up the piece of paper and puts it in the pocket of her overcoat which is hanging on the back of her chair. She puts her hands on the table and interlaces her fingers and smiles. I tell her that she should make the speech at the wedding. She shakes her head.

'All those people,' she says.

'Don't forget to call the sandwiches guy,' she says.

—

So she leaves and goes back to her parents' house in Queen's Park where her wedding dress is hanging on the back of her childhood bedroom door. I tell her that I am going back to my mother's house but instead I walk up to the Heath, to the Men's Pond. I jump over the gate and I walk down the path, past the toilets and the locked door to the changing area, past the lifeguard hut. The water is as black as ink. I clamber down the banks and slip off my trousers and boxers and I climb down the ladder into the water. The skin of the water is covered in small insects.

On the bank there is a bald man, watching me. I plunge my hands into the water and then I plunge my head in and swim downwards, trying not to think about breathing. It's fucking cold. At the bottom of the pond there is a glimmer of light which gets bigger and bigger as I swim towards it.

There is a church glowing with blue sunlight. Everyone is standing in the narthex. Light pours through the stained-glass windows, pink and blue. A boy wearing blue and a girl wearing pink, whom I don't recognize, are running down the side aisle and their small smart shoes are clack-clacking on the loose parts of the herringbone parquet floor. It's a Victorian church, neo-Gothic, but the décor inside is beige and pastel. There are twentieth-century Stations of the Cross hanging on the walls and twentieth-century stained-glass windows. My sister Caoimhe is there, and Father Edward. Caoimhe's current boy-friend is there too. I can see Caroline's parents, huddled together in a corner, trying not to make eye contact with any of my relatives. There are a few other people I don't know: Caroline's colleagues from school. Caroline's American cousin and her husband. Father Edward is still wearing his civilian clothes: a pair of canvas slacks and a sky-blue short-sleeved shirt. The only person wearing a hat is Caroline's American cousin. Caoimhe is wearing a tartan shirt and a pair of high-waisted jeans. She sidles up and nudges me.

'Nice suit,' she says.

'Thanks,' I say.

'Where's Mum?' she says.

'She went to the bathroom,' I say.

'Where's Caroline?' she says.

I shrug.

'Morning sickness?' she says.

I look at her.

'She isn't pregnant,' I say.

And Caoimhe grins.

Now I'm standing at the front of the church, before the altar. The altar linen is rough to the touch from being laundered and ironed too many times. The surface of the altar mantle rustles inaudibly against the ridges of my fingertip. My mother used to launder and iron these cloths. Sometimes Caoimhe or our neighbour, Mrs Evans, would help her. They would stand at the ironing board in the living room on Quex Road, ironing. The next day I would see the same cloths that had been in our living room on the altar, a breeze from the half-open door at the side of the church moving them, slightly. The incongruity would make my head swim.

The congregation rises. I know that Caroline is here now. I don't take a look back. Instead, I pray silently. Please allow me the strength not to desire to convince her that she is shrewish, I pray. Please allow me the strength not to desire to convince her that she is shrewish.

Later on, years later, Caroline will say that I looked so nervous that I didn't even look her in the eye, and I will ask well what is the implication of that and she will just say:

'No implication. You just didn't look me in the eye.'

At the back of the church a baby is lowing. I can hear a low hum coming from inside the priest's chest. The battery pack for his microphone, hidden inside his alb, humming. His eyes are locked on hers. She is trying to remember the words. I can feel everybody looking at us: her American cousin and her American cousin's husband.

'*You* remember,' her American cousin kept saying, over and over, prodding her husband, when we had lunch with them last week. 'You *do* remember.'

'*Allow* him man,' Caoimhe will say to me later, after she has been forced to sit next to him for hours at the wedding breakfast. She is scornful of the shy. 'Simply *allow*.'

'Since when do you talk like that,' I will say.

'*Allow* him,' Caoimhe will say, again.

I should be taking all of this in. I should be listening to the words. I pinch the outside of my thigh, through the pocket of my wedding trousers, with my finger and my thumb.

'I, Pol,' says the priest.

'I, Pol,' I reply.

*

My mother thought that it was contrarian of my father to want to call me Polonius. She agreed only on condition that they would abbreviate it to Pol. But from the day that I was born, my mother started calling me Polly. When she first met my mother, Caroline took to calling me Polly too: first to mimic my mother, and later out of habit. They are the only two people in the world who call me that.

I still don't know why he wanted to name me that. I think he maybe just thought that it would help him to feel sorry for me. He found it difficult to feel sorry for people.

He was teaching English at a Gymnasium school in Frankfurt and finishing his doctoral studies when I was born. He was a Shakespeare man, an Anglophile. When he first met my mother, he assumed that she was English. They were already in love before she told him that she wasn't. She was Irish and shy and spry and younger than he was by a good ten years. She was studying at the art school, the Städelschule. She was studying to be a painter.

I find it hard to separate my own memories *of* him from anecdotes *about* him. Like trying to separate the sight that you have out of one eye from the sight that you have out of the other. He was a pissed-off man, my mother would say, later. He had little round spectacles that he wore even when he was nude. He went swimming in the sea, nude, even when there were other people around, even when we were in Ireland.

'*Teann an fuacht triom,*' my mother would say, shivering, wrapped up in my father's duffle, sitting on the huge boulders that had been brought down to the shore from the quarries by men who were trying to stop the sea from eroding the beach. When he came out of the sea and walked up the beach towards us there was a blue hue to his bald scalp.

Sometimes when I see him now, standing at the foot of my bed, I see him like that: nude and bald and blue.

We moved to Bournemouth in '86, when I was five. My father

got a job teaching German at the Weymouth College of Education, which became part of Bournemouth Poly the year he joined. He hated it. He didn't want to teach German. He wanted to teach English. He just wanted to live in England so badly.

Sometimes I can feel his voice. Like a physical feeling inside my brain. But I can't hear it. An irreducible thing. Like an itch that exists an inch below the skin. Like the very last thing that you can hear in a hearing test.

*

The priest is telling the congregation what is going to happen next. He points to the Paschal candle. He points to the tabernacle. He gestures with an open palm to the little red Formica table beneath the apse where the wedding registry book lies open: a green braided tassel, a fore-edge painting of the wedding at Cana.

I can see that Caroline has crib notes written on her palm in blue ink. I did try to convince her that she wouldn't need to do that. It isn't a test, I told her. I reassured her that the priest would tell us what to do. He would coach us through the ceremony. There was no need to try to memorize any of it.

We'd gone for the marriage preparation programme a few weeks before. We missed the deadline and so we had to do an emergency one. I was expecting it to be like a job interview: like a cold room and a stern-looking priest. I was worried about how Caroline would respond. I was relieved when I saw that it was a nice, soft, middle-aged Polish lady who was running the course.

On our way out of the building, after the three-hour course, the Polish lady asked us what we would be having for the readings

12

at the ceremony and I realized then that we hadn't discussed it. I was worried that the woman would take this as an indication that we were not taking it all seriously enough, that this question was one final, secret stumbling block. Instead, she just smiled and put her hand on my elbow and told us that a traditional choice would be the story of the wedding at Cana.

Actually (I didn't say this to the Polish woman) I wanted to include a reading from Bartholomew Playfere's prophecies, from notebook 9, sometimes referred to as 'The Nightingale Notebook' because of the marginalia: the little scribbled drawings of a nightingale that you can find on verso 20 and recto 25. Later on – when the notebooks were rediscovered and rebound and donated to the British Library – the designers included a gold inlaid design, a drawing of a nightingale, on the front cover.

'Please tell me that you're joking,' Caroline said when I suggested it. She pulled a sassy expression. She always goes to sassy as a precursor to real irritation.

To my face she said that it was nerdy, but to her friends she boasted about my obsession with Bartholomew Playfere.

'He reads this stuff for pleasure mind you,' she would say. 'For *pleasure*! Ima*gín*ate amigo.'

She liked the idea that I was a savant. A member of an invisible empire of the unschooled learned. It intrigued her that I had done nothing by the book because her parents had done everything by the book. They were doctors.

'Do you think that you *love* knowledge?' she asked me once. 'I don't think that I ever knew anyone who really *loves* knowledge the way that you seem to.'

Sometimes, before we were married, she would come over to my mother's house and I would find her in my bedroom leafing through the densely scribbled exercise books that were piled on my desk.

Anyway, we chose the wedding feast at Cana instead.

Only now, sitting next to Caroline in the front pew and listening to Father Edward read the story of the wedding feast at Cana, do I remember sitting next to my father on my bed in the house in Bournemouth – the bedspread with the faded, primary-coloured shapes of dinosaurs on it – while he read from the story of the wedding feast at Cana, and how he got to the word 'steward' and I asked him what a steward was and he couldn't tell me. How days later he told me that it was an attempted translation of an untranslatable Ancient Greek word. A word that must have meant something to the Evangelist, but which does not mean much of anything to anyone any more. A word which might mean something like 'chief party-goer'. Architrinklinos.

'You know who is the Architrinklinos in this family?'

'Who?'

'You.'

*

He meant that I made him laugh. He lulled me into a false sense of security when he roared with laughter at the things that I said or did. Other times he would get angry. Once upon a time my father's sister sent us a jar of raw honey that she had gathered from the beehives that sat behind her farmhouse in Lobbach on the outskirts of Heidelberg. There was a label on the jar, written in Gothic script, which said *Akazienhonig aus der Pfalz*. The honey was pungent. One day somebody left the lid off the jar of honey and by the time we got home from school the pungent aroma had filled the house. I walked into the kitchen and I told my father that the honey smelled like farts. He dragged me out into the garden and made me sit on the back step. I was crying. He told me that my conduct was vulgar. My conduct was intolerably vulgar, he said. I didn't even know what he meant. And – even afterwards, even years later – I *never* understood why he had to take me outside to tell me this. It was as though the jar of honey was an honoured guest, as though he couldn't make a scene in its presence.

I suspect he was just a little worked up, my mother said to me at the time, I suspect he was just feeling a little homesick.

Sometimes I didn't understand what he meant. I didn't understand, either, why the Gospel stories seemed to go straight from Jesus being born to Him being thirty. I didn't understand why Christmas was only a few months before Easter. I didn't understand why – when he showed me the statues of Mary in church – she seemed to be the same age when she was in the stable with the infant Jesus as when she was kneeling at the cross or holding His adult body in her arms. And then when my father read to me from *Treasure Island*, events that seemed to be weeks apart would all take place in the course of one evening, yet events that all took place on the same day seemed to take place over multiple evenings. My father refused to believe that I didn't understand that time is different in books. He accused me of being anally retentive. He turned the lights out early. He closed the bedroom door even though I asked him not to. I lay in the dark listening to the wind battering at the windows.

It was windy in Bournemouth.

'*Teann an fuacht triom*,' my mother said, on the long walk home from the school. I hated that school. The children were all cruel there.

–

'They aren't cruel,' Caoimhe said to my mother, who cradled my head in her arms. 'They don't like him because he tells them that they're all stupid and that he's cleverer than them. That's going to be the same wherever he goes to school.'

*

Caoimhe wanted to do a reading at the wedding, and we were pleased about that until she told us, a few weeks before the day of the wedding, that she had chosen to read a bit from one of my father's poems. In the end we agreed to a compromise. She would read his favourite passage from St Matthew's Gospel.

'And why take ye thought for raiment? Consider the lilies of the field, how they grow; they toil not, neither do they spin: and yet Solomon in all his glory was not arrayed like one of these.'

She looks funny, standing up there, reading from the lectern – so solemn – wearing those jeans and that tartan shirt. The priest looks abashed. I can hear the rustle of Caroline's American cousin's bashful American husband's polyester trousers as he crosses and uncrosses his legs. I don't want to turn around. I don't want to catch my mother's gaze. I reach my hand down and I squeeze Caroline's hand and she looks at me. I meet her gaze and then turn and catch the gaze of the Eugène de Mazenod statue, staring down at us from the altar. I try to visualize my mother's face, her fixed smile.

'Why would it upset her?' Caoimhe had said when she first proposed reading my father's poem.

'Why would it *upset* her?' I had said.

'What did he do wrong anyway?' she had said. 'What did he do to her that was so terrible in the final analysis? You tell me.'

He quizzed her. She would cry when he did.

He was generous but he hated to be asked for anything. That was the main issue. That was also why he always told my mother that she was demanding. It seemed to him, after all, that she was. He had always given her everything and she had always asked for more.

And even when he left he gave her all of his money: the house, the money, his books, everything. He walked out with just the clothes on his back. That was so she could never complain. It was what he had been doing all along. It was his masterpiece.

The day that he left we got straight on the train from Bournemouth to Holyhead. I was nine. The train was orange. The air was scalding. The seats were orange and red and brown and I was wearing my orange corduroy dungarees. My mother bought us cups of scalding orange-coloured tea from the buffet car. Somehow it was all comforting to me. I felt as though we had all been blown into the air by an explosion, and that we might just keep floating, up and up into the universe, untethered by gravity. It was the gravity that I hated. That the family felt like gravity to me at that age. It was 1990.

My grandfather's house in Connemara was white, in a green field. The house smelt like mud and milk and bacon. I ran around outside in the field with the half-mad dog and the girl cousins.

'If you fail to matriculate your son before March then he will sacrifice his place for the new term,' said the headmaster's secretary over the phone from Bournemouth. My granny didn't understand. She called my mother over to the phone, but my mother was already in a state of convalescence.

My grandfather – your great-grandfather – lifted me up and threw me, weightless, into the air above Connemara. He laughed when he asked how old I was and I told him that I was nine. He didn't believe me.

'*Is bréagadóir é!*' he shouted, everyone laughing, hooting, as he threw me into the air. '*Is bréagadóir é!*'

Once it snowed. We got into my grandfather's tractor and drove to the highest point and looked out across the landscape. My uncles dared one another to jump into a hole in the ice where the little lough had frozen over, but neither of them did. They punched each other in the arm. They were younger then than I am now, I realize, suddenly. On the other side of the white field there were two black figures. From a distance they looked like two erect black ants. They were throwing snowballs at each other. And when we got closer we saw that it was priests: two priests dressed head to toe in black, with black cassocks and black, woolly balaclavas. They were from the island, my grandfather told me: the last of the monastic community that lived there.

Another time he took us down to the coast and pointed out the little island for me and Caoimhe. He told us that it was a holy isle, the place where the battle at the end of the world would be fought. Father against son and son against father and brother against brother and mother against daughter and sister against sister. Caoimhe wasn't interested. She tugged at the tongue of her Clarks. But I begged my grandfather to take us out to the island to look at it. When he broached the issue with my mother she burst into tears. I didn't understand why until later.

One of the uncles said, accidentally unkindly, that my mother had been a great beauty. I knew it already. I didn't know about sexual intercourse, but I knew that my father had deflowered her.

Some days in Connemara it rained for just a few seconds: a whiff of petrichor and a damp dapple of dark grey on the tarmac that led up to the house. My mother's bedroom was an extension at the back of the house, built in the nineteen-forties. It had been her childhood bedroom.

'The only thing that stops a person from being a liar is being humiliated,' said Caoimhe, pulling at the loose strand of lace that hung from the armrest of the old pink bergère that sat in front of the fireplace in the living room in Connemara. 'If you don't humiliate a person when he tells a lie, then he'll never learn not to do it.'

My mother considered it precocious when Caoimhe gave her advice about child-rearing. Caoimhe was just a child herself, after all. My mother would laugh angrily, and go pink, as pink as the pink bergère.

'You are so wise beyond your years, *mo mhuirnin*,' she would say, sarcastically.

I would go pink too, but not with anger. I just felt embarrassed. I felt embarrassed whenever anybody said anything critical of my mother. I felt like I wanted to disappear. Like when I was very young, and I really would disappear: when I would bury my face in the folds of my mother's dress or coat or I would run headlong out of the front door and into the street.

'But what will you *do* here?' my uncle – my mother's brother – said, when we had already been in Connemara for two months. 'There is nothing for you *to* do here.'

—

19

I can remember the big mural of JFK and Jackie, painted in black and white, on the wall at Shannon Airport. My mother and Caoimhe both crying uncontrollably. They didn't want to go back to England. They didn't want to go to the flat in Kilburn that my uncle had arranged for us to live in. The one over the road from the Albion Ballroom. The Albion Ballroom which was a dance hall, not a ballroom. Which would eventually become a bingo hall and then a Pentecostalist church and then a ruin. Which they listed so that it couldn't be pulled down except by the weather. Where herons nested in the Art Deco clock tower.

Where, thirteen years after we arrived, at a concert celebrating the fifteenth anniversary of the fall of the Berlin Wall, I met Caroline, who was playing second violin. Who was bookish and smart and deracinated. White skin. A centre parting and two curtains of straight black hair like Patti Smith.

A GALA OF EASTERN EUROPEAN NATIONAL ANTHEMS

'Don't you think that girl is debonair?' I whispered to my friend Edward.

'Debonair?' he answered. 'I'm not sure that girls *can* be debonair.'

I disagreed. I told Caroline.

'Why, thank you kindly, pard'ner,' Caroline said in her cowboy voice, curtseying.

'He's been disappearing his whole life,' Caoimhe said, when I came home the next morning and refused to tell anyone where I had been. Caoimhe was always worried that my mother was infantilizing me, that she was coddling me on account of my condition. I had experienced an acute heterochronous shock a decade earlier and my mother still saw herself as my carer even though I was a grown-up. Because I had the body of an adult when I was only thirteen, she didn't seem to notice that I had become an actual adult.

A few weeks later I introduced them to Caroline.

'You know,' I overheard Caoimhe saying to my mother in the kitchen, after tea. 'No one person can redeem another person. It isn't fair to think like that.'

*

Nevertheless, here she is, next to me, sitting at the little red Formica desk, beneath the apse, in Sacred Heart. A hundred yards from the Albion Ballroom. I glance to my left to see if her hand will shake as she signs the book. Her signature is so vertical. Like a field of wheat, like a barcode. And, looking to her right, she sees me and smiles at me. And just for a few moments, I allow our eyes to meet.

The speeches are meant to be after the dinner, but halfway through the meal my mother stands up and says that she wants to say a few words.

'I never expected to be such a reliant person,' she says. 'But I turned out to be one, so I'm so grateful and relieved that Polly has found somebody who is so reliable.'

I can see Caroline's parents shifting uncomfortably in their seats next to her.

When the meal is finished, me and my mother stand together outside the Mazenod Social Club – me watching her smoke – and she tells me that if my father was here he would be trying to make the whole day about himself.

'Does that resonate with you?' I ask Caoimhe later, next to a pyramid of cocktail sausages. Caoimhe shrugs.

After Caroline and I have done our first dance, Caroline's father and mother approach us and her father hands me a thick envelope and tells me not to open it now.

'Marriage,' he says, laughing slightly uncomfortably. 'Very impressive, Pol. Adulthood I suppose they call it.'

And he laughs again. When they walk away, Caroline rolls her eyes and, looking straight ahead, says:

'I honestly have no idea. Please ignore, I beg of you.'

Afterwards Caroline and I get on the train from Euston to Holyhead and Caroline pulls a copy of the *Daily Mail* – which has a photograph of Mohamed Al-Fayed on the cover – out of her suitcase and exclaims:

'First Brunei buys the Dorchester, and now this.'

It's something that she heard a little old man say on a train long ago. She says it whenever she sees anything about Mohamed Al-Fayed. She is still wearing her wedding dress, but she has changed out of her satin pumps and into her Dr Martens. She is disappointed – leaning out of the window of the carriage door at Crewe – to see another bride climbing on to the train.

It rains every day in Dublin. On the third day, we catch the 14:06 to Westport and it's just torrential the whole way. Caroline stares out of the window at the view but you can't even see the view. All you can see is the torrent, pouring off the roof, pouring across the window.

'We be bein' woven into a goddamn watery cocoon here, pard'ner,' Caroline says in her cowboy voice.

From Westport we have to catch a little ferryboat out to the island. I tell Caroline how Bartholomew Playfere believed that this island was the highest point on planet Earth: that when the flood came, the island would be the only land left, peeking above the risen waters. For that reason, I tell her, the island would be the site of the battle at the end of the world. God's people would be forced to fend off the invading forces of the other nations. I bid her recall that Silly Symphonies *Father Noah's Ark* cartoon where the dove fetches the stick from the olive tree and the little patch of land appears on the horizon.

'Or like *Waterworld*,' Caroline says.

We have three suitcases. One each for me and Caroline and one for the wedding dress. And Caroline's violin case. She has a violin case that straps to her back like a backpack.

'I want to play music in the countryside,' she says. 'I've never done that before.'

The taxi driver carries her violin under his arm and then props it against the door of the cottage. It's an old bothy, converted into a holiday cottage. It's all in one room, with a kitchenette at the side and a little wooden table and a pot-bellied stove for heat which already has a fire in it when we arrive even though the owner is nowhere to be seen. Instructions for the house written on Post-It notes here and there. Leave a couple of euro in the plant pot on the sideboard if you take any of the good whiskey. We park the suitcases inside the door.

When the fire goes out and the sun goes down, we light the fire again. The thick red light fills the place. Caroline stands in the light, naked, and strums at her naked violin strings with her fingers. She picks up her bow from the dresser and she begins to play. She plays 'Bishop Alexander MacDonald's Farewell to Victoria'. When I close my eyes, I can see polar bears roaming through dense Canadian forests.

—

You are my bear, she tells me. We lie on the bed together like Tetris bricks, her legs around my shoulders. She pulls at my long black hair.

'Like a little teddy bear?' I ask her. 'Or like a big, murderous bear.'

'Bears can't commit murder,' Caroline says. 'Only humans can do that.'

'It's good for you,' she says, about the hair pulling. 'Christopher Walken does this for twenty minutes before breakfast every day.'

In the morning we go for a walk across the fields. We find ourselves in a little valley. In the distance there is a hill and on the hill a little bothy, green with ivy against the blue sky. Feel how good the air is. God's green air, clearing all the black thoughts out through my lungs. Perhaps that hill is where Bartholomew Playfere and his community lived, Caroline speculates, and I choose not to correct her. Let's save up enough money and come and live here, she says. We wouldn't need much money to live here forever without working. We could raise some chickens and raise a child who would grow into the shape of a willow tree or would be able to fly or would be able to paint with all the colours of the wind. A long, spindly son who will look after us when we are old.

Later on, on the day that you are born, I will remember that sentence.

When it starts to rain, lightly, we stand under a tree. We watch, concerned, as a blue tractor seems to amble towards us across the field. Here we are, on planet Earth, under a tree, Caroline thinks. Later on, years later, I know that we will reheat our separate meals in microwaves. But that seems like an impossibility here, in this field, in the air greyed by rain, with the blue tractor on the ersatz horizon. Is that tractor coming towards us? Are we supposed to be here? Are we going to get in trouble? Are you the farmer? The air shimmers with mizzle. The tractor turns around and heads in the opposite direction and we are relieved.

She looks up at me, her left eye occluded by the yellow triangle of the corner of the hood of her cagoule. Telepathically we begin to run. And the hoods of our cagoules flap immediately over our heads and begin to pat-pat-pat on the tops of our backs, sending little drizzles of rainwater down our necks. Then, after a while, it starts to stop raining and we slow to a walk and then to standing and then to kneeling and hugging on the stony, pebbly, rocky mud in the field. And while we are hugging, Caroline throws her head back and sings:

'*I am the word for God and boy: the man who searches and destroys.*'

The pub is dark. There is a warm, fat waitress pulling pints, speaking Irish.

'Nice,' says Caroline.

It is warm in the pub. The waitress brings us two pints of Guinness. The beer smells like wood. The kitchen smells like bacon and cabbage. There is peat in the fire in the corner. The waitress asks if we are the honeymooners who are staying in the bothy below and we laugh, all three of us, at the smallness of the place. My parents came to the island for their honeymoon also, I tell the waitress. And Caroline kicks me under the table.

At night in the bothy, I lie awake and I think about bomber planes, loaded with nuclear bombs, flying overhead and nuclear bomb-strength fire pouring through the hole in the ozone layer, burning up all the birds and the trees. Caroline blames the

Bartholomew Playfere books that I have brought with me.

'That's hardly light reading, babe,' Caroline says.

She doesn't think it is healthy for me to be reading about the endless wars and holocausts that lie in store. Father against son, brother against brother.

*

My father brought a copy of Heinrich Böll's *Irish Journal* with him on his honeymoon. My mother found him reading it in the bathroom while she was waiting for him to come to bed. He was making notes in the margins in blue biro. My mother found that worrisome. He was researching the place. He was worried about her having anything that was hers. He wanted this event and this place to be something that they had co-created. Him and his young wife. If only he could co-create something with her, then perhaps he could lasso his timeline to hers. That was what we were for I suppose: Caoimhe and I. We found that biroed copy in his study in Bournemouth when we were clearing out, and my mother kept it as a memento of her marriage. The pages had gone yellow but the notes were still bright blue, biro blue.

He had an oil heater in his study, in Bournemouth, that he would switch on when the rest of the old house was cold, at night or early in the morning. Now, whenever I smell the acrid smell of an old oil heater, mixed with the smell of bookpaper, it always reminds me of that book, of that room.

We weren't allowed to go into that room.

'That room is like my mind,' my father said. 'You wouldn't like it if somebody tried to go inside *your* mind, would you?'

I didn't mean to pry. I was just intrigued by his black notebooks. He would write stories for us in those black notebooks and he would read them to us at bedtime. I had seen those black notebooks on the desk in his office. When I learnt to read, I wanted to read the stories for myself. So I went into his office and took one of the black notebooks and began to read it. But what was written in this particular notebook was not like the stories that he had read to Caoimhe and me. I got scared. I forgot which shelf I had taken the notebook from. I stole it and hid it in the place in our bedroom where the carpet lifted up. He searched for that notebook, angrily, for two weeks. The more angrily he searched, the more determined to keep it hidden I became. I was so determined to keep it hidden, even years later, that I took it with us when we left the house in Bournemouth. I took it with us to Ireland and then I took it with us to Kilburn.

When my father and mother got back from their honeymoon in '77 my father wrote an article for a student newspaper in Frankfurt with the title 'Freedom and Beauty: The Struggle for Ireland'. Ireland must be freed, he wrote, because Irish culture could only be properly protected by a sovereign government. If Ireland was not freed, then Irish culture would be lost not only to the Irish but also to the world. He didn't really know anything about it.

He didn't really have a homeland. He got really angry if people referred to him as German even. He didn't really have a family, at least not one that he wanted.

'I am the beginning,' he said to us once when we asked about his mother and father and grandmother and grandpops. 'Full stop.'

That's why he wanted to invent one. But when he invented one, he realized that the one that he had invented was sort of the same as the one he had just finished destroying in his imagination.

—

27

In '77, on their honeymoon, they – your grandparents – stayed at a William-Yeats-Was-Here house on the island. On the last day of *our* honeymoon we decide to go and visit it. The place is all boarded up now. There is nobody around except for the few villagers who don't even really get what it all means. It's all a bit sad, a bit silent. Perhaps the villagers are put off by the graffiti. There is always a slow trickle of tourists, Armageddon-chasers, making a pilgrimage to the island, inspired by reading Bartholomew Playfere. One of them has daubed some graffiti in white paint on the boarded-up windows of the William-Yeats-Was-Here house.

Be Godded with God.
Deadn't You Realise That You are Alrdeady Dead?

*

In 2010 they will transform this house into an artists' retreat with money from the EU. We will try to book a room here, when you are still a little baby. But they will not let us.

'Are you artists?' the woman will say over the phone when I try to reserve a room. The line will be bad. I will not be sure if I have heard her correctly.

'No,' I will say, hesitantly.

There is a new fire in the pot-bellied stove when we get back to the bothy.

'Who is looking *after* us?' Caroline says, and she chuckles spookily.

We have to pack. We have to put all our stuff back into the backpacks and suitcases. I don't want to go back. But we have to go back. We have to go back to London. We have to get the ferry back to the mainland. We have to get the bus back to Westport. There are three suitcases. One each for me and Caroline and a third for the wedding dress. There is a bus shelter in Westport.

There is rain thundering on the corrugated iron roof. I stroke the roof of her Dr Martens with the sole of mine.

'Everything is going to be okay,' I tell her.

Reading Is Sexy

Caroline is already sitting in the restaurant when I arrive. It's one of those dingy places with dark wood tables and gingham tablecloths and empty Chianti bottles draped with melted, hardened candle wax. Caroline is wearing a blue T-shirt with a photograph of Paul Newman reading a book on it and the inscription *Reading Is Sexy*. The T-shirt is stretched to breaking point over her belly. In three or four more weeks she will be huge, she tells me. She is wearing a *Vote Labour* sticker stuck to her T-shirt. There is another *Vote Labour* sticker stuck to the window of the restaurant. I wonder if Caroline stuck it there.

'They aren't here yet?' I say.

'Don't be irritable,' Caroline says.

She looks up at me for the first time, then reaches into her handbag and pulls out a tissue and dabs it against her tongue and then dabs it gently against the skin beneath my left eye.

'Escalator muck,' she says.

Her parents are only over for a couple of days. They sold the house in Queen's Park last year and they moved back to Dublin. It's a shame. I loved that house. The only thing bad about that house was that it had an upstairs bathroom window that looked over their neighbours' back garden and didn't even have like frosted glass in it so that – if you didn't close the blinds – you could accidentally have a wee in full view of the neighbours. I would always ask Caroline why they didn't just get a frosted pane put in. It would be a day's work, if that.

'It's just not a big deal,' Caroline would say.

When you are born, I shall take you down there – to the house in Queen's Park – and I shall point up to the window that was once your mother's bedroom window. I shall tell you about what your grandparents were like when they were younger.

They have come over from Dublin for the weekend just to knock doors for Gordon Brown. They still love Gordon Brown. Caroline's father, Ted, has set up a group specifically for retired doctors who still love Gordon Brown. Caroline doesn't love Gordon Brown as much as her parents do. But she does have a thing for Alistair Darling.

'There's something Thunderbirdy about him,' she says. 'Let's not even analyze it.'

When they arrive, they sit down at the table and without even looking at the menu Ted announces that he is going to order minestrone soup.

*

The first time Ted and I met I talked to him about how the rising sea levels would lead to an internal refugee crisis in the United States with people trying to escape low-lying areas like Florida and trying to get to the north to New York and how (incidentally) it all matched with some of the predictions that Bartholomew Playfere had made in his prophetic texts. How Playfere had predicted that household would turn against household as the world's resources began to sink below the seas.

Father against son and mother against daughter and brother against brother. Then, when I went to the loo, I overheard him and Ellen talking about 'paranoiac prognostications'.

'He's clever. He's exploring,' Ellen replied. 'He's young. He can take his time.'

Ted is saying that they had come out the previous night to watch the parade. Some kind of Kurdish affair. How the streets were littered with flyers and bottles and plastic bags after the parade had passed. And how they got up in the morning pretty early to find the whole place spotless.

'I do think that nightwork is like magic, isn't it,' Ellen is saying. 'The same quality of experience. Like little magic elves making you think that the whole thing was just a dream.'

'Nightwork is like set dressing,' Caroline says. 'Paying these people to create a stage set for this fricken opera that we call "capitalism" or "civilization" or whatever.'

Ellen is a GP and Ted is a paediatrician. Ted used to take Caroline's temperature rectally when she was a child, which still blows my mind. Neither Ted nor Ellen seem to be particularly passionate about medicine. They always wanted Caroline to be an artist. They got Caroline violin lessons when she was nine years old. She could learn Irish fiddle tunes, they said, but only after she had finished practising her Associated Board pieces. They flat out denied that they had said that, years later. I thought that Ted was going to cry when Caroline pressed him on it.

'It's a question of whether or not you want to make them feel sad,' I said to her later.

It made Caroline feel sad, when she was a child, to think of other people, friends of hers, who had parents who were not as

32

good as her own parents. She would visit her friends' houses and come away struck by the fact that her friends' parents were so thoughtless of each other's feelings and of their children's feelings. Her friends' parents seemed to be so dead, so angry, so like children themselves compared with her own living, thinking parents. While her own parents thought about what they should do to each other, say to each other – discussed it, innovated – her friends' parents all seemed to go through the motions: never changing, never thinking about changing. Either that or they were gone, weren't at home, were working too much, were working too little, were broken up with one another.

Her parents were craftsmen. They were not habit forming. They associated the formation of habit with beastliness and they said so. The joy of being human lay in the fact that you could decide to change the way that you did things, they said.

Caroline did do things. Caroline did well. They were pleased with her. They took her out to dinner to talk about her options. They reminded her that there was nothing that they wanted more than that Caroline should spend her life doing the things that *she* wanted to do. At night, when they thought that she was asleep, she heard them discussing ways that they could strategically avoid unconsciously imposing their own hopes, aspirations, ambitions on to Caroline. So many parents unconsciously imposed their own hopes, aspirations, ambitions on to their children. It was easily done. It was an easy mistake to make, and it would take rational thought and combined effort to avoid making it. She knew that they weren't lying, because they didn't even know that she was listening.

Sometimes when she dreamed, she dreamed that she *was* her parents.

When she would have her angry times – when she would throw her books on the floor or at the wall or would throw a piece of plastic crockery at the wall or would use the kind of language that she knew would upset her dad – it actually upset him so much that it broke her heart to see his face and she would just *try* her hardest not to think about doing anything like that again for a while.

'I think that you might just need to take a little bit of time on your own to cool down,' her mother said. 'I'm sorry that you're feeling so angry. That looks hard.'

There was no point in Caroline's mother instructing Caroline not to have these temper tantrums, Caroline's mother told Caroline. The key was to work harder, to work together, to understand better where they came from. She also wanted to understand better where Caroline's *hard*ness came from. Ellen had always thought of herself and her husband as quite soft, soft-hearted people. And, as such, Ellen had always expected – she admitted – that she would have a soft-hearted daughter.

'You are *quite* hard Caroline,' she said, with a whimsical smile. 'I *do* wonder where this *hard*ness of yours comes from.'

As though Caroline's hardness was a foreign coin that her mother had found floating around in the pocket of a scarcely worn coat. Or a group of fruit flies found floating around the fruit bowl on a hot summer day.

Caroline stood up from the dinner table and flipped the ladder-back dining chair backwards so that it did a backwards somersault in the air and landed with a crash on the tiled kitchen floor.

'Do you think that they were putting all of their anger into you?'

34

I said. 'That you were feeling all of the anger that they felt they couldn't express themselves? To one another?'

'I don't know,' Caroline said, her face getting warm. 'That just sounds a bit science-fictiony to me.'

She thinks that she felt kind of like a unit of currency. The value of her parents' love for one another was expressed in her. Like a currency, she didn't have intrinsic value. Her value was attributed to her by what she represented in the process of the giving and receiving of love that took place between her parents. She knew that they knew that if she was happy, it was because they loved one another. She knew also that if the value of a unit of currency in a society collapses, then the society *itself* collapses. This was not so much of a problem in a society where the unit of currency was coins or beads or pelts or giant stone discs because in those societies the unit of currency was not a conscious being, was not aware that its own collapse in value was directly linked to the collapse of everything else.

'Do you realize that you just said that you don't think that you have any intrinsic value?'

She would get angry.

'Do *you* realize that you are projecting your own shit about your childhood on to me? Do you realize that you're taking things out on me on account of the way that you feel about your *own* parents?'

Another time she said:

'When I think about the carnival barkers that raised *you*, I cannot *believe* that you have the entrails to criticize my family.'

With all that, and despite her bluster and defensiveness, there was a short time, between the wedding and her parents' move to Dublin, when she hardly spoke to them at all.

And it was a relief, it was relieving. She felt herself stopping being so anxious. As her anxiety unravelled, she began to remember things: moments, events. Or perhaps she didn't. Perhaps she just became able to confide in me about them. About when she had walked ten metres ahead of them on the road when they were in Spain that time and they had sniped at each other, whispering, through the sides of their mouths, so that she wouldn't hear them swearing. Or when she had walked out on them during a trip to the movies because her father had asked her to swap places with him so that he didn't have to sit next to her mother and everyone in the crowded cinema looking at them. She would get quite quiet after telling me about these things. It was sad, but good.

We had moved into the house on Iverson Road. We had bought the big TV. The spare room in the new house spooked Caroline.

'What if we can't get pregnant,' she said. 'That room will become so strange. Like an inverted mausoleum.'

So she locked the door. I had started working as a gardener at the school where Caroline was teaching. We were spending all day, every day together, walking to and from work together.

Maybe because at that time I wanted to have some space for my own thoughts, I began to work on a book about Bartholomew Playfere. Caroline had shown me an article about a man who worked as a derrickhand on an offshore rig and who spent his time teaching himself Aramaic and eventually became so expert that he was able to formulate a theory regarding the dating of an important fragment of the Dead Sea Scrolls and as a result was given an honorary doctorate and a teaching post at Yale Divinity School.

'He just presented this brilliant book to them,' Caroline said. 'And they handed him a PhD.'

It was something that I wanted to do anyway. We had studied Bartholomew Playfere at school. It was my favourite day of my whole time at school. The teacher had taken us to the Reading Room at the British Museum and had shown us some of Bartholomew Playfere's notebooks – including the Nightingale Notebook and a copy of *The End of Nightwork and the Sundering of the Curtain in Twayn*. He had told us about the life of Bartholomew Playfere, the soldiering prophet. But I remember at the time being frustrated about the gaps: that his life story seemed to leap from his childhood to his time as a tub preacher to his ill-advised pilgrimage to the island where he and his followers lived out the rest of their lives awaiting the coming apocalypse.

I told Caroline about it.

'Go for it,' Caroline said.

I got a British Library card and I spent my weekends transcribing extracts from the notebooks. One thing that everybody knew about Playfere's output was that it was voluminous. He must have spent all day, every day writing. Some of his notebooks were held at the Collins Barracks, but they were mostly notebooks from the last two years of his life. Most of the writings that he produced when he was living in Cheapside were kept in the British Library, and they amounted to nearly a thousand folios.

Everybody seemed to think that these notebooks were impenetrable, only of interest to New Agers and esotericists who harvested them for weird, gnomic aphorisms or predictions about the future. You could read into them whatever you wanted to read into them, it was suggested. So I was surprised to find that there were still some bits and pieces of overlooked biographical detail. There wasn't much, but every few weeks I came across a tiny reference, a tiny jigsaw puzzle piece, which cast light on the lost years of his life:

My Lord *Oliver Cromwel*, I claim protection from you, by vertue of the Oath you have sworn unto the People, and confirmed it by many reitterations, vowes, and protestations, as that protest at *Huntington* in the Market-house, my SELF there present, and those words I challenge you to make good which you declared, the words were these: You sought not ours, but us; and our welfare, and to stand with us for the liberty of the Gospel, and the Law of the Land.

Caroline was thrilled.

'Imagine if in two or three years you bring this book out and it's like a literary sensation,' she said. 'It's like you're jumping the queue of life.'

One evening, one of her friends – drunk – said to me that she had never met someone who was a true sage like I was.

'You just have this aura,' she said. 'This wisdom beyond your years. It's hard to explain. You are so smart and you just bide your time and do your own thing and stay out of the rat race and all that. I just know that you're going to be famous one day.'

'What about Caroline,' she said to Caroline, later.

'What about me?' Caroline said.

'Will you stay on at the school when Pol is rich and famous?'

'I'm sure I'll need to have something to keep my feet on the ground,' Caroline said, straightfaced.

Once Caroline said that she didn't understand why – if

Bartholomew Playfere believed that the people of God would be protected by Him from the rising seas and invasionary armies on the islands of the West – why he would feel like he had to go there himself. Why did *he* take the initiative? Didn't he think that God would make it all happen? It was a difficult question.

'I suppose it's like curiosity,' I said. 'It's what Popper called "the Oedipal effect". Like Pugliev says about suicide: the only way to allay the crippling uncertainty about how your life will conclude.'

'So curiosity kills the cat,' Caroline says. 'Curiosity kills the prophet.'

*

Caroline is swiping her index finger through the flame of the candle on the table in the restaurant. Her mother slaps her hand. They are talking about school. Ellen wants Caroline to take her maternity leave now. Caroline is saying that she doesn't need to take maternity leave now. She wants to time it right, so that it won't coincide with the summer holidays. Ellen goes quiet and then starts to snap the breadsticks into little pieces, and then to lay the little pieces out in a row on the table next to her plate. Ted is saying something about epistemology. Absent-mindedly, I am picking at the *Vote Labour* sticker that is stuck to the window behind me. I hate sitting in the window seat in a restaurant. It makes me feel as though I'm eating on a cinema screen. Outside, on the windowsill, a sparrow lands and scratches its armpit with its beak and then it lifts its wings and lifts off into the night sky above Kilburn. In the sky, it joins with a mob of sparrows and they disappear behind the railway bridge.

'Was that a sparrow?' Caroline's mother asks. She looks at her watch and pulls a face.

I nod sorrowfully.

'It's out of control,' I say. 'You can hear them singing at two, three in the morning sometimes.'

Ted is reading a book by Eliezer Pomerantz. Humanity has a mania for priesthoods, he says. The whole point of the scientific method – the whole point of Pascal and Bacon and Hume – was not just to tear down the authority of Aristotle and replace it with a different authority, but rather to point out that we can never know anything for sure. That the best we can do is predict. But somehow scientists have become a new sacerdotal class, no different from priests or lamas or shoguns. And that's where the conspiracy theorists come in. They are using precisely the same language as the scientists – scepticism, empiricism, trusting your own senses rather than epistemic authorities – to tear down the priesthood, just as Pascal had done in the seventeenth century.

'How interesting,' I say.

*

That first time I went over there for dinner, Ted told me that he had discovered the secret to living a happy life. The secret was just to not compare your life with other people's. He called this the Paul McCartney syndrome. Paul McCartney was one of the most successful people in history, and yet he was completely consumed by the need to compare himself with John Lennon.

'The scary thing is,' he said, in a tone of voice that suggested he had made this joke before, 'I could easily have called it the John Lennon syndrome.'

He smiled broadly.

'I don't really know *the Beatles* so well,' I said.

Are you thinking about doing a degree, Pol, he had wanted to know. Are you thinking about seeking out a profession? He knew that I was interested in seventeenth-century history? In the Civil War? In climatology? I told him how my condition meant that I had had to drop out of school early. I had started to fall out with my teachers. I think, really, that it was too weird for them to have a fully grown adult sitting in their classrooms. Try as they might, they couldn't seem to help extra-scorning me if I got basic maths wrong or if I forgot to shower. In the end I stopped going in. Maybe I would get back to it one day, I told Ted, but if we were going to get married and have a baby quickly, like Caroline wanted to do, then I would be better advised to get a job rather than doing a degree for the next three years, didn't he agree? Besides, I knew a little bit about how they taught climate science in UK universities and I wasn't convinced that the professors were really interested in the truth. During dinner he went upstairs, and when he came back he was carrying a slim paperback. It was a book by Dietrich Bonhoeffer. Was I familiar with Dietrich Bonhoeffer? I would enjoy this book then. The book was called *Living for Others*.

Ted's physical frailty was caused by treatment for a bout of cancer that he had had as a child. It was touch-and-go, he told me. It gave him a different attitude to life, he said. Caroline wondered when she was a child if her father's cancer explained why he seemed to weep so often. He would well up sometimes when Caroline's mother did something that hurt his feelings.

'It is absolutely *nothing* to be ashamed of,' Ellen would tell Caroline. 'The really sad thing is that some people when you get older and when you are in school will tell you that it *is* something to be ashamed of. *That's* the sad thing. *This* isn't the sad thing.'

*

When the waiter brings the bowl of soup over, Ted dives straight in with his soup spoon before Ellen stops him and warns him to blow on it or else he will burn his mouth. Ted smiles sardonically, first at Caroline and then at me and then at the waiter.

'*Life is a minestrone*,' Caroline sings, softly, under her breath, '*filled up with Parmesan cheese*.'

*

One day, when she was fourteen, she came home from school to find her father sitting alone at the kitchen table, reading the newspaper. He used to read those big old newspapers. He was so small that you could only see his hands when he was reading them. Ellen had gone on a conference. Ted asked Caroline to set the table for dinner. She took the copper-coloured forks and spoons out of the drawer and laid them next to each other on the table. Then she took a chair away from the table and climbed on it to lift down the nice white and blue plates from the top shelf of the crockery cupboard. She carried the plates over to the table and laid them on the table next to the spoons and forks. Then she opened the drawer next to the cutlery drawer, the one with the linen in it, and took out two starched white napkins and laid them on the table. There was no tablecloth on the table. They ate just like that, with the plates and cutlery on the wooden table top. Her father had cooked minestrone soup from scratch. Usually, they had minestrone for lunch on Saturday afternoon, but on this occasion, he had made it for dinner. During the meal, he kept his copy of the *Observer* next to him on the table and he glanced at it now and then between asking her questions about school.

'Thank you, sweetheart,' he said, when she took his bowl away and put it in the sink.

Upstairs in her bedroom, Caroline lifted up her mattress and pulled out a copy of *NME* that was already over a month old. She began to read. When she heard the sound of her father's footsteps on the stairs, she closed the magazine and listened. She heard him begin to walk across the landing towards his own room, then stop and then walk towards her room. She pushed the magazine underneath the covers and folded her arms. Her father knocked on the door.

—

Caroline was supposed to be asleep by the time her mother got home from the conference, but when she heard the car pull into the driveway she climbed out of bed and went over to her bedroom window. She watched her mother walk up the path to the front door. It was raining and her mother was wearing a yellow fold-up cagoule over her smart trouser suit. She watched her mother fish for her housekeys in the pocket of her cagoule.

She was still awake half an hour later, when her mother had finished eating the leftovers from dinner and had moved with her father into the living room. She heard the sound of her mother pouring wine into glasses. She couldn't understand what was being said, but she heard the sound of raised voices. She opened her bedroom door and crept, silently, down the first three stairs and leaned over the balustrade. She could see her parents sitting on the couch in front of the fire, their backs to the open living-room door. Her mother was sitting upright. She could see her father's legs spilling over the side of the couch. She could tell that he was lying with his head in her mother's lap. She could tell, even though she couldn't hear him, that he was crying and that her mother was comforting him. She crept down two more stairs. From there she could hear what they were saying. Her father was complaining. He had tried to socialize with Caroline, he was saying, but Caroline had rejected him. Caroline had been dismissive, he said. Caroline had been aloof.

She could never explain the full horror of that moment to me. The only way that she could express it, she said, was to say that she would have much preferred it if she had walked in on them having sex. That would have been easier. I could tell that she wasn't exaggerating.

—

43

One day in the future I will think about this anecdote while I sit, haunted, on the couch in our living room in the house on Iverson Road and hear the sound of you moving around upstairs in your own little bedroom.

*

After the meal Ted and Ellen ask if we need a ride home and we say no, it's fine, it's only a short walk and Ellen says well then all right, we can't force you. Ellen grabs hold of me and gives me a tight hug. We agree to meet the next day to go canvassing together. Caroline reminds me that I should take my driver's licence and, when her parents look at her quizzically, explains that sometimes people don't believe that I'm of voting age.

'I don't have that problem any more,' Caroline says, dryly.

Caroline's parents laugh. Ted asks if they can give us a lift anywhere. It's only a short walk home we say, again. He asks us if we want a last drink anywhere and we say no, we should probably be getting back. Ellen turns to leave, but as an after-thought she bends down and puts both palms on Caroline's belly and kisses her belly where her navel is.

They go around to the car park at the back of the restaurant and we walk towards the bus stop. When we get to the bus stop, I stop and sit down on the bench. Caroline taps me on the elbow, uncertainly.

'Let's walk to the next bus stop,' she says. 'I don't want them to drive past and see us standing here.'

Later on, when we're at home, Caroline thanks me for being so understanding.

44

I Think That Might Be Your Anxiety

'I always thought that revenge was a dish best served cold,' says Caroline. 'But now I understand that it means *getting your own back on someone.*'

She is brushing her teeth. She jabs me in the arm with her free hand and then hops from foot to foot on the warm white bathroom tiles, like a bantamweight boxer. Toothpaste suds dribble down her chin. I am sitting cross-legged on the lid of the toilet. So spry, as Caroline says, so fucking spry man. Enviably spry. She envies me.

'I don't know why you ever *stop* eating,' she says. '*I* wouldn't.'

The newspaper is spread out on my lap. The newspaper falls apart, falls everywhere, when she jabs me. It is midnight. Caroline picks up the pillcase which I keep all my pills in and shakes it like a maraca.

'Boysoboys,' Caroline says when I tell her that it's midnight. Toothpaste suds spill out of the sides of her mouth when she tries to speak. She spits in the sink.

'Boysoboys,' she says again.

*

'Boysoboys,' my mother said. 'I wish I was half as clever as you are, Caoimhe.'

Caoimhe didn't look up from her magazine.

'Yep,' she said, lethargically. 'I wish that you were too, Mum.'

A shaft of pink light coming through the window of the living room in Quex Road in 1993. Catching the smoke from Caoimhe and my mother's cigarettes and making it look like pink clouds. Caoimhe reading a magazine article about a Greek island where there are no cars. Whenever she came across a joke in her magazines, she would always try it out on my mother, to test my mother's intelligence.

'Did you hear the one about the Italian barber?' she would say. 'Did you hear the one about the Irish skier?'

She never looked up from her magazine. She never gave the punchline. She would take a drag from her cigarette and let the thorn settle into my mother's flesh and turn the page.

*

Caroline has a special pillow to support her back, to stop her from rolling over on to her belly. I'm more worried about her belly than she is. Once she stood behind a set of swing doors in the corridor at school and I scolded her about it later when we got home.

'What?!' she shouted. 'What am I supposed to do?'

'What if somebody had opened those doors quickly?' I said. 'There are two hundred little maniacs running around in that building!'

I make sure that she doesn't take two stairs at a time when she's running upstairs, like she likes to.

'You know that I'm doing these things when you're not around,' she says. 'You are *aware* of that, aren't you?'

I try not to think about that.

'We can do some hugging on your side of the bed,' Caroline says. 'And then I can move over here.'

46

When she sleeps on her back, she snores. I don't tell her, even though she always tells me when I snore.

The morning sickness makes her talk in strained staccato grunts.

'Egg,' she might say. 'Pills.'

This lasts for the rest of the day sometimes. Even after she is dressed and walking around. I walk into the kitchen and I boil the kettle to make some tea. The kettle is broken so that the switch stays pressed down even after the water has boiled. You have to keep an eye on it.

'Why. You insist. Door open?' Caroline wails, softly. '*Why. You insist. Kettle noise. So loud.*'

And she breaks into soft pretend sobs.

It's her last day at work. When we go into the staffroom, there is a hushed silence and people nod at Caroline in acknowledgement of the day. There is a note for me from Edith, the Year Two teacher, written all in capitals, pinned to the bulletin board in the staffroom.

'HELP!' the note says.

There are little creatures living on the tulips in the flower bed behind the Year Two classroom, Edith tells me. Edith's pupils planted the tulips at the start of the school year. One of the children started crying when they saw the little white circular creatures.

I try to find out what the little creatures are, but there is no mention of them in my gardening books. They are tiny and white. They are curled into circles and they sunbathe on the surface of the petals of the tulips.

I spray the tulips with the spray that I used to kill the caterpillars that time. The spray is supposed to work within thirty minutes. My plan is to spray the tulips and then forget about them. But when I spray them, I notice that the little creatures unfurl, straighten, and then wriggle rapidly across the surface of the petal, weaving their way around the droplets of pesticide and down through the sepals. When they reach the heart of the bloom, the creatures drive down into the ovary and disappear completely. I stand in the garden and gaze into the heart of the tulip bloom, baffled. Something about the white shapes on the scarlet petals has upset me in a way that I can't explain.

After work, all of the teachers gather together in the staffroom and they give Caroline some daffodils and a card and then produce a cake. I wrap my arm around Caroline's shoulder as she cuts the cake. I can feel her shoulder blades through her jacket. Everyone applauds. The cake has a picture of a smiling, dimpled baby's face with a single yellow curl, the shape of a question mark, coming out of its head. The dimples are represented by tiny curved strands of black icing. The baby on the cake looks sort of like an alien.

'I think that that might be your anxiety talking,' Caroline says, barely concealing her smile.

We're walking home along the Kilburn High Road. Our house is being painted and the fumes are disrupting Caroline's sleep. She looks tired. Every afternoon, after work, she takes a snooze on the couch in the living room. The couch has a low back. When Caroline lies on her back, her belly shows above the back of the couch, the only visible part of her body, like a mostly submerged sea creature. I make the dinner. When she first got pregnant, I anticipated that she would have all kinds of interesting cravings, but the only thing that she really wants to eat is egg. Boiled eggs with Marmite on toast. Omelettes. I bring her omelette over to the couch and I stroke her hair to wake her up and I place the omelette on the half-size table that stands between the couch and the TV. Do you want to watch TV, I wonder aloud. This rouses her.

'What time is it?' she says. 'I think the smell of that paint might have put me to sleep.'

After Caroline has had a nap, we always stay up late. The light from the TV reflects in the lenses of her spectacles. We channel-flick, speculatively. Cameron and Clegg in the rose garden, chuckling. An aeroplane has crashed in India. They have sent cameras down to the bottom of the Mariana Trench and have brought back footage of a sea creature which lives in a tiny cave ten miles below sea level which has been affected by radiation from nuclear weapons tests. It's not supposed to be phosphorescent, but now it is. And that's just the *good* news, the presenter says, sorrowfully. Then they show footage of a giant glacier calving. The ice crumbles into the sea like a tooth in a bad dream. The light bulb flickers in the kitchen. Specks of dust flicker in the TV light.

'Why don't you climb on a chair?' Caroline says, speculatively.

I climb on a chair and I flick the bulb with my index finger. The bulb continues to flicker.

'Have you been channelling evil spirits again, Pol?' says Caroline, softly, invisibly, from the sofa.

The television screen flicks back and forth between different channels. From my angle, standing on the chair in the kitchen, looking through the kitchen door into the living room, it appears to strobe. It appears that there are some evil demons, some evil entities in our house, and they are messing with our electronics.

Black Planet

I still remember talking to you before you were born. I still remember the feeling of my voice rippling, like waves, through the blackness, through the black amniotic fluid, like ripples in a black blanket, like ripples in an ink-black sea.

Even then I was always envious of you, even when you were in the womb. Especially when you were in the womb. It still keeps me awake at night. Even now. My only saving grace is the knowledge that I was never more envious of you than I was in the moment that you were born. A shrill shriek of envy, emanating from that single moment. Perhaps the years ahead will see a continued softening of that sound, like the softening of the sound of the universe from the moment of the Big Bang until now.

In the hospital room. I am looking down at you. Your eyes are tightly closed. And I feel all of my thoughts around me. Like tails of light. And the tails all knit together into one dazzling beam. Dazzling you as you emerged from the black water inside Caroline. Caroline reaching for my hand. The sound of the voices of the nurses on the ward and the machines. All dulled now. Dulled to a dull, lowing sound, a dull throb in my ears. And all I can do is meet your gaze, through your closed eyes. The light of my eyes. The darkness of yours.

We wrap you up in a white blanket. Your tiny red face peeking out from the white blanket like a glacé cherry on top of a Bakewell tart.

I remember climbing out of the dark black water at Beaghcauneen, rash red with the cold, and my grandfather wrapping me in a white blanket to keep me warm. The cold black water trickling down the inside of my legs. I left a big wet mark on the seat of the tractor when we drove back to the house where my mother was weeping. Caoimhe laughed.
    'Look at Pol's nose,' she laughed. 'It's as red as a cherry.'

I remember the house appearing from behind the land as we drove towards it: the white house mounting the horizon, like the white ghost of a long-dead whale, surfacing for air.

That house is itself really a ghost to me now. Sometimes it stands in my dreams. A white dream, built in a black universe. The dream seems to be built of white, doughy bricks and thatch until I wake up and I look around me and realize that I am in Kilburn, that I am an adult now. Caroline laughs at me. When I wake with a start like that, she says, I make a snorting noise like a startled pig.
    'You make that little wrinkled thing with your nose,' she says. 'Makes you look like Keith Flint.'

*

It was when my mother was fired from her job at Twistleton's in '92 that the trouble started. I remember our neighbour, Mrs Evans, used to look in on us. I thought that it was to check on Caoimhe and me, but later I realized that it was really to check on my mother. Mrs Evans was cool. A long, cool, cooling element. She kept the keys to our house on a key ring, and she wore the key ring like a ring, around her index finger, twirling the keys as she walked down the street, as she spoke. When my mother would wander away from us, as she did at times, Mrs Evans would be on hand: spooling her out into the world and then spooling her back in again. Sometimes she would walk us to school, if my mother didn't get up in time. Sometimes she would knock on our door until we came out. We used to sleep over in her house sometimes, and once, when she went to Mass, I snuck into her room and read her diary. Like my mother, she had moved to Kilburn from Connemara after her husband left her. Later on her husband came to live in NW6 also. He would drive down our road in his yellow Ford Cortina, with his new young English girlfriend next to him in the front passenger seat. He would slow down outside Mrs Evans' house and he would sound his horn and shout until the whole street was awake. Mrs Evans would just stand on the front step and smile and smoke. She never seemed to be rattled by it.

I forgot all about that yellow Ford Cortina until years later when Caroline played me the song 'Janie Jones' by The Clash and the bit about the Ford Cortina which just can't go without fuel.

Caroline was a big fan of The Clash. But the lyrics to that song are hard to understand. Sometimes when Caroline sings along to a song she gets the lyrics wrong:

And he knows when the human comes and his job is done he'll be holding a cigar for youuuuu.

I am the word for God and boy: the man who searches and destroys.

—

Probably for the same reason, Caroline has a bad ear for languages.

'Just repeat after me,' I will say to her one day, standing in the road, with you in my arms, outside the train station that we have to go to to get to Pompeii.

'*Dov'e. Il. Ristorante.*'

'*Goonay. Snuff. Plugnofanti.*'

After the incident with Mrs Evans' diary, I started to keep a diary myself. I bought a hardback notebook with a silvery holographic cover. I used the diary to write down stories about things that had happened in school. In the diary I wrote about all of the girls who were attracted to me and all of the fights that I had had with the older boys and won and all of the commendations and plaudits that I had got from my teachers and peers and all the tries, and goals and sixes that I had scored. I tucked the silver notebook into the gap between the mattress and the slats on my bed so that nobody would find it and read it.

Even from early on, even then, my mother was always worried that I wasn't growing properly. Everybody knew that I wasn't growing properly. Everybody knew that there was something wrong. I was eleven. She went through a phase of trying to get me to drink a pint of milk every day and she went through a phase of trying to get me to tell people that I was eight instead of eleven because she was worried that people would think that she was malnourishing me.

We went to the school uniform shop and the assistant didn't have blazers that were small enough for me.

'It's an error,' my mother said. 'We came here last year. You're embarrassing my son.'

Getting one in special would cost more. We walked home. I will have to wear the ripped one.

'It has a rip in it,' I told her. 'I'll get in trouble.'

'You'll get in trouble for having ripped your blazer you mean?' she said. 'Well that seems fair to me. You shouldn't complain about things which are *just*.'

She regretted saying that and she took me to a café on the way home. The café was in Maida Vale. On the next table there was a young couple interviewing an older Greek lady for a job as a Greek-speaking nanny. It was making my mother anxious.

'How is your schoolwork?' my mother said to me, just barely drinking her strawberry milkshake through a straw. On the next table, the young couple were explaining to the old lady that they would expect to have weekly meetings with her to discuss the quality of their children's nutritional intake.

'I was a dancer,' the old Greek lady was telling them.

'Is everyone kind to you?' my mother said. She signalled to the waiter, and when he arrived, she told him that the milkshake was far too thick and could she have some milk to pour into it. I looked out of the window to avoid looking at the waiter. The old lady stood up and shook the young couple's hands and walked out of the café. The young couple waited for her to leave before agreeing with one another that she wasn't right for the position. They referred back to things that the Greek woman had said during the interview and they did her accent and they chuckled. My mother was inspecting her nails, tapping her foot in a rapid rhythm.

'Come on,' she said, putting a five-pound note on the table even though I hadn't finished my ice cream yet and the waiter hadn't returned with her milk. 'Let's go.'

—

Mrs Evans came over for dinner. Mrs Evans believed in psychosomatics. The power of what happens in your head to affect your physical health, she told me and Caoimhe. My mother continued to carve the ham. Mrs Evans was driving at something.

One night a few weeks later, I heard them discussing it in the living room. If my mother is afraid of me growing up, Mrs Evans was saying, then my body can read those signals. The body knows what she wants. I know what she wants. I want what she wants. My body knows what I want. A self-fulfilling prophecy.

'If he grows up,' Mrs Evans was saying. 'If he becomes a man. Then he will *leave*. *That's* what's on *your* mind.'

'That's why he is the way he is,' Mrs Evans was saying.

*

I'm sitting on the stairs with my head clamped between the balusters, listening in my head to my mother and Mrs Evans speaking to each other in 1992. The windows are open in the living room. It is warm and damp and dark outside. The smell of front-garden grass in the dark hallway. I straighten up and walk upstairs and along the corridor, where I pass Caroline, who is pacing up and down, rocking you to comfort you. But you can't seem to stop crying. You just cry and cry.

He Hakari Nēke

We decide to go to Ireland for a holiday, but Caroline is worried about the plane, about how you will find it. You are still only eight months old. But we need to get out of the city, out of this country. My mother is beginning to get sick. The world is beginning to get sick. We are both sick of Kilburn. Sometimes I stand outside our house and watch an idling taxi dropping off its passengers at two o'clock in the morning and spewing chains of smoke into the air and I just think: you motherfuckers, you motherfuckers.

Mostly because of her illness, my mother is being cruel to Caroline. In her demeanour. She criticizes Caroline's parenting.

'It isn't that I'm worried about the plane,' Caroline says. 'I just want to make sure that everything is healthy before we go on a foreign holiday. I just don't want to be *stranded* there in the back of beyond. That's all.'

And while we're at it, it wouldn't be a bad idea to check if the baby has inherited my condition.

So we take you to see Mac. Dr McCaul. Dr McCaul looked

after me after my first heterochronous shock, in 1994. My 'mega-puberty' he sometimes called it because he thought 'heterochronous shock' was too jargony. Or sometimes my 'mega Bar Mitzvah.'

'Because of it happening when Pol was thirteen and because he really did turn from a boy into a man overnight,' he said.

'I got it,' Caroline said, smiling politely.

He picks you up and he strips you down to your nappy. He has a way about him. Caroline just hands you over without batting an eyelid.

'Now what can we do for you today, sir?' he says to you, all of us laughing, finding it very funny, very relaxing, before he takes you into the other room. We don't see you then for another hour or so. We sit in his office and wait for him to bring you back.

'I remember that he used to have a jar of teeth in here,' I whisper to Caroline, 'like an ornament.'

Caroline nods. After a few seconds she whispers:

'Why are we whispering?'

He has a drawing of He Hakari Nēke framed on the wall in his office. He Hakari Nēke is depicted as a figure with the white bearded head of an old sage and the muscular torso of a young warrior.

Mac brings you back into his office and sits you down, in your nappy, on the edge of his desk. You just sit there, nearly naked, on the big leather-topped desk, cross-legged like a baby yogi.

'There doesn't appear to be anything amiss here,' he says, not looking at us, picking up a stack of papers. 'There doesn't appear to be anything amiss with this one whatsoever.'

—

Caroline says, sheepishly, on the way home from the hospital:

'You really are the chosen one.'

'Why?'

'It's not even in your *genes*.'

We walk all the way home.

'It's just one straight line,' Caroline says.

'It's Watling Street,' I say. 'Park Lane, Edgware Road, Maida Vale, Kilburn High Road, Shoot-Up Hill. And then the A5 all the way to Holyhead and the Irish Sea. It's all just one Roman road. Watling Street.'

Walking up Maida Vale in the sun. The sun bouncing off the brown buildings and making them look orange. Caroline is wearing her large floppy sun hat and shorts and a white T-shirt tucked into her shorts and no bra. She suddenly looks young again, pushing the pushchair, too young to be a mother even. Her sunglasses keep slipping down her nose and she has to take her hands off the handlebars of the pushchair to push them back up again. We walk past the shop that sells the deadstock leather jackets and the jackets with tassels all over them. The leather jacket shop owner has brought a record player outside on to the street and is sitting on an old ladder-back dining chair next to it, reading a magazine. The record player is playing 'Sailing' by Rod Stewart. I love this song, Caroline tells me. She pushes the foot pedal brake on the pushchair and takes her hands off the handlebars and puts her hands around my waist. We begin to slow dance in the street. Caroline goes up on tiptoes and whispers into my ear that she loves me.

*

In 1993: Mr Harrison with the acetate reproduction of the map of Watling Street which he placed on an overhead projector. He placed another acetate on top of it with a reproduction of an Ordnance Survey map of Kilburn and Maida Vale. He explained that Watling Street was one single road that was now broken up into Edgware Road, Maida Vale, Kilburn High Road, Shoot-Up Hill and Cricklewood Broadway.

'See how they overlap?' he said, even though they didn't really.

The previous week he had taken our class to see Bartholomew Playfere's notebooks which were on display in the Reading Room at the British Museum. It was the twelfth of December 1993. A big book and a small book. The man at the museum told us to gather around a large leather-topped desk. He wore thin blue latex gloves. He opened the big book, a copy of *The End of Nightwork and the Sundering of the Curtain in Twayn*. He showed us the picture of the nightingale on the frontispiece. Next he showed us a manuscript text, which he called Notebook 9, catalogued as MS 682424. We couldn't read the writing, but he traced his latex-clad finger along the long, looping hand and read to us from the obituary that Playfere had written on the occasion of his father's death:

'What wails there were, were not for his difference but for our own. For we knew that there was no account to grieve. For death was a happy change in him.'

Then he turned back to the bigger volume. He turned to recto wacb. There was Playfere's own hand-drawn map of London: a cobweb of black ink with one thin red line running like a vein through the centre of the image. Our teacher pointed this out to us and told us that this red line represented Watling Street. Playfere himself had labelled the red line with an arrow:

'The Way to Uttoxeter.'

Playfere walked out of London along that road: what would

now be Kilburn High Road and Shoot-Up Hill and the A5. He believed that the street was an artery in more ways than one. It was revealed to him in a dream that Babylonish London would be destroyed and that the Godly would escape from the inferno by marching together up Watling Street and out of the city. Which is precisely what he and about a hundred of his followers did, Mr Harrison told us. They brought horses and traps loaded with tents and gear along with the caravan. They marched together from the palace of Westminster, up old Watling Street, and they kept going – only stopping to sleep in their tents – until they got to Beaumaris, where they paid a ferryman to carry them over to Dublin. After staying in the Pale for a week, in their encampments, they began to walk again, and they walked across land to Connemara and from there took small boats out to the island.

Mr Harrison had a little book, a Ladybird book, that explored the life of the seventeenth-century prophet in a way that children would understand. It was a way of explaining the landscape of the English Civil War through the eyes of one individual. The book was only about thirty pages long. It had little line drawings in it. There was a drawing of a typical wattle-panelled cottage in Wymondham, where Playfere was born. There was a drawing of a Roundhead in musketeer's uniform: the kind that Playfere himself would have worn when he was mustered into the Parliamentarian forces in 1646. There was a drawing of a preacher standing on a tub in Swan Alley, preaching to a crowd of the intrigued. Next to the picture, the book included an extract from one of Bartholomew Playfere's sermons, printed in a speech bubble:

'And those that said to me why art thou come into Towne to make divisions were answered not by mine tongue but by the

Lord who promiseth such fire as will cuppell His creation. Since the last Days foretold and forewarn'd of by our Saviour, are at hand, wherein iniquity abounds, and the love of many waxes cold; hence Father against Son, and Son against Father, betraying one another, and hating one another; hence the Judgments of Famine and Pestilence; Nation rising up against Nation. So that the whole World seems to be on Fire before its time and the birds of the air will gather in the darkling sky and will tear out the eyes of the slaves of Sathan.'

The most interesting picture in the Ladybird book was the one of the carved wooden model of Jerusalem that Playfere and his companion Christopher Poole had constructed in the year 1655. Playfere spent the summer of 1654 having visions and dreams about the New Jerusalem that would be built on the islands of the west, on the eve of the Millennium. He would return from his visions in a fever and would write down as much as he could remember in his notebooks. He filled his notebooks with details about alleyways and barracks and fountains and emerald-studded buildings and plumes of smoke. He wrote descriptions of the uniforms that would be worn by the halberdiers and musketeers who would guard the walls and portcullises of New Jerusalem against the incursions of Gog and Magog. He described the complex system of hypocausts and aqueducts which would keep the sons of Israel warm and watered. He spent the winter reading these notes and replicating the images in sketches and designs. Only when he befriended Christopher Poole, who was already a famous wood-carver and sculptor, did the plans for a prototype emerge. Poole had heard Playfere preach at the intersection of Swan Alley and Old Jewry and was convinced of the veracity of Playfere's prophecies. As an act of piety, he spent two years carving a model of Jerusalem that was based precisely on the scales and measurements and sketches that Playfere had produced. It was about five feet by five feet in proportion and was carved out of the wood from a single giant oak. In the picture in the Ladybird book the model had wheels. Actually, the wheels were only added later. Poole and Playfere got the idea of moving the model from site to site so as to act as an aid for Playfere's tub-preaching. The model became an attraction in itself. Poole and Playfere added iron wheels and an iron handle and it was the job of Christopher Poole's seventeen-year-old son – Do-Right Poole – to manipulate the wheeled model and to steer it through the streets around Paternoster Square, Swan Alley, Coleman Street and Old Jewry. In the 1970s, Christopher Hill called it the greatest ever portable work of art.

On the very last page of the Ladybird book there was a picture of an abandoned monastery on top of a cliff. The monastery was on the island. The island which would be attacked by all the nations of the world but which would hold out until the floodwaters rose and drowned all the enemies of the people of God, and all their chariots, and all their foreign territory, leaving only the little island peeping above sea level. The people of God squatted there, in the abandoned monastery, for nine years, until the crops failed and they all died. Shortly afterwards, the cliff began to subside, and the monastery fell into the sea. The flood still hadn't come.

I stole the Ladybird book. I took it home. I took it everywhere. It was a frightening book for a child, really, because it contained within it prophecies concerning the end of the world. My mother turned to the page with the picture of the monastery on the cliff.

'Your father and I went to this island on our honeymoon,' she said. It was only then that I remembered her tears when my grandfather had proposed taking us out on the boat to the island.

I remember where we were when I showed my mother the Ladybird book, the little drawing of the doomed monastery. We were sitting in the waiting room of the GP surgery. The GP surgery is in an old Georgian townhouse off the Kilburn High Road. I think it's called Cambridge Avenue. White paint flaking off the walls, off the pillars and off the heads of the little rampant lions that stand atop the pillars. Back then, the interior was all dark-wood panelling. The clock was stopped. There were letters engraved into the wood panelling and painted in gilt, saying: *Either Help Or Do No Harm*. There was a Bangladeshi woman with a huge Alsatian on a leash. My mother leaned over and whispered in my ear.

'I didn't know that they liked dogs,' she said. After a while, she leaned over again.

'I didn't know that dogs were allowed in the waiting room,' she said.

The doctor had told her off once before.

'Have you been administering enemas to your son?' the doctor had said. My mother saying nothing.

'It's advisable not to do that,' the doctor had said. 'It's really highly advisable not to do things like that.'

He had stood up and walked around the room. He had told my mother that administering enemas could rupture my rectum because the enemas were adult-sized enemas, made for adult-sized anuses. The doctor told my mother to tell him who had given her the enemas. Whoever it was had nearly caused great harm to me and had the potential to cause great harm to some other child. My mother kept her mouth shut. She wasn't going to be bullied.

The enemas were actually from a Chinese doctor on the Edgware Road. The Chinese doctor had told her that they were herbal remedies. He'd told her that my condition was common in China, much more common than in Europe, and that he recognized the symptoms and knew of a ready-made cure. The only downside was that the ready-made cure had to be administered rectally. Anyway, it turned out later that they were just rehydration medications which you could buy over the counter in America and which the Chinese doctor had smuggled into the country on his way back from a holiday in Florida.

'Your mother didn't give you an enema,' Caroline says, doubled over with laughter, when I get to this part of the story. 'She was probably just taking your temperature rectally.'

She can laugh but it's true. It really was enemas.

'What did it feel like then?' Caroline says. 'When your mother was administering these mysterious enemas.'

I shrug. I remember all of these surrounding details but I have no recollection at all of my mother administering them. I suppose I must have blocked it out.

'*Enemas*,' Caroline chuckles, scoldingly.

On that particular day, when the doctor let us into his office, I could tell that he was frightened of my mother. He was young, with light blond hair and a downy light blond moustache.

'I know that it is frustrating,' he said. 'But there really is not much more we can do at this stage. It really isn't uncommon for puberty to be quite delayed in boys.'

'Delayed?' my mother said. Her voice became very Irish when she was angry. 'This boy is nearly fifteen years of age. You don't see anything uncommon here?'

He squirmed. I could tell that he didn't want to point out

64

that I was actually only thirteen. He glanced down at my notes and then looked back at us.

'If you're really worried, perhaps I can refer you to a neotenics consultant. It might take a long time. Would you like me to do that?'

When we got back from the GP, Caoimhe was on the swing in the back garden that my mother's brother made for us when he came over to build the Jubilee line. I had a special kind of disease that only one in ten billion people in the whole world have, I told her. Caoimhe went higher and higher on the swing.

'What did he *really* say?' she asked.

My mother came out into the garden.

'My God Caoimhe!' she exclaimed. 'You look like an angel.'

*

It is dusk by the time we get back to the house. It's taken us nearly an hour and a half to walk the length of Watling Street. Summerdusk. Makes you sleepy in your pram. We lift you out of the pram and put you into your crib. We've brought the crib down into the living room. It has four white pillars from which the actual crib part is suspended. The wind from the open window swings the crib back and forth. The wind blows through the darkness of the unilluminated room.

'Wooo!' says Caroline and pushes the crib a little bit. You laugh: a sweet, gurgling giggle. I walk over to the TV and turn it on. The room turns blue from the light from the big TV. More plastic surgeons have been assassinated in Afghanistan. Caroline keeps one hand on the crib but switches her attention away from you and towards the TV.

'Have you heard about this?' she says. I nod, but don't turn to face her.

'Blacked-out Humvees turning up outside people's houses,' Caroline continues. 'These little suburban bungalows.'

I make a joke about feminists and jihadists having some common cause in their shared objection to plastic surgery.

'Put your head inside a box of poisonous insects,' Caroline says. 'And let them bite you.'

II

There Is a Giant Head You Can Walk Around Inside Of

At the Wellcome Collection there is an exhibition about brains that is designed for children. There never seems to be anywhere to sit. I always end up getting a pain in my coccyx.

'It's from all the bending down,' Caroline says. 'Toddlers are such a bad design. Why are they so much shorter than adults? And given that they're so much shorter, why can't they climb up us? Why can't they scramble up us the way a marmoset scrambles up a tree? Other primate babies scramble up their parents, don't they? I *think* I've seen that.'

'I feel as though I've been scrambled up plenty,' I say, and Caroline laughs.

But it's true that you ask to be picked up and carried more than other three-year-olds. I'm pretty sure of that. I'm pretty sure that I've seen other three-year-olds that don't need to be picked up like several times per hour. After a few minutes Caroline always passes you over to me and – because I can – I end up carrying you around for afternoons at a time.

'It's good for my core strength,' Caroline says, shrugging defensively, whenever Caoimhe asks how she manages.

'Yeah,' Caoimhe says. 'Really handy if you ever want to give up teaching and become a shot-putter.'

'Or a postman,' Caroline says, refusing to be laughed at.

In Connemara, at the end of the nineteenth century, postmen would arrive in villages with sackfuls of mail, only to find that the entire population had disappeared. Goats would wander down from the mountains and would sit on the roofs and nibble at the rotting thatch. Nobody knows where the people went.

'Don't you think that that's probably a myth,' Caoimhe would say. 'A cultural memory to do with trauma passed down from – like – the famine or whatever?'

'*Like – the famine,*' my mother would repeat, doing an impression of Caoimhe's voice but mixed with Californian. As she got sicker, she would do unflattering impressions of her children more and more.

There is a giant head you can walk around inside of. There are synapses that light up when you touch them. There is a vat of gloop with a rubber replica of a brain suspended in it. The vat is sealed with a lid, but there are rubber gloves attached to openings in the lid so that you can reach in with your hands to touch the surface of the brain. I bring you over to the vat and show you how to do it. I guide your hands, by your elbows, towards the artificial brain. You chuckle and then begin to whimper, and then you wriggle out of my grasp and run over to the other side of the gallery. On the other side of the gallery, you sit down at the feet of a twenty-year-old woman who is reading aloud from a giant-sized picture book about the life of Oliver Sacks. I reach my hands down into the rubber gloves. The gloop is cold. When my fingers touch the surface of the replica brain, they instinctively shrink from it. Slowly I glide my fingers over the soft, cold, grey ridges.

—

Caroline comes over and nudges me. She has her hands plunged deep into the pockets of her overcoat and her elbows out and her knees bent. It gives her the vibe of a rationing-era black marketeer or an illegitimate turf accountant.

'Live long and prosper,' she says, pulling one hand out of her pocket and making the Vulcan sign with her fingers. We walk over to where you are sitting with the other children, listening to the young woman read from the storybook.

'How much do you think one of them makes?' I ask Caroline.

'I think they're drama students,' Caroline says.

One of the drama students takes the children on a guided tour of the inside of the giant head, and we hand you over to her and then go into one of the other rooms. This room is separate from the children's exhibition and there are only adults in here. There is a social dreaming workshop going on. There are people sitting in a circle around a facilitator. The facilitator is explaining what a social dreaming workshop is. Caroline and I sit down in the circle.

Nobody else in the group is speaking so I decide to go first.

'I have a recurring dream,' I say. 'That I'm playing a football game on the PlayStation with my son, but then I try to move the controls and the players don't respond to my instructions. Then after a while they start crouching down on their haunches and putting their heads in their hands or looking up towards me through the screen with disparaging looks on their faces.'

Nobody has anything to say about that. The silence is only broken by the sound of a woman, on the other side of the gallery, who is arguing with somebody over the phone.

'I don't care that you're expecting me to be there,' the woman is saying. 'I'm telling you that I'm *not* going to be there.'

We all wait for a museum attendant to usher the woman out of the gallery. The woman sees the attendant approaching and walks briskly towards the exit, her high heels clacking on the hardwood herringbone floor. Caroline says:

'Do recurring dreams exist? Isn't it more likely that we just *dream* that the dream is recurring? And then, perhaps, when you wake up and tell people that you've had a recurring dream, it becomes like a self-fulfilling prophecy? Like you start to dream about it because you start to obsess about it?'

She laughs. There is another silence. An older woman, wearing a blue shawl-collared cardigan, turns towards me and says:

'I think that your dream might have something to do with feelings of masculinity.'

The facilitator holds up a gently reprimanding hand and says:

'Our objective here is not to analyze each other's dreams, but rather to talk about the elements of other people's dreams, as they describe them, which resonate with our own dream experiences and thereby to collectively come to a fuller picture – a fuller understanding – of the society in which we live. Let's try to confine ourselves to making contributions which are only concerned with what you have been dreaming about recently or what the dreams of the other people in the group remind you of.'

She smiles beneficently at the woman in the shawl-collared cardigan, who avoids her gaze. There is another silence. The facilitator says, softly:

'Let's try to be free-associative here.'

'The worst dream I have,' says an elderly man in a worn-out leather jacket, 'is I wake up in the morning and the ceiling is coming towards me.'

Once I dreamt that I was in a house in Connemara. It was similar to – but not the same as – a house that my uncle had taken me to when I was a child. I was eight. The house had no internal walls. There were leaves on the floor. There were holes in the thatch through which we could see the sky. There was grass where the floor should be, but the grass was wispy and anaemic. The grass had died and dried in places and had been uprooted and blown around the house in the wind.

But in the dream, there was an upstairs. There was even dry grass on the floor upstairs, in the bedrooms. This was my house, I realized: my mother's house. In the dream, my uncle tried to reassure me. There is no one here, he told me, but that's all right. He didn't feel the absence of people. But the people who didn't live in the house were as real as ghosts to me.

After the Wellcome, I drop in on Caoimhe while Caroline takes you home. Caoimhe has moved back into the house where we grew up, to look after our mother. Caoimhe is afraid that our mother is immortal.

'I don't know,' she says. 'I know it sounds crazy.'

'Not in a supernatural way,' she says.

'Not in a supernatural way?' I reply. 'Well that's good to know.'

On the wall in the kitchen they still have that framed picture of me standing on stage in the committee room in the Mansion House in 1994. The little sign – Pol Meyer, Aged 11 – in my hands. Caoimhe taps the pane.

'Your finest hour,' she says.

I remember my mother, sitting on the worktop stirring the beans. She: carving a triangle of cheddar cheese into the beans, making the mixture salty and translucent. Going out of the room to call Caoimhe. Calling back into the kitchen to tell me to check on the fish fingers under the grill. My mother called fish fingers 'fished fingers'.

While we were eating, she sat at the end of the table smoking and reading the paper. No food, just cigarettes. Outside in the garden a bird was pecking at another bird. The other bird was lying on the ground. It looked dead. The garden in that house was long and thin. At the bottom of the garden there was a white fence. Beyond the fence was the communal garden for the mansion block. The mansion block towered over us like Vesuvius. It was the summer. In the bright sunlight, the bricks were white and orange, bright white and bright orange. The first bird shambled into the air. My mother: following my line of sight and then looking at me and then smiling quizzically. She weighed five or six stone at that point. She was wearing a cornflower blue summer dress with a white watercress pattern. She placed the newspaper down on the kitchen table in front of me. She smoothed out the paper and tapped on it with her index fingernail.

'See,' she said.

But I was too old by nine months. The competition rules said six to twelve years of age. She told me that it didn't matter.

'Don't be such a Pisces, Pol,' she said.

'Pisces Pol,' said Caoimhe, laughing, reading her magazine.

'We'll say that we misread the rules if anyone asks. Nobody is going to ask. It's not really cheating. It's not as though everyone suddenly gets better at writing short stories on their thirteenth birthday. Nobody is going to ask anyway.'

'Nobody is going to ask for your birth certificate Pol,' Caoimhe said. 'They're not going to ask for your passport.'

'He doesn't even have a passport.'

'I know that. It's a figure of speech.'

'Nobody is going to think that you're over twelve. Believe me. And if anyone *does* ask, you just tell them it doesn't matter.'

The invitation came in the post. It was on thick card, with an illustration by Quentin Blake, who was one of the judges.

You have been shortlisted.

Lord Mayor's Young People of London Short Story Prize.

Mrs Evans didn't even know the word shortlisted.

'I thought that it might mean that you were in trouble,' she said, with a flush of relief. My mother laughed at her.

'Jesus, Deirdre,' my mother said. 'What in God's name would he be in trouble for anyways?'

The two of them picked me up, each taking one arm and one leg, and paraded me around the kitchen.

My story was about a village on a hill. The villagers on the hill are suspicious about their neighbour who lives on his own in a little house at the bottom of the hill. He is likeable, but the villagers are troubled by his choice of lifestyle. The villagers decide to play a prank on their neighbour by rolling a giant snowball down the hill towards him. But they underestimate the girth and power that the snowball will gather when rolling at speed, and they accidentally destroy the neighbour's house and kill the neighbour. When they discover that the neighbour is dead, they hold a commemorative service for him. They remember, together, all of the good things about him.

'You wrote this?' said Caroline, years later, when she read the story.

'Yes.'

'*You* wrote it?'

'Because it's good or because it's bad?'

75

'Neither,' Caroline said. 'I'm just surprised that a thirteen-year-old wrote this.'

I remember the footlights. From where we were standing, at the back of the stage, I remember the heat that came off the footlights and the way that the light from the footlights glinted and refracted through Quentin Blake's glasses and how it caught and changed the colour of Quentin Blake's hair and formed a halo of dust around his head from behind while he was making a speech from the podium about the stories that we had all written.

All of the stories demonstrated remarkable maturity for such young writers, Quentin Blake said. He had no doubt that we would all go on to become great writers in the future. The audience was laughing. I didn't understand why they were laughing. Quentin Blake turned and smiled at us a little awkwardly. The Lord Mayor, in his chain, in his big wooden throne, turned around and smiled at us also. The boy to my right whispered out of the side of his mouth.

'What school are you in?' he said.

'It doesn't matter,' I said.

'What year are you in?' he said.

'It doesn't matter,' I said.

'How much do you think his chain costs?' he said.

Outside I feel like there was an oompah band playing. My mother bought me an ice cream. She said that she was proud of me.

'You never told me where the idea for the story came from,' she said.

She lit a cigarette. The smoke mixed with the music in the air. The smoke tangled in her hair and the wind blew strands suddenly across her face and she was then reaching up with her free hand to free herself. There was a patch of empty scalp at the back of her head which the wind was exposing. We walked down to the river, to Southwark Bridge. We leaned over the rail and looked down at the pillows of sudsy white flotsam billowing in the wind and rocking on the surface of the black water.

When I look at the small photo of all the young writers standing in a line on the stage, I can't believe how small. How small the stage is. I remember it was called committee room B or something. It looks more like a parish hall.

A man in the picture was later in a dream that I had, walking around the city all night with a piece of chalk in his hand, marking on all the buildings the expected point that the Thames would rise to, changing the property values forever. The Thames already up to his armpits as he stretched up to draw the Plimsoll line, higher and higher.

That row of children. They made us hold signs in front of us with our names written on them and our ages. I wrote '11' on mine, even though I was really thirteen. None of them became writers of course. Or at least I don't recognize any of the names. All the fathers wearing suits, I notice. About half of them seem to have those thick square-framed glasses, those thick black square cameras in their hands.

You can't see it in the photo, but I'm standing on the edge of a cliff. I'm standing on the side of a hill, the ground giving way beneath my feet, like slurry. I was starting to have bad dreams. White toothpaste streaming down a hillside. White blood cells streaming through a city. Nightmares screaming in the night cells. Church bells pealing in bridewells.

—

Caoimhe goes to the kitchen and comes back with a plastic jug of water. The plastic jug is translucent and is decorated with pictures of multicoloured balloons all around the side. Except the balloons are faded and scratched away. The white ceiling in the house is yellowed with fag smoke. I glance through the open door into the kitchen and I can see the marble painting that you and Caroline made for my mum's birthday Sellotaped to the door of the fridge. On the worktop in the kitchen there is a pair of electric hair clippers. From her bed, which is set up on the other side of the living room, my mother says, softly:

'*Wir müssen diesen Ort verlassen. Die Leute hier sind so provinziell.*'

'There's no such thing as dying of old age,' Caoimhe says. 'She eats like a horse. She never leaves this room. The doctors says that her heart is immaculate. She's not going to get hit by a car or catch a virus or have a heart attack.'

'*Wissen Sie, wann wir am nächsten Bahnhof ankommen werden?*' my mother says. '*Der regen fällt so stark.*'

'Want to make it interesting?' I say, reaching into my pocket for two folded fivers. I hold the two fivers up and rub them together between forefinger and thumb and smile, temptingly. Caoimhe pretends to be shocked and then breaks into a scandalized laugh, covering the bottom of her face with her hand.

Just before I leave, I think about asking her about the clippers on the worktop.

'What?' she says, as I pause on the threshold.

'Nothing,' I say.

'Spending a lot of time with somebody who has dementia,'

Caoimhe said to me once, 'is not so different from being able to read somebody's diary.'

'I can see the appeal of that,' I said.

Later on, when I get home, I tell Caroline about my mother's condition and about how my mother believes that she is on a long train journey, somewhere in Germany. She thinks that she is twenty years old. It's interesting how you can almost tell from her facial expressions that she thinks she is young. It's the only way that she can put together the glimpses of different places and people, that seem to flit through her consciousness, into a coherent narrative. Caroline is clipping your toenails. Somehow you have developed a fungal infection on your feet and your toenails are yellow and cauliflowery. You cry out in pain whenever the clippers get too close to the cuticle. But your nails are so small, there's barely anything to cut.

'Is that what your mother thinks,' Caroline says, 'or is that what Caoimhe *thinks* that your mother thinks?'

I hang my rucksack on the coatrack in the hallway.

'I suppose she's just trying to make sense of the things that Mum is saying,' I reply. 'Sometimes it's hard to make out. She speaks so softly.'

Caroline said once that she and Caoimhe were opposites. I think it was a subtle way for her to say that she and *I* are opposites. When we first moved into the flat on Iverson Road, we found a chest of drawers, that the previous people had left behind, standing in the middle of the living room. Actually, it must have been there for some time because the flat had been unoccupied for a couple of years at least. The walls in the living room, when we first moved in, were a kind of a greenish white and the carpet was green too, with a large reddish-brown stain in one corner.

—

The chest of drawers was made of pine. It looked as though somebody had tried to move it but had given up. The drawers were lined with wrapping paper. The wrapping paper was matt and faded. It was blue with pictures of Donald Duck and Mickey Mouse on it. When I touched the paper it was sticky in places. In the third drawer down, I found a small piece of cotton wool. When the cotton wool unfurled in my hand I could see that it was wrapped around a tooth. It was a milk tooth. It was yellow and white and it glowed yellow, like a bead of amber, when I held it up to the light. In the socket part, where the tooth had once been attached to the root, in somebody's mouth, there were three minuscule reservoirs of grey lint. I took the tooth to show Caroline. She was exasperated with me. She was busy stripping the woodchip wallpaper off the walls in the room that she would later lock and later still unlock and decorate in preparation for your nativity.

'Why are you showing me this,' she said, not turning to face me. I didn't know how to answer.

'Doesn't it give you a strange feeling?' I replied.

But I could tell, even without her saying anything, that she didn't know what I meant.

But it gave me a strange feeling. It invaded my dreams that night. Yellow teeth, pouring out of a cereal box, into a white bowl. White toothpaste streaming down a hillside. White blood cells streaming through a chilly city. An ambulance hurrying through the night in 1994.

Charlie Manson Cunt

When the ambulance arrived, that night in 1994, the paramedics said that my mother could ride in it with me and I couldn't say that I didn't want her to because the oxygen mask was covering my mouth. I was only thirteen years old. They all would have forgiven me.

I know from the dates that only a few days before the attack I had been standing on the stage in Mansion House, but that timeline feels intolerable to me. Those days, in my memory, are like a chasm, with one me standing on one side staring at another me standing on the other side.

My mother saying that she will pray for the rest of her life and that she will just spend the rest of her life saying sorry to everyone – to me, to Jesus, to the doctors, to the government – if anyone can prove that this is all her fault.

The doctors ushering her into a different room.

'Can't you see that you're upsetting him?' she was screaming. I can't remember anything else from that night except for the smell of the shaving soap.

—

The nurses came in to shave me every day. The sweet and memorable smell of the shaving soap. The mixture of pain and oblivion like vodka mixed with milk. The white porcelain tiles like an old-fashioned butcher's shop. The spatter of blood on the white porcelain tiles. Now and then my mother's voice, echoing towards me down a long corridor.

They had to shave me every day, because the beard and body hair growth was so rapid that it was getting in the way of the doctors who were trying to operate on me.

'The Play-Doh hair salon. Do you remember that?' my mother said, years later. 'It was like that.'

But other than the shaving, the doctors got everything wrong. They were trying to stop my heart from stopping. They were trying to stop my head from growing too quickly. They were cutting me open to get to my heart. My heart was just adapting to the task of pumping blood around my new body. That's why the monitors were going haywire. They should really have been trying to administer drugs that would act as growth hormone receptor antagonists. They should really have been trying to do something to dam the amount of somatotropin that the anterior lobe of my pituitary gland was secreting. That's what was causing the rapid beard growth. They weren't to know really. They just saw a thirteen-year-old boy who seemed to be growing a full beard every two hours and whose limbs were almost discernibly extending and whose skull was expanding. A boy turning into a man before their very eyes. The neotenics experts should have been called. But they weren't. The neotenics experts were only called in on the second or third day. By that point they couldn't help. They could only comment. They just came up to the ward to marvel at me, because I was so strange and new.

—

Sometimes long processions of people appeared to be walking through my room and I would hunt around in the crowd for a policeman who could divert the crowds away. The crowds were cheerful, they carried placards with funny phrases on them.

You Have Made a Deadcision, We Have Deadcided.

None of them looked at me. Later on I will see those signs again outside Mornington Crescent tube station while watching a Kourist protest, trying to pick out Cynthia in the crowd. Cynthia.

At other times it would just be my father, standing at the foot of my bed, sometimes clothed, sometimes naked. Blue of scalp.

They didn't let anybody except my mother see me until all of the surgery had been done. The first time Caoimhe saw me, she burst into tears.

'Jesus Christ,' she said. 'You look like the Exorcist.'

There were hushed conversations on the new ward. After the worst had subsided, I was moved into a public bed, but they didn't know where to put me so in the end they put me on a paediatric ward because technically – or chronologically or whatever – I was still only thirteen years of age. They wheeled me down the ramp on to the ward in my wheelchair. The other parents on the ward looked confused at first, and then they became disturbed.

'That's not a patient,' one of the mothers said to the orderly who was wheeling my wheelchair. 'That's not a patient on this ward, I gather?'

Usually it was just mothers on the ward, but when the controversy started I began to see more fathers on the ward. The fathers were in charge of having the hushed conversations with the nurses. I remember one who was especially angry, especially disturbed. He said that he wasn't going to leave his ten-year-old daughter to sleep on the same ward as that giant Charlie-Manson-looking cunt. That six-foot hairy cunt. It wasn't my fault. They wouldn't give me a haircut on the ward and they tried to tame my beard but it kept growing back every single day until they finally gave up. But I sympathize with the man in retrospect. When I think about *you* being in that situation in particular. I wouldn't want you to have to share a ward with a Charlie-Manson-looking cunt if you were in hospital.

In the end they had to move me back into the private room again. My presence on the children's ward, even though (in chronological terms) I would be a child for another five years, was too controversial.

'Is this your daughter,' a nurse said to me, unthinkingly, when Caoimhe came to visit.

'Do you recognize me, Pol? Do you know me? It's me. Caoimhe.'

'You have to see the pictures,' Caroline says, these days, when we have people over to dinner. 'Let me just get the pictures.'
    'This is you, when?' our guests say. 'Last year? Last summer?'
    And I tell them that it is a picture of me from 1994, when I was thirteen years old. And Caroline points out that not a single line on my face had changed, from that day to this. And the guests all remark on the rare and curious nature of my condition before moving on to a different topic of conversation.

When the neotenics experts came to examine me, they were better able to explain what had happened.

'Isn't it always the way,' Mrs Evans remarked. 'They can explain everything *after* the event. But at the time they can't explain *anything*. Retrospect.'

They had spent days poring over the details of my case. It was a constantly evolving picture, they said. Caoimhe and my mother sat at the other end of the room on wipeable plastic wingback armchairs. The neotenics experts stood in an arc around my bed. There were nine of them. The science around human heterochrony was all very new, the neotenics doctors said, but there was a small handful of precedents. What I had experienced, in very simple terms, was a kind of radically expedited pubescence. In the course of a few days, my body had decided to undertake the same task that most human bodies undertake over the course of a few years: usually between the age of twelve and around twenty-two. The doctors were pointing to areas of my body using one of those lecturers' pointers, like a slender pool cue, while describing the radical changes in my musculature, my beard and general body hair, the size of my feet and hands, the shape of my genitals. I remember thinking that this was all a little redundant.

'We can expect a similar event to happen again,' one of the doctors said, hedging. 'But when it will happen – ten, fifteen, twenty years' time – we can't know. And how severe? It is possible that Pol can expect to have an attack in future that will cause him to age by another thirty or forty years. Unless the correct somatotropin inhibitors are used. Between now and the next attack it seems likely that his body will not undergo the same ageing process that you or I experience.'

'After it's already happened they'll know,' said Mrs Evans, later on, in the car on the way home. 'After it's already happened they'll explain why it happened then.'

—

'Think of this as like tectonic plates,' another doctor said. 'When tectonic plates move properly they just gently glide along nice and easy. This is what life is like for you and me: we gradually age, very gradually, over a very long period of time. With tectonic plates, sometimes something blocks the tectonic plates. Then there is a lot of friction building up, building up, building up. When finally the tectonic plates move, it is not with a smooth, gradual movement. It is with a quick, explosive type of movement. And then what happens? An earthquake happens. This is what happened to the somatotropin in Pol's body. It is supposed to flow easily and consistently. But something was blocking it. When this blockage couldn't resist the flow of somatotropin any more, there was a huge torrent of somatotropin flowing through Pol's system. The amount of somatotropin that you expect to be released in a decade was released in only a few hours. Earthquake.'

So not like an earthquake, Caoimhe wanted to clarify, but more like a flood. More like *the* Flood. My mother clipped her ear.

My mother came in and out of my head like a dream. Like a tide. The sound of the cars in the street like a tide. The sounds of the old-fashioned medical machines. The sound of the medical footsteps along the tiled floors outside my room, like a clock. The perfume of the disinfectant that filled the ward. The perfume of the nurses' perfume. The mouthwash and shaving soap and all the years afterwards, forever and ever.

And for all the years afterwards forever we would have to check in with Dr McCaul and the neotenics specialists every fortnight or at *least* every month.

'Don't think of it as being like a guinea pig,' one of the foreign specialists said, even though we didn't. 'Think of it as being like a *privilege*.'

86

But other people did seem to see me as a guinea pig. Letters and little packets of literature started arriving from all over the world. There was a whole group of people – a 'community' they would call themselves – who believed that people like McCaul were crooks, that the whole concept of the condition that he had helped to discover was a lie, was invented to cover up some secret experiments that government scientists had been conducting on pregnant women during the Cold War. The Americans, the West Germans and the British had injected a select number of women with special hormones that were intended to make their unborn children into a kind of master race. This group called themselves the Independent Scientific Platform. I still get letters and pamphlets from them to this day:

'When you look at the history of the pharmaceutical and medical establishment. When you think about the ways in which governments have used the priesthood of medical so-called science. When you think about the Tuskegee Syphilis Study or Operation Whitecoat or the so-called MMR vaccine. Then I wonder why you would ever choose to put your lives in the hands of these people.'

'Did you hear the one about the Whore of Babylon?'

My mother, ignoring Caoimhe, putting on a new skirt suit that she had bought from M&S. We were getting ready to go to my appointment.

'So now you're going to try to marry the *neotenics doctor*?' said Caoimhe from behind her magazine. '*Good* plan.'

Dr McCaul told us to call him Mac. He was tall and broad and chieftainly with a broad, chieftainly smile. He was still young. There was a brass plaque next to the door of his office. There was a jar of teeth on a shelf behind his head.

'Ignore the jar of teeth,' he said, smiling. 'Somebody's idea of a joke.'

He sketched out what the future would look like for us. There were no technologies available to us that would allow me to live a normal life, to age at a normal rate. In a way, the medical team planned to augment the disorder, to give me drugs that would further impede the secretion of somatotropin, prevent me from ageing at all for as long as possible. Maybe it would work for ten years, maybe twenty or thirty. But it wasn't a long-term solution. Some day, something terrible would happen.

The teeth were old, like antiquarian, and the jar was not polished or medical looking at all. It was more like a Kilner jar; more like the kind of thing that you might find in a rustic kitchen, filled with cereal, or in an Edwardian sweet shop.

'What a beautiful view,' my mother said, trying to ignore the jar of teeth, looking instead out of the window, at the many trees of Queen Square.

Everywhere Looks Literally Exactly the Same as Everywhere Else

Caroline only stopped playing the violin properly when you were born. She played all the way up to the day you were born.

'I never appreciated how hard it was on the stomach,' she said, 'until that goddamn C-section.'

She even brought her violin with her to the island when we went on our honeymoon. It annoyed me at the time. It seemed like a burden. That makes me sad to think about now. She had a violin case that strapped to her back like a backpack.

It is our fourth wedding anniversary.

'*Back to the island*,' Caroline sings, from the Vengaboys song, over and over, even when nobody else is in the room.

But I couldn't face the train. The idea was so depressing to me somehow. Instead, even though it was more expensive, we flew to Knock and got the bus to Westport and the ferry from Westport. You didn't like the smell of the boat. It smelt of sheep and salt. The ferryman was an evangelical.

'Did you know that God Almighty had a Son?' the ferryman asked Caroline.

'Sort of a when-did-you-stop-beating-your-wife-type question,' Caroline said to me later, recounting the conversation.

We wanted to stay at the house that my parents had stayed at for their honeymoon – the Yeats-Was-Here house. It had been redone with European money. But they wouldn't let us.

'Are you artists?' the woman said over the phone. I didn't understand the question.

We settled on a little hotel that my uncle knew the owner of. The owner was a big, friendly woman. She looked after you one night so that Caroline and I could have a romantic dinner together. We left you with her at reception and she took you into an adjoining room which was the family's living room. We went through to the restaurant. We ordered bacon and cabbage, but the waiter came back and said that they had run out of bacon and would we have steaks instead for the same price. We both ordered steaks.

'There goes everything,' Caroline said, when the waiter left.

'Stop,' I said.

One day I will see her form, made out of the darkness, perched on the end of my bed, and she will speak to me. And then, after that, occasionally. Sometimes you will be there, next to her, your back turned towards me. And when I sit up in bed you will be gone again.

When we first visited the island, on our honeymoon, we barely explored it. This time, we want to see the beauty spots. The woman who owns the hotel gives us the card of a man who does tours. They let us phone the number on the card from the telephone at reception because there are no telephones in the rooms and our mobile phones don't work on the island.

—

A Jeep pulls up in front of the hotel. A man called Anthony, with greying, tufty hair and a reddish complexion, jumps out of the Jeep and shakes our hands and helps us to put our stuff in the boot of the car. In the back seat of the car there is a little boy, a few years older than you, seven or eight, playing on a Gameboy.

'Say hello, Duncan,' Anthony says, following my gaze. The boy waves, without turning around to look at us.

'I'll just need to drop him off at his mother's,' Anthony says. 'Then we'll start the tour.'

We get into the car. You sit in the back with Caroline and Duncan. I sit in the front next to Anthony. You are transfixed by Duncan's Gameboy. You stare and stare. Duncan notices your plaintive expression and he turns his shoulder to block your view of the screen. Anthony keeps one hand on the wheel, and he reaches behind his seat with his other hand and punches Duncan twice on the legs. He never takes his eyes off the road.

By the time we reach Duncan's mother's house, Duncan's face is wet with tears. Anthony parks the car in front of the house. Duncan opens the car door and jumps down and runs towards the house, the Gameboy clutched tightly in his hands. Anthony sounds the car horn twice and then drives off, leaving Duncan standing on the threshold. You crane your neck to stare at Duncan through the back window of the Jeep as we drive away, saying nothing.

We drive out of the town and into the countryside. The branches and high grasses which form the hedgerows on either side of the narrow road whip against the windows as we drive. You don't like the sound. Caroline covers your ears with her hands.

'Do you live here, Anthony?' Caroline asks, loudly. Anthony glances at her in the rear-view mirror briefly and then nods. A few seconds later he asks:

'And ye are from England?'

We nod.

After a while Anthony pulls off the road and drives on to the land which forms the perimeter of the bog. He brings the car to a standstill and then tells us that we can get out to stretch our legs. Caroline opens the door and you climb out.

You push down on the ground with the tip of your shoe, testing the sponginess of the surface. Anthony lights a cigarette.

'The people from hereabouts still dig their peat here,' he says. 'For fires.'

I point at the ground. I say to you:

'Some people a long time ago thought that there was going to be a huge flood which would cover everywhere on the planet, just like in the story of Noah's Ark. And they thought that this would be the only place which *wasn't* going to be covered with water. And so they came to live here.'

You look confused.

'Jesus Pol,' Caroline says, under her breath.

We get back into the car and drive down towards the sea. We drive down the narrow coast road for twenty minutes. Whenever the long grasses by the side of the road whip against the windows, you clamp your hands over your ears. It irritates me. Anthony lights a cigarette and opens the window and blows the smoke out. The wind thumps loudly through the half-opened window. I turn to see if Caroline is looking at me and I see that she is. I turn back to face the windscreen. You stretch your seat belt out and clamp your arms over the top of it. To stop it from strangling you, you tell Caroline. Caroline wrestles you back into the seat belt. You do it again. You start to whimper.

'Maybe we could just stop here?' Caroline says, pointing out of the window at one of the idyllic sandy coves that seem to flit past every few minutes. 'It really is beautiful along this stretch of coast. Any of these places look like they would be nice places to stop.'

I can feel her, in the silence that follows, glaring at the nape of my neck. Either Anthony really doesn't hear her or else he just pretends not to and continues to drive.

'Perhaps we could pause here for a breather?' I say, my voice raised over the throbbing percussive sound of the wind through the car windows. 'I think we'd like to have a look at some of these spots.'

Anthony doesn't react. Then, after a minute, he shouts:

'We're just around this bend in the road ahead. Five minutes now.'

There isn't much I can say to that. I glance at you and notice that you look a little green at the gills. I feel a little green at the gills also. I sit back in the seat and try not to think about Caroline looking at me.

I remember when we came here on our honeymoon, that we went down to the sea one day and we took our shoes and socks off and let our feet sink into the sand. The water seemed black to me. But Caroline told me that it was transparent.

'Suffer the little sea creatures to go around your feet, babe,' Caroline told me, closing her eyes.

That night, on our honeymoon, I lay in bed while Caroline played 'The Black Water of Beaghcauneen' on her violin. She instructed me to close my eyes, and I did until the white duvet felt like warm black water immersing me.

It isn't five minutes. It is fifteen minutes. We turn off the coast road and drive inland. The sandy coves are replaced by anonymous, endless grey and yellow fields with poor soil and jutting rocks. Every moment that we spend driving in the opposite direction from the sea feels like an eternity, like an inappropriate speech at a wedding. Finally, we pull on to a verge at the side of the road. Next to the verge there is a rusty gate leading to an overgrown and inauspicious gravel driveway. Anthony climbs down out of the car and, with a great deal of effort, hoists the rusty gate open. We wait in the car. Anthony beckons to us and I get out. Caroline doesn't move. She says, through the half-open window of the car:

'I think that maybe Jesse and I should wait in here. It looks a bit dark up there.'

'It'll be fine,' I whisper. 'The tour is part of the hotel.'

She nods and I open the car door and I lift you out of your seat. You scream quietly. I set you down on the ground and then – when you scream quietly again and pick up your knees to prevent your feet from touching the ground – I lift you into my arms and then up on to my shoulders. The gloom is beginning to set in. There is a dim film of grey rain in the air.

We walk up the driveway. The driveway is on a slope and the gravel gives slightly as I try to get a footing. Whether by livestock or by humans, the gravel has been kicked away in some places, revealing the dark brown ground underneath. I look down the hill that we have just driven up and see the little knot of cottages at the bottom, by the sea, where we turned off the coast road. I suddenly have a feeling that we have been here before. I ask Caroline if she thinks that this might be the field that we ran across when we were on our honeymoon.

'Who knows,' Caroline says. 'We don't even know where we

are. Everywhere looks literally exactly the same as everywhere else.'

At the top of the drive there is a small house. The house is low: a single storey with a low roof. The thatch is filled with holes and inside there are stacks of mouldy thatch piled up here and there on the floor. The smell of the mouldy thatch fills the small space. The windows have been smashed in, but Anthony reassures us that this must have just been cows or weather but certainly not vandals.

'You wouldn't see many vandals in this part of the world,' he says.

There is a cold, clammy feeling inside the house. We can hear the wind whistling through the windows. The darkness is almost black. We can feel the damp reverberating through the walls, through the air. You start to cry and I pass you to Caroline. You press your nose deep into Caroline's neck.

'Ow,' says Caroline.

'Don't worry, Jess,' I say. 'It's just a house. Just an old house.'

At the front of the house there is a raised row of loamy soil. I know that it is just an abandoned flower bed, but it really does look like a grave. The grass is poor: yellow and wispy. Behind the house the hill increases and there, at the top, is another structure. It is small, it doesn't look as though it is big enough to stand upright in. From a certain angle, it looks almost like an accidental heap of stones. Moss growing, in heavy green beards, from the side of the building. Anthony tells us that this is a bothy and that it is also part of the property. Thunderous clouds amble across the sky, making stripes on the grass on the hill of dark grey and black. As the sky turns grey and swirls, the little grey building turns black against the clouds.

'Now this,' Anthony says. 'With good land here and the sea down beyond. Wouldn't this be a nice spot for a holiday place?'

Caroline wants to berate the hotel owner when we get back but I convince her not to. She has been so kind and it was so nice of her to have looked after you when we'd had our romantic meal.

'She's probably his sister-in-law,' Caroline says. 'You said that this place was too small to have scams like that.'

'We're here for another week,' I say. 'Really what would be the benefit of alienating the hoteliers?'

Caroline looks aghast. Hotels is a service industry, she tells me.

'*We reeeeeeallly don't want to alienate the hoteliers,*' Caroline says in a mocking tone. 'So now we *really* don't want to alienate the hoteliers. And before that we *really* didn't want to alienate the religious nut on the boat, the fucking ferryman. And then it's the head who won't give you a raise after five fucking years and the waiter in that shitty Indian restaurant who brought a bottle of Evian when we asked for tap and the driving instructor who charged you for the lesson when he left you waiting outside his mother's house when he went in to check if the carer had come.'

'*Big* man,' she says. 'Big, *big* man.'

We look at each other in the hotel room. Caroline looks tired. After a while she says that she just wanted it to be nice. She wonders why it feels like carrying a Ming vase across a slippery floor sometimes.

'It isn't like that,' I say. 'You worry too much. It isn't always like that.'

'I said *sometimes*,' Caroline says, calming down.

'I understand,' I say.

'I worry too much?' Caroline says.

'It's not illegal to try to sell somebody a cottage, Caroline,' I say. 'It doesn't make you a criminal to try to do that.'

She sits down on the bed and then drops her hands from her head down to her sides and then rests her hands, palms down, on the bed. She sighs, a long, yogic exhalation.

'You're right,' she says.

She goes into the en suite and closes the door. The en suite makes a loud humming noise when she turns the light on. She stays in there for ten minutes or so. When she comes back out she says:

'I never want to come back here again. Okay?'

That night, my mother comes and stands at the end of the bed. Her face is pitiless and confused. I know that it is just a ghost. But in the night-time it seems plausible that she has woken up in Kilburn and has wandered out of her house and tottered across land and sea to find her way here, to somewhere she knows and recognizes and knows the way to, only to realize at the end of her journey that she doesn't know where she is.

'It's okay,' I tell the ghost, softly, even though I know that it can't hear me. 'It's just a dream that you're having. Everything is going to be okay.'

Caroline shakes me.

'You're waking the baby,' she whispers. 'When you shout like that you wake the baby and then we're all up all night.'

'He's not a baby,' I say.

'You're right Pol,' Caroline whispers. 'He's not a baby.'

North Korea

After we got back from Ireland, the year seemed to drift away, like flotsam.

'I've given up on this year,' Caroline said one Sunday afternoon at the end of March. 'I'm going to just learn from this and try again next year.'

We did your fourth birthday. It was your first-ever birthday party. We didn't really know who to invite. You hadn't made any friends at nursery yet. All the other children seemed to shun you. I worried that it was to do with your lisp. Caroline looked exasperated when I mentioned it.

Now it's June and I'm having problems with my sleep.

'The new medication doesn't have that side effect,' Caroline says. 'Call Dr McCaul if you don't believe me.'

Maybe it isn't the cure, I suppose. Maybe it's just the illness.

The sun is rising earlier and earlier every year. I check my diary and I show Caroline when she doesn't believe me. I wake up in the middle of the night and go downstairs. In the hallway I can see that somebody has pushed litter through our letter box again. It just sits there in a pile, a jumble of old baked-bean cans and wet old newspapers on the carpet.

'I know who's doing it,' I told Caroline last time.

'No Polly,' Caroline replied. 'You don't know who's doing it.'

A few hours later you and Caroline wake up and get ready for nursery. I make you your cornflakes. You paddle in them with your spoon until they are mushy and then tell me that you don't like cornflakes.

I never wanted you to go to the nursery. You're so young still. Just a baby really. But the nursery is attached to the school and it's really better for us to bring you to work with us in the morning than to leave you with Caoimhe. Caoimhe has to look after my mother.

My mother's condition got worse over the winter. I had to take a few days off work before Christmas to help out.

'Early-onset dementia,' said the head when I asked for leave. 'How old is your mother? That seems like terribly bad luck.'

'Believe me,' I replied. 'When it started, we thought that she was putting it on.'

The head looked at me a little strangely.

She only used to whisper, and in German, but at least it was audible. Now when she speaks it sounds like a ghost is speaking.

'It's the only option,' Caroline said, applying her mascara. 'And it also happens to be a good option.'

She was so beautiful and thin when she was younger, standing on stage at the Albion Ballroom playing her violin. She was so lithe.

'*You* are *so* thin,' I remember she said to me on our wedding night. '*So* thin.'

When we first got to know each other, Caroline thought that I was basically a miracle, rather than a medical case, rather than a guinea pig.

'You are the miracle boy!' she said in a sonorous voice, like Charlton Heston playing Moses, standing bolt upright, naked, on our bridal bed in the bothy, pointing down at me with a straight, quivering arm. 'You are the *chosen one*!'

When we first got to know each other, and even when we were first married, Caroline was never guarded about my condition the way other people were. She would joke about it. She would show pictures of me from when I was a teenager to anyone who would let her, when we had people over for dinner even.

'This fucking cretin,' she would say, pointing a fork at me, everyone laughing, me laughing, 'eats and eats and eats. And no exercise. They need to cut out his chromosomes and boil them up to make an elixir of youth.'

And when we were younger, before my mother got sick, it caused disharmony between my mother and Caroline. Caroline would refer to my being lucky. My mother would shout at Caroline. Caroline didn't know what it had been like, my mother reminded her. She hadn't been there during the really bad times. There was one time – when we were at Caoimhe's thirtieth birthday party in the Coopers Arms – when Caroline pushed back.

I remember her recounting the conversation with my mother later on that evening when we were getting ready for bed.

'I said "Listen you,"' Caroline recounted. 'I put my finger right in her face and I said: "Listen you. Don't go down memory lane with me, *you*."'

She grimaced, ferociously, like a pirate. I waited for her to finish.

'Don't you think that was good?' she said, suddenly clambering on the bed, kneeling, bouncing on the balls of her feet.

'What do you mean "good"?'

'Well, you know: funny?'

When we get to school you take your coat off and you go through to the nursery and hang it on your special hook. The hook has a label above it with your name, Jesse, written on it. Caroline goes into the staffroom and hangs her coat up in there. I keep my coat on. Nick, Caroline's line manager, is leaning against the door frame in the staffroom. Nick and I exchange nods. I know that some of the Year Two students – because I spend a lot of time in Edith's room and because Edith and I talk to each other – speculate that Edith and I are married. They don't know that Caroline and I are married because Caroline didn't change her name to mine when we got married.

'Well, I think it would be a nice thing for my mother,' I'd said at the time.

'Well, yet another fucking reason why I'm not going to do it,' Caroline had said, licking her index finger and making an invisible mark in the air.

Sometimes my friendship with Edith makes Caroline jealous, but she expresses it in slightly circumlocutious ways.

'I think,' she says, nursing her cup of tea cosily, 'that you like hanging out with her because at the back of your mind you're unconsciously strategizing about hanging out with young people in order to stave off the next heterochronous episode.'

Caroline submitted that almost everything that I did or said was part of an unconscious effort on my part to stave off the next heterochronous episode.

Edith went to either Oxford or Cambridge. She could have got a much higher-paying job but she is a socialist so she decided to work in a primary school. She teaches Year Two.

'I think that's great,' Edith said when Caroline first told her about my interest in Bartholomew Playfere. 'I'm so admiring of autodidacts.'

Three years ago or so, when Edith started at the school, two other trainees started with her. The leadership took everybody out for a meal. At the meal, all of the senior teachers sat together at one end of the table and all of the trainees and support staff sat together at the other. I sat with the trainees while Caroline sat with the senior teachers. I told Edith about my condition. Edith said that she knew when she first saw me that there was something wrong with me, something a tad askew. I told her that there was actually nothing visibly wrong with me. That there was no way of discerning that somebody had He Hakari Nēke syndrome purely from their physical appearance. It was an invisible disability, I said. She thought that I might have been physically traumatized by something, she told me, she thought I might have been burned badly. One of the other trainees widened her eyes and cackled, scandalized. I could tell that she was joking.

'*Burned* badly?' I said, laughing and balancing a pint glass on my upturned forehead, like a seal (we were already drunk): 'Could a burned badly do *this*?'

Later that night Caroline said that she wanted to go home but that if I wanted to stay out with the younger teachers then that was fine.

'Is she your girlfriend?' Edith asked when Caroline left.

'Wife,' I said, smiling.

'*Wife?*' Edith said, 'How old *are* you?'

And I told her that I was thirty and she pretended to fall backwards off her chair.

Edith and I spent the rest of the night talking about my Bartholomew Playfere project. I told her that I had parked it for a while because I was so busy with the maintenance job at school plus looking after my son. I would get back to it one day, I told her. I had boxes and boxes of meticulous notes that I had made. It was my life's passion, I told her. I wanted to write something about the prophet's intuitive awareness of climate change and ecology. You don't have to believe in the metaphysics of it all to believe that these old prophets had some things to say which are relevant to us now. There was so much about his life that hadn't been written about, I told her, so many notebooks and journals that the Poole estate had bequeathed to the British Library but which had never been read.

'And if you go to the island itself,' I told Edith, 'you can feel it. Everyone can feel it. Not just me.'

'Wow Pol,' Edith said. 'You know that you beam when you talk about this stuff?'

She told me that if I was passionate about it I could make time for it. All it needed was an hour or two per day. I could get up earlier or go to bed later. She herself was doing something similar. She was writing a novel, she told me. Her flatmates all thought she was crazy, she reckoned. They all wondered where she found the time. All the great thinkers and artists had other gigs, she said. That wasn't an excuse. I asked her what her novel was about. She told me that it was a science fiction novel about a futuristic world in which people who are suffering from Alzheimer's upload their memories into computers and are turned into holograms.

Caroline came and picked me up from the pub a couple of hours later.

'Boy are you loaded,' Caroline said in her *Sopranos* accent when I got into our little car. *'Boy* are you loaded.'

She laughed. She didn't mind. Once, when we were younger, she put both of her palms on either side of my head.

'I don't want there to be any elephants in the room,' she said. 'Not now. Not ever.'

It's a long day. I have to prune the high purpurea in the garden behind the Year Two classroom. The walls of the classroom are all glass. I watch Edith through the glass, picking up plastic blocks from the floor of the classroom. I wait for her to turn to look at me and then I give her a hearty wave. I really want to plant things in the garden, rather than just pruning things. But every time I plant anything a fox comes in and digs it up. I assume it's foxes anyway. How they get into the garden I will never know. The gates are all locked, I always check. Someone told me that foxes can dislocate their bones to get through small gaps.

The plastic blocks are all different colours: red, yellow, green and blue.

'Bit by bit,' Edith said to me once, 'I want to eliminate all of the active learning from my teaching, until they just sit on the floor and stare up at me in silence.'

On the walk home from school, Caroline says:

'It's your turn to cook.'

'Would you mind if you cooked tonight?' I say. 'I'm feeling a bit morose.'

'I would mind very much,' Caroline says. 'It's your turn to cook.'

When I cook pasta sauce I use all of the ingredients that I can possibly think of. I use all of the savoury ingredients that we have, plus some not-so-savoury ingredients too. I fry up some onions and garlic. Then I add butter, chilli flakes, basil and oregano. Then I add red wine, pepper, Lea & Perrins, sugar, mushrooms, balsamic, salt, soy sauce.

'Don't put too much salt in,' Caroline says from the other room. 'And don't put soy sauce in like last time. Soy sauce and salt are the same thing.'

She comes into the kitchen wearing a dressing gown and a towel wrapped around her head like a turban. In my mind's eye I envision the white hairs on the white tiles on the bathroom floor. If she plucks them out of her scalp it means that they aren't real, but picking them up from the floor and putting them in the bin would mean acknowledging that they *are* real. It would be a little too much time in their company. So the only solution is to pluck them out and then leave them on the floor. You are doing your numbers at the kitchen table. She leans over you and she takes the pen out of your hand and corrects a backwards number 5. She gives you the pen back and then, with her index finger, draws the shape of a number 5 on your back. She catches me smiling at this.

'It helps,' she says blankly. She plods out of the kitchen, leaving bathwater footprints in a trail across the floor.

'Ladies and gentlemen,' she says as she leaves, 'the world's foremost authority.'

—

Caroline is the opposite of me. She puts nothing at all in the pasta sauce. She puts: a can of tomatoes, a huge slab of butter, a half of an onion. I have to admit it tastes nicer. It tastes meatier.

'That's the difference between me and you,' she says.

The difference between me and her is now, technically, twelve years. Technically speaking. Physiologically speaking, I should say, rather than chronologically speaking. She's physiologically around thirty-five while I'm physiologically twenty-three.

'I've never understood that,' she said one time to McCaul. 'Like how old is Keanu Reeves *physiologically* speaking?'

McCaul smiled.

'It's a compendium statistic,' he told her. 'It's a compendium of the median points on a whole range of indices. *Almost all* things about Keanu Reeves would indicate that his physiological and chronological ages match up, even if *some* things do not. Almost *all* things about Pol do not.'

The kitchen is the best thing about the house on Iverson Road. The previous people had done it up in order to sell the place quicker. It has an island.

'Not even Mohamed Al-*Fay*ed has an island,' Caroline said when we first saw the kitchen.

When we moved into Iverson there was a front garden that belonged only to us. A long time ago someone had tried to grow blackberries there or else the blackberries had grown by themselves. But they had gone wild. There was a tangle of brambles covering half of the garden.

'*Blackberries. Gone. Wiiiiild*,' Caroline said, wading towards the front door in her wellies.

The stems were dark green and thick as cables with military-grade thorns all along them. The berries, when they grew, were not juicy and black but grey and ungleaming.

'Don't ever eat them, *ever*,' Caroline said to you, squeezing your cheeks until the blackness and the seeds mixed with saliva spilled out of your mouth into her open palm. 'They have chemicals in them.'

She thought that the dullness of the berries was because of the fumes from passing cars.

These days, the front garden is all paved over. I can't even remember whose idea it was. These days, when you have gone to bed, Caroline and I watch TV shows and Caroline points out her physical defects.

'Do you remember?' she says. 'Do you remember how I used to have a concave belly?'

'Now look at me.'

'Now look at this.'

'Look at this.'

'Look at this.'

She lifts up her T-shirt and pinches her belly fat between forefinger and thumb, like a pair of callipers. Or else she points out the stretch marks on her flanks.

'It's just part of having a baby,' I say, and then Caroline goes pink with quiet rage and within twenty minutes or so we are having an argument.

'Why do you say that if you only want me to contradict you?' I say and she says:

'Because that's called being in a marriage.'

And then I say:

'No it isn't, that's called being in North Korea.'

Carmela Soprano says:

'When you ignore me, Tony, when you trivialize things that

are important to me like this family's financial security, it makes me feel unloved.'

And then Tony replies:

'Well that's your problem right there, because you equate love with money.'

And then Carmela shouts back:

'No! *You* equate love with money.'

Caroline, with a mouthful of Häagen-Dazs, lying on the sofa, points her spoon at the screen and says:

'You know what that is? That's us.'

'Why do you have to run down our marriage all the time?'

'No, *you* run down our marriage all the time.'

When I Look at These Ancient Heroes
It Makes Me Think What Am
I Doing with My Life

We're going on holiday to Pompeii with Nick and his family in the first week of the summer holidays.

'We're not going on holiday *to Pompeii*,' Caroline corrects me. 'We'll *visit* Pompeii while we're there.'

She laughs. Nick smiles pityingly. We are standing in the corridor outside Nick's office and Nick is telling us about who will be coming on the trip. Nick's wife Shirley is older than him and she has grown-up children from a first marriage. Angela is nineteen, Tess is twenty-five. Tess has a husband called Mark who works in the city. He is closer to our age. Thirty-four or thirty-five. Tess and Mark have a newborn baby called Julia. The only child that Nick and Shirley have together is Cynthia. Cynthia is adopted.

'Why do they want to go Italy with *us*?' I said when Caroline first broached it with me.

'Because,' Caroline said. 'They. *Like*. Us.'

We hire two big cars at the airport. Nick offers to put me on the insurance and I remind him that I can't drive. Mark and Nick drive us from the airport to the place. I go in the back of Nick's car with Caroline and you. When we get to the place, there is this long driveway with a gate at the top. A man comes down the driveway and unlocks the padlock on the gate and waves for us to drive through.

Later on, while we are giving him our passports to photocopy, the man introduces himself to us as Mario. He has thick black hair and black stubble.

'He looks *so* like Pol,' Angela says. 'I mean he is the *double* of you, Pol.'

We knew that it would be hot. We thought that you would be able to cool off in the pool. But you aren't able to cool off in the pool because the water in the pool is basically warm, basically bathwater temperature. Above ground. A big canvas thing. A big blue oblong. I think they just fill it with a hose. The house is beautiful: a crumbling old palazzo carved into holiday apartments, a huge raised veranda at the front. Caroline and I are on the ground floor and our bedroom has French windows which open on to the veranda. Upstairs there is a big kitchen and a dining room with three bedrooms leading from it. Nick and his extended family are upstairs. Outside there is a terrace next to the pool. On the wall, there are portraits of the people who used to live in the palazzo when it was a palazzo. Big twirly moustaches. I look at the portraits and I try to figure out if there is any resemblance between the ancestral faces and Mario's face.

'I'm sure he just works here,' Caroline says.

There's no air conditioning in our room. There's a kind of long cot for you with low rails around the outside. When you wake up in the night, you can't get out of the bed because of the rails and you scream until we come and get you.

—

Mark thinks that everything is stupid.

'Politics is for people who don't like the idea of getting things done,' he said to Nick on the drive over from the airport.

But Tess is nice. Tess is sort of angelic. She is so much younger than him. She feels that he is tolerating her naivety, when in reality she is tolerating *him* without even knowing it. Why does she tolerate him, I wonder.

It isn't really your fault that Julia – Tess and Mark's daughter – is so well behaved. You can't settle. You run around in the hot sun, like a hot little red pig, and become exhausted and grumpy and shout at Caroline during dinner and fall asleep at five and wake up in the middle of the night, in the ink-black, oil-black, sweaty, greasy night. And all the time Julia, a newborn baby, chuckles and gurgles and smiles and holds on to everyone's fingers until wet tears bleed out of our eyes. Let's put a frilly bonnet on her head, which will keep her cool. Let's get her to clap along to a pop song with sexually explicit lyrics. We try to get you to wear your baseball cap with the Gaillimh GAA logo, but it falls off every time we put it on your head.

Nick was in his late thirties and Shirley was in her early forties when they met, and both came from unhappy previous marriages. They had IVF to try to have a baby together. When that didn't work they adopted Cynthia.

On the first night, we all sit around together on the veranda for a big dinner. The veranda is right in front of our bedroom, so it's difficult for us to make an exit before the very end of the meal. From the veranda you can only see the fields which stretch down to the sea. But the topography hides a coast road, with cars driving down it, and the sound of the cars from the road drowns out the sound of the crickets on the farm at night.

After dinner, when the coffee comes out, the table separates into two camps, with the younger generation congregating at one end and Nick, Shirley, Caroline and me at the other. Nick and Caroline discuss the capitation for the school and the affordability of the SEN provisions that they want to introduce.

'How are you finding the heat?' says Nick, turning to me.

He is short and balding on top and there is a little red glow appearing on his scalp after one day in the sun. He is from one of those towns around Manchester. He has a gruffness to his voice which he got from years of smoking. He wears little round glasses, too.

I go back into the house to get another coffee. There isn't any fresh coffee left, so I go through the cupboards and find a jar of instant and make that. When I come back out I hear Tess say, from the other end of the table:

'I bet Pol would know.'

She pulls a chair away from the table for me. When I sit with Tess and Angela I feel more relaxed. Tess and Angela want to know about the differences between Hinduism and Buddhism. Mark looks bored. I tell them that I don't know anything about either Buddhism or Hinduism. Tess smiles at me.

'What made you think that I would know anything about the differences between Hinduism and Buddhism?' I ask her and Angela says:

'Nick told us that you know everything about everything.'

Angela is studying classics at Bristol. She has had three or four glasses of wine. I get the sense that she isn't used to being drunk around her family, that the novelty of it is exhilarating to her.

'It's so amazing,' she says, 'to meet someone who is actually interested in knowledge for knowledge's sake, rather than just to get a piece of paper out of it.'

When she says 'knowledge's' she apostrophizes twice. Knowledgeses. She raises a glass. Everyone is laughing now. Nick and Shirley and Caroline pause their conversation and look down the table at us, trying to overhear what the merriment is about.

'Pol,' Angela says, laughing, 'we salute you.'

The next day we all go outside to sit on the terrace by the pool. You are being particularly difficult. Everyone politely averts their attention. You put your feet in the water and you start kicking the water on to the terrace. Caroline gets up from her lounger and goes to get you. You start to scream.

'I'm going to take him indoors,' Caroline says. I offer to help but she doesn't hear me. She pulls you by the arm up the steps that lead from the terrace to the house. You pretend to fall over and then scream even louder.

What am I reading, Tess wants to know. I tell her about the research that I have been doing about the life of Bartholomew Playfere. I show her the scanned printouts of the notebooks that I got from the British Library. I consider telling her about how extortionate the price of scanning the documents is but I decide against it. Tess vaguely remembers the name Bartholomew Playfere from an episode of *In Our Time* that she heard once.

'So these are the real, actual notebooks?' Tess says. 'This is his real handwriting?'

She is walking towards me with a bottle of Estrella in her hand. She moves as though to take the pages out of my hands but I place them back on the sun lounger behind me.

'Pol is going to be famous one day,' Angela says over the top of her book. 'You can just tell. A famous public intellectual or whatever.'

I glance inadvertently over at Mark.

'Oh my God,' Tess says. 'You should talk to Cynthia. My mum and Nick's daughter. She's studying the Civil War for her A levels. She told me that she was finding it really difficult.'

Cynthia. Cynthia who was adopted. Her real name wasn't Cynthia. She had an Angolan name. Both of her birth parents had been killed in the civil war there. They had been killed by a landmine. Cynthia had survived but was confined to a wheelchair. She was left alone in the world, with no siblings, no mother or father. Later on, when we meet, I will notice that you can tell that about her.

She had been put in an orphanage in Luanda. Nick and Shirley went to Luanda and adopted her when she was six. Caroline and I argued about it when she told me that. I told her that I thought that it was strange that people could go to less economically developed countries and adopt children with no proper oversight. Caroline said that we knew Nick and Shirley and that we knew that they were good parents and so therefore there was no bad outcome.

'You have to *try* to *start* being a little less deontological, Pol,' Caroline said. 'It's no kind of life otherwise. It's suffocating.'

'They made her change her name,' I said.

'*She* chose that name,' Caroline said. 'It's just a *name*.'

She is sixteen now. She is doing a week-long residency training on activism as part of her role as a member the UK Youth Parliament, which is why she hasn't come on holiday with us.

Nick is having therapy over the phone while we're in Italy. He is having a full analysis, a few days a week. While everyone is sitting by the pool, I go upstairs and pretend to be doing something in the kitchen. There is a window in the kitchen from where you can see down to the terrace and the pool. I can see if anyone is going to come upstairs to the kitchen from the terrace. The door to Nick's room, where he is having his therapy session, is locked. I can hear his voice, a few snatched words here and there. I sit down at the table in the kitchen and listen.

Later, over lunch, Tess and Angela tell Nick that I should tutor Cynthia for her Civil War topic. They remind him that I know everything about everything. Nick had said so himself. Nick is a little too eager to agree to the plan. I don't want him to think that I'm a charity case. I don't want the others to think that I'm a charity case either.

'That's settled then,' Nick says.

'Do you work out, Paul?' Mark says.

'Pol,' I say.

This evening is our turn to cook. We cook aubergine parmigiana. It irritates me that Caroline insists on calling it eggplant parmigiana.

'It's from *The Sopranos*,' Caroline says, cheerfully.

'It's from Italy,' I say. 'It's not from *The Sopranos*.'

I laugh lightheartedly but I know that she knows that I'm irritated.

'Then shouldn't it be *zucchini* parmigiana?' Caroline says.

'That's courgette,' I say.

I go outside and start setting the table on the veranda. I bring out seven large white plates. Each plate has an intricate blue and yellow design on it: images of a blue bearded man emerging from yellow waves. The knives and forks are silver with multicoloured plastic handles. Tess comes out on to the veranda. She is wearing an expensive-looking black dress. Her hair is wet from the shower. She looks at the stack of plates.

'Oh dear,' she says. 'Didn't my mum tell you?'

She looks a little flustered. She puts one hand into her hair and frisks it to shake out some of the moisture.

'We aren't eating here tonight,' she says. 'My mum is babysitting Julia so that Mark and Angela and I can go into town for dinner.'

She grimaces apologetically. I feel anger bubbling in my stomach. I can tell that she's worried that she might have upset me.

'She didn't tell us,' I say. 'But it's absolutely fine. You can have it cold for lunch tomorrow. I think it'll still be nice.'

I run my fingers down the stack of plates and lift up the three that we won't be needing any more and I carry them back into the kitchen.

'Oh God, I'm so sorry,' Tess calls after me.

'Why are you apologizing?' I call back.

Over dinner, the talk is all about politics. Where had it all gone wrong, we wonder. Maybe when Brown refused to go to the electorate back in 2007. Nick had liked Brown. Brown was good, he says. History would judge Brown kindly. Nick says that the Iraq War has been blown out of all proportion. You will always have people who complain, he says. The world is an imperfect world, he says. He and Shirley are worried about Cynthia, their adopted daughter. She goes down these rabbit holes on the Internet, reads a lot of radical tosh. He spoke to her on the phone earlier and she was telling him about an anonymous Greek anarchist writer that she has been reading. They are sure that she will grow out of it. The world seems like such a volatile place these days, even compared with only a few years ago. He asks me about my work.

I tell him, a little unrepresentatively, that I'm putting together an application for funding for a PhD based on the research that I've been doing over the past few years. Caroline glances at me. Nick nods slowly, a little ruefully.

'Impressive,' he says. 'Now's the time to do it. While you're young. Take risks.'

We decide to have coffees and then we decide not to have coffees because it's too late. You have already gone to bed and Caroline wants to get some solid hours in before you wake up at five. I'll stay up, I tell them. I'll wait for the others to get back.

'I think they've gone out for the night,' Shirley says after a pause. 'I think they mentioned something about a nightclub.'

I nod ambiguously and carry the plates back up to the kitchen.

It's later. Nick and Shirley have already gone to bed. I'm sitting on the veranda where we ate. I know that there is a bottle of vodka in the freezer. It's Angela's, but I know that she didn't buy it herself: she put it on the list with the groceries when Nick did a supermarket run on the first day of the holiday. I creep upstairs. There are no sounds coming from Nick and Shirley's room. There are some glasses drying on the rack next to the sink. Now that the traffic has died down you can hear the sound of the crickets in the fields outside. The moisture sticks my feet to the cold tiles in the kitchen and my footsteps make a faint slapping sound. I take the bottle of vodka out of the freezer and I take a glass from the rack and I pour myself a glassful, almost to the brim. I place the bottle back in the freezer and I head back to the veranda. At the top of the stairs, I look back and see the trail of my condensatory footprints evaporating behind me on the cold copper-coloured flags.

—

I sit on the veranda and sip at the ice-cold glass of vodka. There are no sounds coming from the house behind me. I think about *The End of Nightwork*.

'I saw the world and its divisions resolved against me. And such was the clanging noise that they made with their lyres that I fell down. And upon returning to my feet I saw the divisions dissolved into an indistinguishable dust. And there stood my Lord who held within his hand that same instrument which had made that clanging noise. And he bid me play the thing. Whereon I plucked all of the notes together. And the sound it made was a clanging sound. Whereon my Lord indicated with which fingers I should pluck which strings. And the notes played thus were transporting to mine ears. The Lord spoke then directly into mine heart and told me that the first was called HISTORY and the second was called PROPHECY.'

He stood on a tub in Old Jewry and told people this and told them that they would have to leave their families behind – their parents, their wives, their husbands, their children, their friends – and follow him. It wows me, that story. Ever since I was a little boy it's wowed me.

At midnight there are sounds in the driveway. It's dark. I stand up and I see the headlights from two cars speeding towards the palazzo. The cars pull into the drive, sending up a small spray of gravel. I expect to see Mark, Tess and Angela climb out of the car. Instead, three men get out. I recognize one as Mario, the man who gave us the keys to the house when we first arrived. He is twenty, with long, dark curling black hair.

Mario is wearing a vest and shorts. He sees me on the veranda and recognizes me and waves.

'Enjoy!' he says, gnomically. 'Enjoy!'

I watch the three men as they walk from their cars to the little prefab at the top of the driveway. The prefab houses the reception where we picked up the keys on our arrival. The lights come on. I can hear them laughing, exchanging anecdotes. I am three sheets to the wind. I stand up and stroll across the driveway to the little prefab. My footsteps are noisy on the gravel. I can hear the voices from the cabin quietening as I get closer. I knock on the door. Mario opens the door a crack. He looks concerned.

'Speak English?'

'Of course,' he says. 'What seems to be a matter?'

I tell him that we have run out of alcohol and is there anywhere open at this time of night where we could buy any. It is a bad lie. He knows that I know that there is nowhere open for miles around. He knows that I know that I am in no condition to drive. I'm inviting him to conspire with me. He laughs in a comradely way. Unfortunately, no, he says. But there are bottles of the palazzo's own limoncello, made right here on the farm in the traditional way, that he could sell to me. He could put it on our bill. Better yet, he thinks he could call it a free gift. Mario doesn't care. Mario just works here.

I know about the limoncello already. I saw the high shelf with all of the limoncello bottles behind the receptionist's desk when we checked in. They also have calendars made of photographs of the palazzo taken throughout the seasons: the palazzo in winter, cloaked in snow; the palazzo in summer with trestle tables laid with plates and glass jugs in rows in the courtyard, awaiting the spectacle of an opulent wedding breakfast.

I enter the prefab. I can see that Mario and his friends are already enjoying some limoncello. Mario goes to fetch a bottle from the storeroom. I smile at his friends and they smile back. They are huddled around a computer monitor watching YouTube videos. When he comes back, Mario offers me the bottle and then – anxious to be friendly – proposes that I share a drink with him and his friends. His friends are called Paolo and Gianni. We all shake hands.

They offer to turn the videos off, but I won't hear of it. I don't want to interrupt them, I say. They are watching videos about a survivalist group living in Montana. Every time YouTube takes the videos down, the survivalist group puts new videos up, under a different account name. The group is called The Primitivist Alliance. They are heavily armed. They say that they are at war with the American government. They say that the American government is intent upon replacing the white population of America by importing Latin American migrants. They say that the United States is headed towards a race war. It won't be the first race war, they claim. At various points in American history, a cabal of international Jews has orchestrated the importation of alien groups in order to create the conditions for conflicts which are intended to prevent the population from consummating the American dream which is their birthright. It had all started with the slave trade, followed by the Catholic Europeans, and now the Mexicans. The camera follows the Primitivists as they trudge through thick, crisp white snow to the wooden longhouse where they keep their arsenal.

Mario and Paolo and Gianni like the videos. They really want to be like the Primitivists. The Jews are doing the same thing in Italy they tell me. The Jews hold all the power in the north and they want to prevent the working people in the south from improving their lives, by importing Africans who will then start a race war with the Italians. The Africans come over on boats that are paid for by George Soros, Mario tells me. I nod.

After a while they leave. They get into their cars and drive back into town. They all live in town. I thought that Mario lived here on the farm, but he just works here. He has a flat in town. They give me big hugs before they leave and Mario tells me that I am a legend, a word that he learned from some Englishmen who came to stay at the palazzo for a stag weekend the previous summer. The palazzo is silent again. My mouth feels as though it is coated in honey. I breathe into my hand and then smell it and it stinks. I feel sick.

At about two I come back to the room where you and Caroline are sleeping.

'Are you awake?' I say into the darkness. You shift in your single cot-bed.

'Are you awake?' I say again, louder this time. Caroline sits up in bed.

'Jesus,' she hisses. One eye is scrunched shut. 'What are you doing?'

I sit down on the bed beside her.

'I want to go home,' I say.

'Where home?' Caroline says. 'London? What are you on about?'

'I'm going to book a flight tomorrow and go home,' I say. She is awake now.

'Are you okay?' Caroline says. 'Did something happen with your mother?'

I stand up again and walk towards the door. I tell her that I don't feel comfortable being around her and Nick. She laughs at this. She asks me what I am referring to. I tell her that I think Nick has feelings for her. Caroline asks me how much I have had to drink. Caroline starts to cry. She doesn't know what I am talking about, she says. I am being crazy. Why am I being so crazy. She doesn't want to have this conversation in the middle of the night. Maybe I should try to get some sleep and talk about it in the morning.

Neither of us hears the taxi pull into the driveway. We don't hear the others come up to the house. I only notice that the others are back when I leave Caroline, who is still in tears, and step out of the French windows of our room on to the veranda and find them there, seated in a circle, eating from a corrugated aluminium container of cold pasta. I can tell from their expressions that they heard us arguing.

'I just need to get a glass of water,' I say.

I'm still wearing the clothes that I was wearing at dinner. Mark gives me a thumbs up and grins. The girls look upset, but they too say goodnight. I walk up the steps to the kitchen and run the tap. It runs and runs but it never gets any colder.

In the night I wake up to find Caroline's hands on my face, her palms pressed against my cheek. Her face is above mine, looking into my eyes.

'Pol,' she is saying, 'look at me. Don't you know me. Don't you recognize me, Pol?'

Her tears fall and brush against my skin.

You wake me up a few hours later by crying. My head splits open like a volcano in a monster movie. Caroline is already dressed and has had a shower.

'We're going to Pompeii,' she says blankly.

On the train to Pompeii, the train doors don't reach down to the floor. The grass and the railway and the stones and sometimes even the sea hurry past. The blur of grass and railway lines and stones makes me feel nauseous. The gap is big enough for you to put your arm through. Nobody else seems to notice. I turn away and try to focus on not vomiting.

We walk around Pompeii. I volunteer to look after you. I never knew that Pompeii was so big. I always thought that it would just be a few piles of stones and a visitor centre where everything would be explained. When we took you to Vindolanda there were just piles of stones here and there and it was left up to the guide to paint the bigger picture, to show us how these piles of stones were actually just the few remaining jigsaw pieces, were actually evidence of a large temple. But Pompeii isn't like that. It's an actual town, with actual streets stretching off in each direction in punishingly straight lines. You hate to have your sun cream put on. I have to sit on my haunches to do it and my haunches start to ache in the heat.

We start out walking through the town together. Mark and Tess have baby Julia in her expensive-looking pushchair. I manage to avoid talking to them by talking to you. The Romans had prophets who foretold that this would happen to the city, I tell you. Your laces come undone. The others take their cue from Caroline and keep walking as I kneel down to do them up for you. Now they are ten yards ahead of us. Now twenty. When I have done your shoelaces, I straighten up. We walk a few yards further. You say that you want to go home. You start to cry. Caroline hears you crying and comes jogging back to speak to you.

'We can't go home yet chicken,' Caroline says, kneeling down and looking you in the eye. 'We have a few options. Either we can look at some of these buildings and things and I can tell you about them, or you can sit here with us and we can wait for the others to finish. Which of those would you prefer?'

'Don't trick him,' I say. 'He'd *prefer* to go home. But he can't. So he has to do what we say right now. He doesn't have a choice. Don't trick him into thinking that he does.'

Caroline straightens up. I can see in her eyes that she is tired of me. For a moment she looks like one of the Pompeiians, her mouth slightly agape, sucking in great dry gusts of dry ash and dust and sand until it fills her lungs. Then she says:

'You know what, Pol, I'm going to leave you to deal with this.'

She walks away from us. She looks happy to see her friends when she catches up with them. From twenty paces, I can see Tess placing one hand on Caroline's shoulder. I hate you Tess. My eyelids feel like razor blades. I look down at you. We are on the children's table, I say to myself. I have to look after you, and you don't have to look after me. My hung-over lungs feel like they are shrinking. I look at the old buildings and I suddenly feel like I am an old building too. Like I am an old painting of an old person on a gallery wall. I feel like if somebody took a photograph of me at this moment, it might damage the fabric of my being irreparably. I run an index finger along my forehead and gather a thimbleful of sweat. I look down at you again, and again I feel my lungs contract. You're trying to tie your shoelaces again. You don't even know where to start.

They are striding away from us now. Quicker and quicker. The town is very big. They are talking about us, Caroline and her friends. There are as many streets in the town as there are in any other town. Some parts of it are not in a grid. There are wide-open bits of grass and amphitheatres and bathhouses. We won't find them, I know, if we lose them. If we wait for them to turn a corner or to disappear over the horizon, we'll be stuck. I can feel the sweat turning into blisters on my heels, my toes, inside my sockless sneakers. Why didn't I wear the sandals like

Caroline told me to? Why didn't I wear socks? I push my hand into my pocket and I take out my phone. You push your finger into your nose. With my free hand, I nudge your hand away from your nose. You start to cry. I attempt to pull up a Google map on my phone but all that comes up is a grey soup of pixels divided into squares by a white grid, like graph paper. When I try to refresh the page it directs me to a Free Wi-Fi invitation with a picture of the museum building where we bought our tickets for twenty euros. You are really crying now. I try with one hand to type in my name and address and postcode and email address and national code for my phone and my phone number in order to get access to the free Wi-Fi. The little circle whirrs and whirrs.

What if the Gorgons were actually real and actually all that happened was that a squad of Gorgons came down from Vesuvius and froze everyone in the town to death? I mentioned this theory to Caroline once before, when we were much younger, and she told me that it didn't pass the smell test.

'Ockham's razor,' she said sombrely.

'That's probably what the Pompeiians said when they were warned about the Gorgons who lived on the mountain,' I said.

'Anyway that's Greece,' Caroline said.

Later that year (I remember now) she gave me a postcard that she'd bought at the British Museum. It had a picture of a petrified Pompeiian on it. Caroline had drawn a speech bubble coming from the man's mouth. In the speech bubble she had written:

'I was not turned to stone.'

I knew that he wasn't actually turned to stone. It just looked that way because his body had been covered in *melted* stone. And for a fraction of a millisecond after his body had been covered in melted stone, he had lived inside there: an infinitesimally tiny portion of life, lived inside a perfectly rendered statue of himself.

When we eventually find the others, they are standing in a semicircle around a half-destroyed statue of a centaur.

'Bronze,' says Nick, pointing at the statue when we arrive. 'Amazing.'

The crown of the head has come away. It is a clean line around the head, passing just above the eyes, just above the ears, and just above the nape. The eyes are gone too, so that you can see the sky where his eyes are meant to be. The centaur looks straight up into the sun, blank and brainless and blind. It reminds me of Randle McMurphy at the end of *One Flew Over the Cuckoo's Nest*.

'When I look at these statues of these ancient heroes,' says Mark, 'it makes me think: what am I doing with my life.'

The Eusocial Network

When we got back from Pompeii I was partly hoping that Nick would just forget about the plan for me to tutor Cynthia for her history coursework. I wondered if the story of the argument between Caroline and me had somehow filtered through to him. I tried to put myself in Angela or Tess or Mark's position and to imagine whether, if I was them, I would decide to tell Nick or Shirley about it. But then one day in September, Nick did actually call the house and he asked Caroline to ask me if I was free the following week to do a trial session with Cynthia. And then after the trial session he asked me to come back every week.

Cynthia fans the books across the table in the dining room like a tail of peacock feathers. The living room is at the front of the house and it has a big bay window looking out on to the street. In between the detached houses on the other side of the street, you can glimpse the Heath. The sun is shining through the window. It's the very last bits of the summer. Cynthia places her left hand on the joystick of her electric wheelchair and she idly rotates the joystick around in her palm. She points with her right index finger to the books that she's read so far. I ask her which ones she enjoyed. She points to the Peter Lake book, and then she smiles.

'Seriously?' I say. 'You didn't enjoy the Christopher Hill?'

Cynthia looks at me, trying to suppress her smile.

'Dude,' she says.

Behind her, hanging on the wall, is a portrait of her in her wheelchair, with a peacock perched on a log beside her. She painted the portrait herself for her art A level. For her birthday, Nick and Shirley had it elaborately framed.

They – Nick and Shirley – bought her the peacock when she first came to live with them. They asked her what animals she liked and she told them that she liked peacocks, so they bought her a peacock. She named the peacock Liberty. Later the peacock died and Nick paid a taxidermist to pull out all of its feathers and he had the feathers preserved with some kind of special spray and made into a headdress. He mounted the headdress on the back of Cynthia's electric wheelchair. After a few months, Cynthia asked that it be removed.

Then, after the peacock, they got her some bees. The bees live in a beehive in the back garden.

Cynthia likes bees, she tells me, because they are eusocial. We can learn something from bees, she says. Which is probably why we seem hell-bent on destroying them, I tell her. Bees are not subject to the Fall. These bees are the direct descendants of the perfect bees that were created by God in the Garden of Eden.

She can use her special cane with a brass hook on the end to take the honey supers out of the hive. She has become quite adroit at using this stick. She can use it to open doors, or even once I saw her latch the hook around the handle of a teapot and pour a cup of tea. A friend of hers designed it in their design class at school and they tried to patent it and market it but to no avail.

'People don't like the combination of disabled people and sticks,' Cynthia told me. 'They like disabled people to have high-tech equipment. Otherwise it just seems a bit almshouseish.'

Another time she used almshouse as a word was when we played Scrabble together. I said that she thought about the word almshouse a lot and she replied that that was because she lived in one.

After we've finished our discussion of Christopher Hill, she tells me that she has to go and take out the honey supers for cleaning. The summer is over, she tells me.

When we have these breaks, she asks me to tell her about my own interests. As she is unloading the supers, I talk to her about the book that I'm trying to write about Bartholomew Playfere and climate change. I stand at the bottom of the garden to avoid being stung by the bees. How long have I been working on it for, Cynthia wants to know. I shave a year or so off either end and I tell her that I've been working on it for ten years.

'Is that normal,' Cynthia asks. And I tell her that it is.

I talk to her, while she hooks the honey supers with her brass hook, about John Eaton and *The Honey-combe of Free Justification by Christ Alone*:

'For the better discerning whereof: first I set downe the sweet, powerfull, and forceable Scriptures, as the flowers containing the honey; then I adde the expositions, testimonies, and consent of the learned Writers, as the honey it selfe; which they, like the laborious *Bees of the Lords garden*, have, by faith, sucked and gathered out of the said flowers of Scriptures; setting the sentence and saying of each Author by it self, as giving to each Bee his own and (as it were) proper *cellulam* of honey: I changing nothing in the substance of their sayings, but only the connecting conjunctions, that may most fitly conjoyn the coherence of their testimonies together.'

Did Bartholomew Playfere ever write anything about bees, she wants to know. And I tell her that he did, that his whole understanding of providence was linked to the metaphor of bees. If bees only knew that their fathers and grandfathers and great-grandfathers and great-great-grandfathers – all the way back to Eden – had also spent their lives doing the same exact things that they themselves spent their lives doing, he wrote, then the bees would stop making honey.

'What knows the laborious bee of the profit of his labour other than that he must do it or else he be not a bee. To know this knowledge out of his own deed is to the bee what it is to be a man knowing of the busy dispensations of providence.'

When we get to the word 'providence', Cynthia wants to know what it means because it seems to come up a lot. I tell her that providence is a way of seeing reality as a story. Some people look at reality as just a series of meaningless events, but some people pick and choose some of those events and put them all together to make a story. And it's only by choosing the right things that we make the story make sense, Cynthia observes. And it's only by leaving out the right things too.

I tell Cynthia the analogy that Bartholomew Playfere used to describe his study of history and prophecy. Like a man walking through a windswept terrain who comes across a field with bricks and sod strewn across it and knows that it is the remnants of a destroyed dwelling. Who finds a stone here and a stone there and is soon able to rebuild the place and then to live inside it. And from inside he is sheltered from the vicissitudes of history. There is a mark on the page of the manuscript here, and I like to think – although there isn't any evidence for it – that Playfere spat on the page as he wrote the dreadful word 'history'. He saw history, the tedious trudge through days, as the opposite of prophecy, which was a dance. He saw history – his own and humanity's – as a burden to be shrugged off, and the only way to shrug it off was through prophecy: doing it and being obedient to it.

I tell her about the device that Christopher Poole would use to read the Bible. Shapes would appear to him in a dream and he would cut the shapes out of a piece of parchment. He would place the latticed parchment over a page of scripture and he would note down the words that appeared through the holes. He would write down those words and try to assemble them into a sensible order. I shrug.

Coming home, coming down from these discussions, is sometimes difficult. Sometimes sad even. Caroline only wants to talk about work. I want talk to her about the things that Cynthia and I have discussed.

'Was Nick there?' she asks. 'Or Shirley?'

I kneel down to pick up the bits of Lego that are strewn around the kitchen floor.

Once, recently, I brought up something that Cynthia had told me and Caroline said that I should think about trying to get some grown-up friends.

'Like Nick and Shirley?' I asked.

As the weeks go past, the deadline for Cynthia's coursework gets closer. She is stressed about the dual deadlines for her history and her art coursework. She had wanted to do a nude self-portrait but the school said no, which was fucked up because a different student – a non-disabled student, she noted, waggling her eyebrows – had been allowed to do one three years earlier. One day she tells me that she is thinking about submitting the history coursework as her writing sample for her Oxford application. It's really important that it's good, she tells me, and it's really important that it's innovative. Only then do I come up with the idea of her writing something about Bartholomew Playfere. She could use some of the research that I've been doing, I tell her.

'Are you sure that you don't mind?' Cynthia says. 'That sort of feels like cheating.'

'Why would I mind?' I say.

She smiles. Her face goes slightly red. I wonder if she has been hoping that I would suggest this.

'All right,' she says. 'Okay.'

It's a warm day, so we decide to have a brainstorming session while taking the air on Hampstead Heath. Whenever we go outside together, we invariably get on to the subject of politics. Cynthia is immersed in political discussions that are happening on Reddit. She calls herself a Kourist. The Kourist movement takes its name from the ancient Greek word for youth.

Over the course of the past year, a pseudonymous theorist calling himself Adonis Dolofonithikos has been posting a series of essays on a subreddit. The essays postulate a new kind of historical materialism. All economic and political and social and cultural events, Dolofonithikos writes, are part of an aeon-long struggle between the old and the young. In order to maintain their power in society, the old have pillaged and raped the young, both literally and figuratively. Dolofonithikos calls it the 'historical overthrow of the youth right'. Eventually, though, this conflict will reach a head. On the subreddit all the people believe that the stage is being set for a final battle, a revolutionary denouement. When the interests of the youth are too much in conflict with the interests of the old, Dolofonithikos writes, then revolution becomes inevitable. In our own era, because of the pauperization and disenfranchisement of the young by the old, and because of the scandals that seem to be gripping the world of politics and media and culture, the public is beginning to wake up to the reality of this thing. The time for revolution and the restoration of the youth right is nigh.

'Father against son and son against father,' I say, sometimes, when she brings up the question of the Revolutionary Restoration of the Youth Right.

'Well,' Cynthia says, sardonically. 'Quite.'

'And how many people are part of this subreddit?' I asked Cynthia once.

'Millions,' Cynthia told me.

'No there *aren't*,' I said, really believing that there weren't. But then afterwards I went home and looked it up and discovered that there were.

We meander over the Heath, from the entrance by the Men's Pond to the Vale of Health. When we get to the Vale of Health, Cynthia points to one of the big houses on the other side of the water. She tells me that the man who lives there is a politician, a member of the House of Lords, and that he is a paedophile. No case has ever been brought against him, and when an investigative journalist threatened to expose him, the man took out a super-injunction so that nobody could write about it. Even still it remains an open secret, widely discussed in online forums.

'Fora,' I say, humbly.

'And you know how come he's so wealthy?' she asks. I shake my head.

'He's a landlord,' she says. 'Student housing.'

Out of the corner of my eye, I spot Caroline and her friend Dawn walking towards us from the other side of the pond. I note that Cynthia hasn't clocked them. Cynthia has only met Caroline once or twice and probably won't recognize her from afar, I calculate.

'Let's go this way,' I suggest, and I steer us both up the path towards East Heath Road.

Later on, when we get back to the house, Cynthia says:

'Why did you run away from your wife earlier?'

She smiles smugly. I can feel myself reddening slightly.

'I actually remembered that I was supposed to have picked my son up from my sister's house already,' I say. 'I thought it best to avoid a conflict.'

Cynthia nods and then glides easily across the room towards the bay window in her wheelchair.

'I didn't know that you had a son,' she says. 'That's good. One of the consequences of the overthrow of the youth right is infantilization. Young people can't afford to have any space and so they can't afford to have children and so they live long into their thirties in a kind of lifestyle that we used to expect only of adolescents.'

On the way home these days I go to the Lidl on Kentish Town Road and I buy two croissants and a packet of discounted chorizo because we're supposed to be being vegetarian in our house now. I find a side street and I unpackage everything and I make a chorizo sandwich between the two croissants and I eat it on the walk home. I fantasize about Cynthia one day becoming prime minister and about me somehow getting a serious boost to my self-esteem off the back of it. Isn't it conceivable that she does a press conference and tells the world about the quiet, nice man who helped her to get her start, who sparked her interest in the world? And wouldn't it be the case that my history of doing nothing of note would in that moment be transformed from a failure into a triumphant declaration of modesty and unworldliness? What an enigmatic character: so clever and yet so disinterested in the glories that would otherwise have been bestowed upon him had he only had the un-Zen-like desire to reach out and clutch them. I push a red wodge of chorizo into my mouth and dump the plastic wrapper from the packet of chorizo in the bin and then walk home.

I lie awake and think about Cynthia. How sometimes, for all her physical disadvantages, she seems to move so freely through life. Her thoughts, her movements are in straight lines, like a bishop moving across a chessboard. It seems almost miraculous to me. Almost as though she might wake up one morning and leave the house and travel in a straight line until she gets to wherever: to Oxford, or to the Houses of Parliament. And how I seem to be the opposite. Like I seem to be tethered to a post, running around in a circle, running so fast that I am corkscrewing down, tunnelling down into the centre of the earth, throwing up festoons of soil in my wake.

Cynthia has asked for an extra session this week, so the next morning I go over to the house. Before I even knock on the door, I feel like I can hear someone shouting in the vicinity. As soon as Cynthia answers the door, I can tell that the shouting is coming from inside the property. Can't you hear that, I ask her.

'I've had music on in the big room,' she says. 'It sounds like Nick.'

The shouting is coming from the garden. Curious, Cynthia follows me out of the room and down the corridor to the kitchen. The Bialetti bubbling and whining on the hob. A cold and blackened piece of toast protruding from the toaster. Outside, Nick is on his knees in front of the French windows, the palms of his hands pressed against the glass. He is wearing only a towel around his waist. He is screaming. A swarm of bees surrounds him. There are bees stinging his hands, his face, the soles of his feet. Between screams, he gags and spits to try to get the bees out of his mouth. Naked, he looks tiny: his arms spindly and flailing and small, protruding from his flabby, anaemic torso.

'Open the door!' he screams when he sees me, and I notice immediately that the door is locked from the inside by a Yale lock. It must have slammed shut behind him when he went out into the garden.

'Help me!' he is crying. 'Help me for fuck's sake!'

I pull open the door. Batting away the bees with one hand, I pull the hood of my hoodie over the top of my head. I bend down and I lift Nick up like a baby, with one arm under his calves and another under his arms. A bee stings me, and then another one stings me right on the eyelid. I wince with pain. I carry him over the threshold into the kitchen. All the time, the sound of the bees is drowned out by the sound of Nick screaming expletives into my ear. His face is red and swollen now. The bees are also stinging him on the crown of his bald head. The bees follow us into the kitchen, and with Nick in my arms I career towards the kitchen door. Cynthia is in my path and I roar at her to move out of the way. I pile into the living room, Cynthia slamming the kitchen door behind us, and I dump Nick on to the sofa. I break to my knees with exhaustion. As the adrenaline subsides I begin to feel the pain of the stings on my face.

'Fucking, fucking fuckers!' Nick is screaming, his voice catching slightly with emotion, as though he is about to start crying. 'Fucking, bloody, fucking hell.'

'Quite a day?' Caroline shouts over the sound of the front door closing when I get back to the house.

'Shirley called you?' I say, coming into the kitchen, where Caroline is making gnocchi from scratch.

'Did you stay for the ambulance?' Caroline says, giving me a kiss on the cheek.

'I left as soon as Shirley got there. I didn't know that they called an ambulance.'

'He has to stay in overnight. The poor man can't even walk. They counted four hundred bee stings on him.'

'I've never seen anything like it,' I say.

I go over to the sink and I run myself a glass of water. I wonder if Shirley told Caroline that I rescued Nick, that I carried Nick to safety.

'That's not all,' Caroline continues. 'They think that the poison from the bee stings has made him delirious. He kept accusing Cynthia of setting the bees on him. All the way to the hospital in the ambulance he was roaring about her putting a *curse* on him.'

She shakes her head. She sniffs at the air.

'What is that smell?'

I lift my shoulder towards my nose and I sniff at my shirt.

'Like shit?' Caroline says, wrinkling her nose.

'It might be the honey supers,' I say. 'They have that weird smell.'

'It's coming from your shirt,' she says, coming closer to sniff me.

Upstairs, I take my jacket off and I put my wallet on the dressing table. I take my shirt off and look at myself in the mirror. Here and there on my body I can see raised bumps from the bee stings. I look a little bit closer and my pectoral muscles twitch and flex involuntarily. I take a step back and raise my arms at right angles and then, looking in the mirror, I flex my right biceps and then my left. I step away from the mirror and then put a different shirt on and walk back downstairs.

'Did you say that Nick is still in the hospital?' I ask Caroline. Caroline is cutting large plum tomatoes into quadrants.

'He's there overnight,' Caroline says. 'Shirley is staying over with him, I believe.'

'Who is staying with Cynthia?' I say. Caroline shrugs.

'Maybe she's staying with a friend,' she says. 'Why?'

'Well,' I say, 'she's vulnerable.'

Caroline doesn't turn around. She carries on chopping. I pick up a quadrant of tomato and pop it into my mouth.

'I don't know, Pol,' Caroline says. 'I don't really know whether I'm supposed to know, frankly.'

I go into the living room and pick up the remote and switch the channel.

'Stop changing the channel,' Caroline shouts from the kitchen. 'I'm watching that.'

On the TV screen the news reporter is interviewing a shirtless man in Bangladesh. The man is the superintendent of a temple that was built five centuries before Christ. The temple has been in constant use since it was built. But now it is at the bottom of the sea. The screen switches to a shot of a flotilla of little boats encircling an object which protrudes from the surface of the water. It looks like a buoy. But the voice-over tells us that the object is the uppermost bauble on the top of the temple's shikhara. One by one the boatmen paddle towards the bauble and they reach out and touch it and then they run their hands over their faces, dousing themselves in its ancient holiness.

Later on, in bed, we have an argument about me changing the channel. It made me feel less-than when Caroline didn't praise me for rescuing Nick. Caroline doesn't turn around to face me.

'When I'm watching something and you change the channel,' she says, 'it just sends me a signal. That's all.'

'I didn't know that you were watching it,' I say.

'It sends me a signal, Pol,' Caroline says. 'Just like the TV sends me a signal without knowing that it's doing it. Whether you choose to know it or not, that's what it does to me.'

III

The Nakba

But then there was the *nakba*, the disaster. The thing that I had spent the previous two decades half-heartedly dreading.

'You shouldn't call it the *nakba*,' Caroline says. As though I should feel the terrible anguish of strangers on the other side of the world more keenly than I feel my own terrible anguish.

One thing that was strange about the second attack, shortly before my thirty-fourth birthday, was that it was preceded by the same dream that I had had before my first attack, which happened when I was thirteen. Yellowy-white teeth pouring out of a cereal box into a bowl. I try to tell McCaul about it.

'Probably just your brain retrofitting some kind of unconscious thoughts somehow,' he says. 'Nothing mysterious about it necessarily.'

We are sitting in my bedroom, me propped up on the triangular pillow that we bought for Caroline when she was pregnant, and McCaul and Caroline sitting at the end of the bed on chairs that they brought up from the dining room. McCaul has asked both of us to write down in careful detail what exactly happened on the evening of the attack.

I start reading from my little piece of paper. The morning with the terrible headache. Caroline cancelling dinner with Nick and Shirley. Me lying down on the couch and falling asleep. Waking up screaming in agony, ripping my body apart. Reaching down to the floor so that I could crawl to the bathroom to get some of Caroline's co-codamol that she takes for her back and feeling my wrist snap in half. Caroline coming into the room and then calling for the ambulance.

There is a silence. Caroline looks at me.

'It's interesting to me that you would choose to leave some things out,' she says, her own piece of paper in her hand.

'What parts?'

She holds the piece of paper up to shield her face from McCaul's view and mouths:

'Your pants…?'

I turn back to face McCaul. My neck hurts just from turning it a few inches.

'I shat my pants,' I say. McCaul nods, unflustered, and taps a few times on the screen of his iPad.

'Very predictable,' he says, without looking up. 'Your body is realizing the rapid changes in your metabolism and is trying to get rid of things that it doesn't need.'

He coughs and then smiles, wanly, at Caroline. After a pause, he says:

'Similar to what happens at the point of death.' And then abruptly reddens as though embarrassed, as a medical man, at having to utter the D-word.

He asks us a few more questions. How is the wrist healing, he wants to know. Have I noticed anything bruising more easily. As the conversation goes on I can tell that he doesn't feel comfortable looking at me. It surprises me, given all of the terrible things that he must have seen over the course of his medical career. Strangely, I seem to find it easier to look at myself than other people do since the attack. Caroline didn't even want to let you see me at all when we were in the hospital. How is that a sustainable solution, I wanted to know.

'I know this is hard to hear, Pol, but you are on a lot of drugs right now and it's making you see things in a much rosier light than you might be doing otherwise.'

'You think he'd be scared?' I'd wanted to know. 'Horrified? Is it that bad?'

She'd shrugged. I could see the glaze of tears in her eyes.

'Crazy gaunt,' she'd said, tearfully. 'Sort of like the Nazi in *Indiana Jones* when he sees the Holy Grail.'

McCaul finishes typing his notes into his iPad and then moves over to the bed and crouches down and takes hold of my hand.

'I'm sorry,' he says, awkwardly. 'I *knew* this was going to happen.'

He shakes his head sadly and straightens. He draws a timeline on his yellow, blue-lined pad. He points to the timeline with the tip of his pen. He points to his temple to indicate taking care of my Mental Health, and Caroline also taking care of her Mental Health. The point of the medication was never to keep me at the same age forever, he reminds me, it was just to prevent the kind of heterochronous shock that I had experienced when I was thirteen, with all the comorbid issues: the pain, the weakening of bones, the threat of coronary failure. To this extent the medications had done their job.

'Don't look so downhearted,' he says. 'You're still younger than me.'

He laughs.

'I'm not looking downhearted,' I reply. 'This is just how I look now.'

As he is walking out of the door, Caroline asks about my hair.

'What about it,' McCaul says.

'He had such a beautiful, thick head of hair,' she says. 'Is there anything that the hospital can do about it?'

McCaul pauses, tolerantly.

'Like a wig?' he says.

Caroline starts to cry.

'Don't get me wrong,' she says, between sobs. 'I know that some people can pull it off really well.'

It's funny the things that you get hang-ups about. Only a few months ago I was worried that I looked pale if I hadn't been out in the sun for a while or if my face looked puffy after a few days of boozing. Now it's the thick blue veins that protrude from my shins. Caroline wants me to shave my head completely.

'I'll look like an alien,' I tell her.

She folds her arms.

'You can't keep these little white fluffs,' she says. 'You look like a baby bird. You look mad. What's worse: looking like an alien or looking like . . .'

She searches around for the name of a celebrity.

'I can't think of anything funny to say,' she says.

The days pass by, blendered into one another.

'Are you here for a papal audience?' I can hear Caroline saying in the hallway, and the sound of Caoimhe's laugh. I can hear her sending Caoimhe up to my bedroom.

She tells me that Donald Trump has said that if he wins he

will introduce a database of all the Muslims in America.

'I haven't been following it,' I say. 'Too strange.'

'Feels like the end of the world,' Caoimhe says.

'Don't stay for too long,' I tell her. 'The new medications make me feel exhausted.'

'You know who you really look like, don't you?' Caoimhe says. 'That baldy head? That belly? All you need is the little round glasses and the German accent.'

Caoimhe says that our mother has become convinced that she is immortal.

'We talked to a psychiatrist who says that it's common among people who suffer from dementia,' she says. 'Apparently their experience of time can become very elasticated. She feels as though she has been alive for a thousand years. She thinks that she was present at various historical events, including the Battle of Lepanto and the bombing of Hiroshima. She thinks that her pills are an elixir of everlasting life.'

'The Battle of Lepanto?'

'Remember the painting that her dad had over the fireplace in Connemara.'

'Golly.'

My father thought he was immortal. His life just seemed to go on and on, he said. I remember the stack of densely typed pages on the floor next to his armchair in the living room in the house in Bournemouth. He didn't want her notes, he told my mother, smiling, just the grammatical corrections. He was holding one of the typed white pages with blue biro written in the margins in his hand, holding it aloft like Neville Chamberlain. She was spooning ground coffee into the funnel of the Bialetti.

He had a friend who was going to help him to get it published.

I remember the friend coming and sitting in our living room and paying my father compliments. I don't know what his name was: tall and thin and younger than my father. He had come up from London on the train. My mother was embarrassed because she thought that my father was rude to him.

'You have this *way*,' she said. 'The *way* you get sometimes.'

'I should try to impress him?' my father saying. 'It's a business relationship. A relationship of *equals*. We both have things that the other wants.'

But the man obviously never came back.

Years later, long after he had left, when my mother and Caoimhe and I were living in Kilburn, mysterious letters began appearing. About once a month my mother would read a letter from my father, translating it from the German as she went along. In the letters my father would commend me for my academic engagement. When I got interested in Bartholomew Playfere, he sent a list of books that he said that I should read about the Civil War. When he found out about the short story competition, he wrote to my mother to tell her that I would one day be a great writer. And he would castigate Caoimhe for going out with boys.

I can't remember if I knew at the time that it was really my mother who was writing the letters. It's funny to think, now that I think of it, Caoimhe is saying, but she was trying to do the right thing. Is it really so different from telling your kids that Santa won't bring them toys if they're naughty, she wondered.

'I don't know why I was so angry about it,' she says.

But she was angry at the time. *She* knew all along, and more infuriating to her than the betrayal or the mendacity was my mother's belief that she could so easily pull a fast one on Caoimhe.

—

At the time, Caoimhe expressed her anger by writing her own letters from my father, pretending to find them on the door-mat and then reading them out to us over the breakfast table. My mother would be forced to listen and to help Caoimhe translate them. Obviously my mother knew all along and I am sure that she knew that Caoimhe knew that she knew. To call Caoimhe out, I suppose she thought, would be a little too thought-planting a thing to do. It was just one of those strange miniature Cold Wars that families create together. Mutually assured destruction. Caoimhe's letters were written in immaculate German. She must have written them in English and then got a friend of hers at school – or even a German teacher – to translate them.

'Don't tell Caroline about any of that,' I say to Caoimhe as she is leaving. 'About the letters, I mean.'

'What world are you living in?' Caoimhe says, laughing.

It's only after Caoimhe has left that I remember about the event which put an end to it all. Caoimhe handing my mother a letter purporting to be from my father's sister who lived in Lobbach: a letter saying that my father had passed away, that he had been hit by a bus in the centre of Heidelberg and that he had died. Then there were no more letters after that. It was pretty hardcore in retrospect.

The last person of all to visit is Cynthia. She is home from Oxford for her reading week. Her parents must have told her about my episode. She never really got a proper chance to thank me for my help with the coursework. After she handed in her coursework we just sort of lost touch. In the intervening period I would google her and look at her Facebook page every now and again.

Caroline shouts upstairs. I don't reply. I wait for Caroline to tell Cynthia that I must be asleep and that I shouldn't be disturbed and then I hear the front door close. I hear the sound of Caroline coming up the stairs and I sink down under the duvet and I close my eyes and pretend to be asleep. Caroline creeps across the room towards the bedside table and I hear her place an object down on the table next to my head. I wait for her to leave and then I open my eyes and I lift myself up in the bed. There on the bedside table is a small stack of books. All of the books have plain blue covers with the name of the author written on them in white Helvetica: Adonis Dolofonithikos.

Over the next few days I go through them all. The books are printed collections of the essays that Dolofonithikos posted on Reddit, with the addition of explanatory prefaces. Some of the explanatory prefaces are written by famous people like Noam Chomsky and Tariq Ali and David Graeber. They don't agree with all of the analysis – they invariably say – but they acknowledge that it's an important or significant or provocative contribution to the discourse.

The longest and the most interesting is called *The Nightingale's Song*. *The Nightingale's Song* is written not like a work of political theory but rather like a parable. It is adapted slightly from the first long post that Dolofonithikos ever posted on Reddit. It is a retelling of the myth of Adonis. Adonis is the epitome of youth: he is handsome, athletic and virile. Up until the birth of Adonis, the ancient gods and their youthful offspring had been able to live side by side. The young enjoyed life and they paid homage to the gods. The old gods lived from these propitiatory tributes. But the birth of Adonis destroyed this ecology. The old gods were no longer happy with the propitiatory offerings of the young. They were consumed with envy at the dignity that Adonis enjoyed. They destroyed Adonis and they set about hunting for the elusive joy of youth. Wherever they found it, they both consumed it and destroyed it.

It's interesting. I suppose it's an origin myth, a story about the natural order of things. In the natural, prelapsarian order of things, a Division of Dignity existed within society. Natural Dignity was enjoyed by the young because of their ability to live life fully: to work, to play, to have sex, to have children. Compensatory Dignity was given to the elderly in the form of care, support and financial help. So a natural ecology was established. But with the advent of agriculture, the development of the concept of property, of ownership and wealth, two things happened. First, the young no longer had to work as hard or to take so many risks. They no longer had to fight and hunt, but the Natural Dignity afforded to them remained the same. Second, the elderly developed the ability to *store* the Natural Dignity that they had created in their youth. That is the purpose of wealth: stored work, stored youth. The line became blurred. At that point, the elderly grew to resent the young, while at the same time becoming able to retain an autonomy which in the natural order of things they were deprived of. They resented the fact that the young were able to enjoy Natural Dignity without having to risk death or without having to undergo hardship in order to gain it. The Compensatory Dignity was not enough. They wanted to have both. But the only way that they could seize the Natural Dignity of youth from the young was through violence. They had to disrupt the natural order of things. And they did so. And they do so. They do so through the rape of the young, the sexual exploitation of young powerless women by old powerful men. They do so through the pauperization of the young. They do so through the disenfranchisement of the young. They supplant the young. They usurp the young. And because the young will always be stronger than the old, the old have to resort to more and more extreme forms of violence in order to maintain their control.

From ancient times to today, the old have had to fight constantly to maintain their counter-intuitive ascendancy over the young. This need to fight, to conquer, to conjure a mythology of superiority has taught the elderly not only how to treat the young, but also how to treat each other, how to treat the planet, how to treat God. It is a habit of violence.

Every problem that exists in society, Adonis Dolofonithikos wrote, is brought about by the hatred of the young by the old. The overthrow of the youth right is an ongoing, violent insurrection, and in one way or another it has brought about the defilement of the planet, of the atmosphere, the exploitative practices of capitalism, homelessness, the rape culture, child abuse, materialism, incest, depression, status anxiety, imperialism, impotence, domestic violence, the extinction of the species. All of these things have come about as a result of the violent overthrow of the natural power of the young by the old.

The desperation of the elderly to suck the pleasures of youth out of the bodies of the young has destroyed the planet and has destroyed humanity. It is incumbent on all, young and old, to plunge a stake into the heart of the system.

'I *will* read it,' Caroline says, 'I promise. I just have a lot on my plate right now.'

She places the tray of food on my lap and asks me to lean forward while she plumps my pillows.

'I don't quite understand why they had to make a book out of it if it's already online though,' she says. 'Cutting down all those trees? How does *that* help the planet exactly?'

It's Such a Joke That It Needs to Be Destroyed

By the end of the year I am back on my feet. The only lasting problem is with my colon. Due to some of the explosive shitting that had been going on at the time of the attack something had ruptured irreparably, and it means that I can now no longer control my bowel movements. It's not so terrible really, even if it does sound really terrible. Instead of finding a toilet and then going to the toilet, I go to the toilet and then find a toilet. The only real issue is in the night-time. Sometimes I don't wake up and in the morning I find that I have filled my diaper in the night. That's how Caroline puts it. *Filled my diaper*, in an American accent. If I roll around in the night, sometimes the shit sort of cakes my waist or sometimes it can even come out of the sides and get on to the bed. The first time that happened, Caroline made a strange face: a mixture of pity and disgust and annoyance and weepiness. If she wakes up first, which she usually does, she just changes it for me now. More often than not I just sleep through it. The first time, I woke up in the middle of her changing me and for a moment I thought that she was going down on me. I could see her crouched at the bottom of the bed and could feel her hands clutching at my hips.

'What are you doing?' I said, drowsily.

'Hush,' she said. 'Let's. Just. Get. This. *Done.*'

Even if I do wake up, now, in all honesty, I just pretend to be asleep.

'Gross as it may sound,' Caroline said, 'isn't it possible for you to accentuate the positive. You have your disability money. You don't have to work at school any more. This is the moment, surely, for you to start working in earnest on your project, your writing.'

And I started to. There's a little bus with disabled access that picks up pensioners from the Kilburn High Road and takes them into central London. I got a special pass that let me use facilities for old people. McCaul got it for me. For a few weeks I got into the habit of waking up with Caroline, and when she took you to school, I would get the bus into town and go to the British Library and work on my book. Every day, the first thing I would do was send an email to at least one person who works in a university to ask if I could get admitted on to a PhD course, and then I would spend the rest of my day doing my research.

After a while, though, it got too tiring. I would wake up later and later, and then after a while I would convince myself that the journey into town was a wasted hour and that I would be better off working on the book at home. Caroline agreed.

'You have a ton of material that you can work through in those notebooks,' she said. 'Maybe you've done the research part and now you just need to do the writing part.'

One evening, Edith comes over for dinner. It's the first time that I have seen Edith since my attack and when I answer the door I can tell that she is unprepared. She almost doesn't recognize me. She takes a step back from the door, almost as though she instinctively thinks that she has come to the wrong place. Then she collects herself:

'Pol,' she says. 'You look well actually.'

'Thanks,' I say, and then smile, as though sharing a joke.

After a few glasses of wine with dinner she begins to acclimatize. She had an aunt who had a particularly aggressive form of motor neurone disease, she tells us. She knows what it's like to have your body begin to waste away. Caroline noisily collects the ramekins from the *Bonne Maman* crème brûlées and carries them into the kitchen. Edith blushes.

'I'm sorry,' she says. 'I don't know what it's like. That's not what I meant. The words just came out wrong.'

After Edith leaves, Caroline blows her cheeks out like Dizzy Gillespie and then exhales and says that she's been ready for bed for an hour. We take turns to brush our teeth and then go upstairs to bed, but I can't sleep. Next door has his cousin from Quebec staying and the cousin takes phone calls in the middle of the night, angry phone calls, swearing in French. I can hear him shouting something about '*m'est égal*'. I think about going out into the night-time street and banging on the door and then instead I think about popping a note through the letter box in the morning, but then I think about probably doing nothing, just hoping that the cousin goes back to Quebec soon or that his business or family problem gets resolved soon. Caroline says that when I can't sleep I should accept it rather than panicking. Just act as though it's normal to be awake. I think about going downstairs and opening my laptop and doing some writing, and as soon as I begin to contemplate this I fall asleep.

In the morning I wake up and come down to find you and Caroline already eating breakfast.

'I didn't want to wake you,' Caroline says from behind a spoonful of porridge. 'There's porridge in the pot if you want some.'

I walk over to the sink and I run myself a glass of water. I'm supposed to keep myself extra-hydrated because of the new medication. I wake up every morning with a clammy feeling in my mouth.

When you leave to go to school, I go back upstairs and lie down on the bed and allow my eyes to close. There's no point trying to write if I'm too tired to even keep my eyes open. The *Today* programme is still on downstairs and the soft sounds lull me off to sleep again. I wake up an hour later and go downstairs and brush my teeth and run a bath. Caroline has left her laptop on the kitchen counter. I open the laptop and scroll through some recommended YouTube videos. They are mostly interviews with Keanu Reeves on late-night talk shows. I wonder if Caroline has been watching interviews with Keanu Reeves on the Internet. I click on one of them. Keanu Reeves is talking about a goldfish which he has had for sixteen years. The talk show host makes a joke about Keanu Reeves' parents sneaking into his house to replace the dead goldfish. The audience laughs. I take a spoon out of the sink and dry it by wiping it on my pyjama bottoms and then scoop a spoonful of cold porridge out of the pan and eat it standing up, watching the screen and Keanu Reeves. I drop the spoon into the sink and I pick up the laptop and I carry it into the bathroom, where I perch it on top of the closed toilet lid. I strip off and climb into the bath, carefully avoiding catching sight of my naked body in the bathroom mirror. Keanu Reeves is saying that it is a common misconception that goldfish have a short life expectancy. In actuality goldfish can live for up to twenty years. I slip my head underneath the water so that the sound of the interviewer's voice becomes a semi-audible waw-waw sound. I close my eyes and try to float in the black-ness. When I come back to the surface, the interviewer is asking Keanu Reeves how old he is and Keanu Reeves is saying that he is fifty-one and the audience whoops. The host pretends to fall off his chair in astonishment. I wonder if Keanu Reeves is joking.

I climb out of the bath and towel myself off and I bring the laptop back into the kitchen. I make myself a coffee and I open up a new Word document on the laptop. While I'm waiting for the coffee, I open a new Internet window and search for goldfish and discover that it is true that they can live for twenty years. Then I search for Keanu Reeves. It seems that he *is* fifty-one. I scroll down the list of results to gauge how surprised people are at this fact. The fifth result down is a subreddit for people who don't believe that Keanu Reeves is fifty-one after all. I click on the link.

The description of the subreddit seems to suggest that it was originally set up for light-hearted reasons, to discuss the seem-ingly miraculous lack of ageing of Keanu Reeves. There are a handful of memes which suggest, jokingly, that Keanu Reeves may be a vampire. But the majority of the thread seems to have been hijacked by people who believe in something called adrenochrome and who believe that Keanu Reeves belongs to a special group who have access to secret therapies which use the plasma from young people in order to preserve youth. There is a link to an article in the *Lancet* which posits that adrenochrome therapy is viable. They used mice in an experiment and they managed to concoct an elixir of mouse youth, using the blood from younger mice. The person who posted the link has written underneath:

'The name of this blood is called Adrenochrome. They scare the heck out of a little child before killing it and as the fear-based death happens, adrenaline is pushed into the neck which they either extract using a needle or they outright cannibalism the child killing her with their teeth like a wild animal. An Illuminati slave once blew the whistle on Queen Elizabeth for killing a child during a Satanic ritual using this method.'

Somebody else has replied:

'As a recreational drug user, someone who regularly extracts their own mescaline and works with medicinal bud, I can't stand this answer. Adrenochrome has no known psychoactive effects and it has been experimented with quite a bit. Nice way to feed the Christian fear mongering of "drugs are the devil" to the sheep mindsets out there. Much more reasonable explanation has to do with the alchemical process of calling a god down into an oracle, children the easiest vessels to occupy, then torturing said god to have effect on this plane.'

I click on the profile of the man who has written this reply. u/Mescalean. Most of his posts are part of a different subreddit called r/Retconned.

I click on the link to the r/Retconned subreddit. This subreddit is even more interesting. There are references to Keanu Reeves here too. The people on the r/Retconned subreddit have a totally different perspective. They notice that their collective memories of the past don't match up with recorded evidence of the past. They think that this is evidence that the past has been doctored in some way or else that some event has taken place which has caused the old world of their memories to die and to be replaced by a new world or else that this existence is a simulation of some kind. There are certain features of this new world that don't seem to match with the world as it was before. In the old world, the sun seemed larger and more yellow in colour. Nowadays, the world seems to be populated not by real people but by NPCs: non-player characters.

'I don't know why but I vividly remember my life feeling more real before this time. The interactions were joyful. There was a feeling of purpose. I could connect with people on just about everything. People had distinct personalities. People weren't completely absorbed by social media. People wanted to do things. Since then life has been the complete opposite. I don't connect with anyone. I just sit around at the office and look at my phone in between working since it seems like everyone is the same NPC.'

'Nowadays, something has been changed which means that time is sped up.'

'I'm only 31 and time has been moving faster since 2010 or so. It's not just the weeks and years either the days also feel rushed or sped up. The seconds on the clock move faster. Every year just goes by faster and faster. Didn't think I would be experiencing this so early if it really is just an age thing. 25–30 isn't even that old.'

I sit there at the kitchen table scrolling through the subreddit, stopping occasionally to read when something catches my eye, usually capital letters. I feel myself quivering for some reason as I read the subreddit. When the members of the subreddit realize that the reality they are experiencing is fake, or is being orchestrated by some malevolent force, they get depressed.

'I have nothing left to lose. I would NEVER birth kids into a thing like this and don't see a point in contributing anything to this realm when everyone here is such a pathetic empty demonic carbon copy of their old selves and this entire "construct" isn't even real . . . I struggle every day just to get things done . . . I cannot take this place "seriously" anymore because it's literally ruled by a trickster. It's such a joke that I feel like it needs to be destroyed.'

I can hear the key turning in the lock and the sound of Caroline telling you why it's dangerous to look straight at the sun during an eclipse. I look up at the clock and realize that it is three-thirty already. I close the laptop gently and I slope out of the kitchen and up the stairs before Caroline sees me. Upstairs, in the bedroom, I hurriedly take my pyjamas off and throw on a jumper and a polo shirt – the shirt already inside the jumper from the day before – and a pair of jeans.

'All okay?' I shout down the stairs. There is no reply. Caroline is still talking to you about the eclipse. You tell her that she's wrong because you once looked straight at the sun when there was an eclipse and you could see fine.

'Oh chicken,' Caroline says, 'I think you must be making a mistake. There hasn't been a solar eclipse since you were a little baby.'

When my attack happened Caroline had some sort of mental block. She didn't understand that my treatment was intended only to prevent the effects from getting worse. She seemed to think that the doctors were going to try to reverse the changes: to iron out the wrinkles in my skin, to make my hair grow back and grow back black, to build up my muscles to the way they were before. That everything would be made to go back to normal. It seemed impossible to her that things would never be the way they were before. They were that way before, it seemed strange that it would be impossible for them to be that way again. She cried down the phone to Dr McCaul.

'I think this is all about expectation management,' he said to her.

After dinner we watch a bit of TV and then go to bed, but for a second night in a row I can't sleep. The Quebecois seems to have put his phone on silent, but I can still hear it vibrating on his bedside table like a vuvuzela, hour after hour. I look at my phone and see that it is one in the morning. I slip into my tracksuit bottoms and trainers and creep downstairs and out of the front door.

Outside, the streets are filled with ghosts, as thick as fog, the colour of wine. The wine-coloured fog is just smoke spilling out of the exhaust of an idling lorry, mixing with the red light from its hazards and the blue light from the stars in the night sky. The idling lorry is standing outside the twenty-four-hour Hilal Food Centre.

Inside the shop I walk down narrow aisles and watch as the staff load packets of unfamiliar grains and unfamiliar spices on to the shelves. A patriarchal proprietor stands behind the counter, wearing a gold watch, his arms crossed. I walk down the narrow aisles and feel the souls of dead human beings (and human beings whose souls have wandered out of their bodies, leaving their bodies lying on hospital beds and gurneys, or sitting, rapt, in high-backed wipeable armchairs, having the sides of their mouths dabbed by nurses and carers) close in around me. I squint to see the spirits of the dead, wading, their torsos just reaching above the ground beneath my feet. Their legs are sunk far below, their feet still walking the streets of the previous decades and centuries, the streets that are still down there, deep beneath our feet, beneath our streets. So many layers of tarmac and tiles and cobbles. Layer upon layer upon layer. Building and building and burying all the time. Why do human beings do such things.

In the last aisle there is an expanding puddle of deep scarlet blood. The patriarch's scion, wearing an apron, chasing me down the aisle.

'Not please sir,' he says, waving me away. 'Not here.'

And when I look down I see that it isn't blood at all but a bulbous bottle of expensive tomato juice, broken, shards sticking out of the soggy red liquid like the fins of sharks in a blood-filled sea. The tomato juice sods deep into the treads of my boots.

I buy a small bottle of Glen's vodka and I slip it into my coat pocket. I walk around the little warren of winding side streets that lead off the Kilburn High Road. Every now and then, I take a slug from the bottle. Suddenly there is a house that is completely covered in jasmine. I can smell the aroma of the jasmine from the other side of the street and it mixes with and sweetens the taste of the vodka in my mouth.

A man standing on his doorstep, almost on the street, wearing a nightgown and smoking a cigarette and calling over his shoulder, into the gloomy recesses of the house behind him:

'Where does he get that from anyway? Where does he *get* it from? He doesn't get it from *me*!'

For some reason it makes me think of Cynthia.

'Did you hear about Cynthia?' Caroline said a few nights ago. 'Athens. Nick and Shirley are worried sick. She's living in a commune with only other disabled people. Something to do with that political campaign that she is involved with.'

I didn't feel like I wanted to think about Cynthia at that moment. And now for some reason I feel like I do.

Here Lovely, Be Sick Into This

There's one week to go of term. You say that you don't want to go in and that you actually don't have to go in anyway because Edith says that they will just be playing games and making Christmas decorations.

'Come on me old china,' Caroline says, hoarsely. 'Just put your shoes on so we can go.'

You fold your arms crossly and say that you don't want to wear those shoes because they pinch your feet.

'Let him wear his Crocs,' she says. I put my cup of tea down on top of the marble-topped table and tighten my dressing gown.

'He'll freeze in those,' I say. 'They aren't warm enough. It's freezing out there.'

'We'll take the proper shoes in a bag and if he gets cold he can change into them,' Caroline says.

'Hey J-dog,' I say, 'this is the best part of the whole year. You can bring in your DS. They might even let you watch a movie.'

Caroline shuffles into her Merrells and – with her heel still spilling over the heel of the shoe – takes a last swig of tea and puts the cup on the marble-topped table and reaches for your hand.

'I'll be back usual time,' she says.

Ted and Ellen call to say that they are going to come over for a couple of days before the end of term and that they will then go back to Ireland to celebrate Christmas on their own. It's something they've never done before and they think it will be nice. They can look after you a bit while they're here: pick you up from school and so on. They feel bad that they haven't been able to be on hand to help since my attack. After she has hung up the phone Caroline looks into the middle distance and nods slowly and pulls a fishtail frown like Marlon Brando.

'So,' she says. 'My own parents don't want to spend Christmas with me and their only grandchild.'

'That's really priceless,' she says. 'That's really the ego boost that I needed.'

I come down for breakfast a couple of days later to find Ted, already dressed, sitting on the bottom stair, reading to you. You have your fist resting against your forehead and your eyes follow Ted's index finger as it chases the words across the page. He turns and sees me and laughs. He tells you to go and fill your water bottle from the tap in the kitchen. He points to his bald head.

'You're one of us now, Pol,' he says. 'I must try and find some time to do your initiation rite.'

'What's the initiation rite?' I say.

'Just a joke,' he says, still smiling.

When you come back from the kitchen, he tells you to wave goodbye to me and then he leads you by the hand out of the front door and down the garden path. I close the front door and go into the kitchen.

In the kitchen, Caroline and Ellen are sitting at the island with

166

cups of coffee. They look serious. Caroline says:

'We need to have a chat about Jess.'

I sit down on one of the stools and look at them expectantly.

'He's being bullied,' Ellen says. 'I asked him why his coat was covered in mud and he told me that the other boys had taken his coat and had dropped it in a muddy puddle. He wouldn't tell me which boys.'

I stand up and go over to the kitchen counter and put the kettle on.

'He shouldn't know that we're talking about it,' Ellen continues. She raises her voice a little to be heard over the sound of the boiling kettle. 'So we asked Ted to take him for a walk while us three have a little chat.'

I pause for a moment.

'Am I allowed to say "boys will be boys"?' I ask. Ellen says nothing for a few seconds. She purses her lips and looks down at the black surface of the coffee in her coffee cup.

'You are *allowed*,' she says, 'to say whatever you feel.'

Later in the afternoon, I find Caroline lying on the bed upstairs, crying. I sit down on the bed and stroke her hair.

'Maybe it was a mistake, them coming over,' she says.

'I'm not sure that you worry any less about what they think when they're not here,' I say.

'That's not what I meant,' Caroline says, pushing my hand away.

Ted and Ellen say that while they're here we should have like a mini-Christmas morning and exchange gifts. That sounds like a nice idea I say. We gather all together around the kitchen table and Caroline gives her parents their gift from us. Ted sits and watches as Ellen unwraps the gift. Underneath the wrapping paper there is a little shoebox, which she opens.

She examines its contents, a little baffled.

'What is it?' I say.

Caroline smiles sheepishly.

'Remember those three little tin knights that you brought back from Germany that time? I found a whole set of them online.'

'That's wonderful, sweetheart,' Ted says. 'Thank you so much, sweetheart.'

He leans across the pile of wrapping paper and gives Caroline a kiss on the cheek.

'Now we can give you our present,' Ellen says.

You say that you want to unwrap a present.

'I'm afraid that this isn't really an unwrapping kind of present, chicken,' Ellen says, sorrowfully. She pulls an envelope out of her jacket pocket and hands it over to Caroline.

Inside the envelope is a card with a photograph of an icy landscape on it and inside the card there are three plane tickets and a reservation for a hotel in Lapland for three nights: the twenty-third, twenty-fourth and twenty-fifth of December.

'Oh chicken!' Ellen shouts, suddenly. 'Isn't that exciting.'

You look up at Caroline quizzically.

'This is where Santa Claus lives!' says Caroline in a smiley voice, even though she isn't really smiling. 'We're going to go and visit Santa Claus!'

Afterwards Ellen tells Caroline that she's felt just awful the whole time not being able to explain why they wouldn't be spending Christmas together and Caroline tells her that she needn't have worried at all, and that even without the Lapland trip it was completely understandable that Ted and Ellen would want to have a child-free Christmas for once.

'Bye!' Ellen shouts, sticking one hand out of the car window and waving as they drive away from the house in their hired Toyota. 'Enjoy!'

We go around to my mother's house and tell Caoimhe and Jamie about the Lapland trip. Even though they have only really known each other for a few months, Jamie seems to have moved into my mother's house with Caoimhe.

They met at Caoimhe's life-writing class. Jamie is training to be a psychotherapist at the Tavistock Centre and is also working on a memoir. Jamie's father was a prominent restaurant reviewer and a bit boozy, and when he died, Jamie discovered that he had kept two wives, two families. Jamie went into psychoanalysis then and eventually quit his job in advertising in order to start his training. He has this closely cropped but very thick black hair and this aerobicized physique. He has a yogic way of moving, a suppleness about him.

We were originally planning to have Christmas with them at my mother's house and so we apologize for the late notice.

'No worries at all,' Jamie says, when we tell them about Lapland. 'I think that's lovely. What a lovely gift to be able to give to a child.'

Caoimhe says nothing. I know that she thinks that it's all a bit flashy. I know that she doesn't like Caroline's parents.

'I'll tell you what,' Jamie says. 'Why don't I drive you to the airport. What time are your flights?'

Over the next couple of days, you get very excited about the trip. You ask Caroline to take you round to your friend Andrew's house so that you can tell him that you are going to go and visit Santa. Caroline tries to explain to you – in children's terms

– that this would be a gauche thing to do. You talk so much about Santa that he begins to invade my dreams. I wake up in the middle of the night short of breath, to find Santa sitting, cross-legged, on my chest with Caroline next to me in the bed making half-asleep soothing noises and stroking the length of the back of my forearm with the tips of her fingernails.

The twenty-first is the last day of school. The next day, you have a day off, an INSET day, but Caroline still has to go in.

'You can let him sleep,' she says. 'Just give him his breakfast whenever he gets up.'

'I think he's coming down with something,' she says. 'He's got the same thing as you. He's dry coughing. There's some Calpol and stuff out on the side in the kitchen if you need it.'

When I wake up the next morning, you are already sitting at the end of the bed.

'Good morning budski,' I say. 'What would you like to do today?'

You tell me that you would like to get a Christmas tree. Andrew has a Christmas tree. We thought that we would skip getting a Christmas tree this year on account of not being at home for Christmas. But when you suggest it, it does make me feel a little sad. Maybe we should get a Christmas tree, I think.

'I was thinking that we might have a bit of a lazy day,' I say. 'Mummy will be back in a few hours. Maybe we could watch a Christmassy movie?'

You say nothing. You walk out of the room with that angry, stalking walk that you do sometimes.

I go to the bathroom and get some cough medicine. I can't seem to shake this tickly cough. I take a swig from the bottle. The bottle is cold in my hand and the pink swill coats my throat with a sharp, saccharine taste, like sweet sick. Downstairs I can hear you talking to yourself, pretending to be a pirate. Being a bit violent. The sound gives me a tight feeling in my chest.

I put on my socks and trousers and I pull a duffle coat on over the T-shirt that I slept in and I go downstairs. I tell you to put your shoes on.

'Where are we going?' you say.

'It's a mystery,' I reply. 'Just get your shoes on.'

We get the bus down Kilburn High Road. There is a shop near the school where I remember seeing some Christmas trees for sale. But when we get there, there aren't any left and the man laughs at us for not coming sooner.

'Very late,' he says.

The man tells us that there might be a few trees in the garden centre up in Cricklewood. But he doesn't know if there are. My feet are like icicles. I thank the man and then take you by the hand and walk you up to the bus stop.

'My feet are tired,' you say. 'And my hands are tired. Where are we going?'

'We're going to find a Christmas tree,' I say, giving up on the surprise.

We get on the number 16. There is some water on the floor of the bus. A woman stands up to offer me her seat and we sit down. You want to sit on my knee but I have to stop you because my legs hurt too much. At St Cuthbert's the bus stops. An electronic voice says that the bus is now on diversion. Two passengers rush down the stairs and jump off the bus. Perhaps we should get off, I think. Diversion to where? I take your hand and we climb down off the bus and we watch as the bus pulls away and takes a right up Mill Lane. I look up at the digital display board in the bus shelter. It's ten minutes until the next bus.

'Come on,' I say. 'We can walk.'

When he walked up this stretch of Watling Street, Bartholomew Playfere carried a long staff. He marched at the head of an army. People came out of their houses all along the way to watch them pass. Some threw stones. He sang a psalm unto the Lord as they walked:

O God, to whom vengeance belongeth.
Render a reward to the proud.
How long shall they utter and speak hard things?
How long shall they boast of themselves?
Understand, ye brutes and ye fools.
My Lord will not cast off his people.
He will rise up for me against evil.
He will stand up for me against kings.
The Lord is my strength and my refuge.
My Lord shall cut them all off.
Yea, the Lord our God shall cut them all off.

If you did that today people would throw stones too. If you left your family behind, left your children, left your elderly parents to fend for themselves. I remember that some separatist feminists did things like that in the 1980s. Linda Bellos for one. I'm sure they had stones thrown at them by people.

After we have been walking for a few hundred yards, it begins to rain. You don't have your raincoat on. The rain is soaking you through. It is icy cold. It is making dents in my skull. Outside the Beaten Docket we stop to hide underneath a bus shelter. I look up the digital display board. Eleven minutes. Two men are standing under the awning outside the boozer, smoking. They're speaking to each other in broad Scottish accents. One of them is wearing a Lonsdale windbreaker, the hood pulled down almost over his eyes, a large Union Jack on the back.

'What's the matter pal?' one of them says, laughing, barking. 'Come out without your brolly?'

Both men start to laugh. I try to avoid eye contact but you turn to look at them, slightly bemused. The man sticks his tongue out at you and smiles. His teeth are a little snaggled. The rain is blowing horizontally, still getting us, even inside the bus shelter.

'Don't look so downcast buddy,' says the second man, wheezing with laughter. 'Don't you know that you can't have the rainbow without the rain?'

'Come on,' I say. I take your hand and hurry up the road away from the men. I can hear them protesting that they are only joking as we walk away.

'Teann an fuacht triom,' I can hear my mother saying, the wind whipping our faces in Bournemouth. Walking to school. Stomach in knots.

There was a rainy, windswept sports field in Bournemouth. There was a dim, gentle grey sky. There were plastic bags blown about in the air. People brought their football boots in in plastic bags and then they dumped their sports kits in their lockers and they just dropped their plastic bags on the ground by the benches. You know: they don't *go* anywhere. You know that don't you? They'll be there, drifting about in the wind, long after we're dead. In the middle of the sports field there was a concrete cube the size and shape of a garage, with a pull-down door like a garage, where the cricket equipment was kept. They called it The Bunker. I was small for my age. They ganged up on me and they made me go into The Bunker and then they pulled down the door and locked me in. There were spiders in there, and nightly creatures and mildewing cricket bats and cricket pads that were burst and damp and blue and spewed damp, blueish foam and straw.

When the teachers came to let me out they were unsympathetic. It was a stupid and dangerous thing to do to go into The Bunker, they said. It was immature. I needed to act my age. The teachers could hear in my voice the traces of my German accent and one of the older masters chuckled unkindly when he saw a cut on my scalp one time. Boys will be boys. The other boys called me a Nazi or did Nazi salutes when I walked past. This was ironic because it was them, rather than me, who were behaving like Nazis. I tried to explain this to them.

'You're not helping him to be a better person when you tell him that he's a victim,' Caoimhe told my mother.

When we get to the garden centre, the gates are locked. There is a buzzer next to the gates which I press. The rain continues to pour. My T-shirt underneath my coat is soaked. I look down at you. You look as though you have been for a bath in your clothes. You sneeze, pitifully, without covering your mouth. I'm shaking. After a few minutes a man comes to the gate to let us in. He runs down the driveway towards the gate, sploshing in puddles in his heavy boots as he goes. The man is stocky and is wearing black dungarees and a blue cagoule. He looks frantic.

'What are you doing out there?' he shouts, over the sound of the rain. 'You'll be soaked.'

'We were told that you had some Christmas trees,' I say.

He looks at me with his mouth agape, calculating.

'It's just that we're closed now,' he says. 'We close early on

Fridays. We're just here for the stocktake otherwise nobody would even have heard the buzzer.'

He doesn't know what to say. He looks down at you and you look back at him with a sodden, windswept angelicness. He puts his hand palm down on the crown of his head.

'Listen,' he says. 'Just come inside. We'll figure something out.'

Inside there is a covered area, a corrugated iron roof which roars with the rain.

'Jesus you're soaked,' he says. He sounds sympathetic but I can tell that he's judging me. Underneath the corrugated iron roof, there is a row of Christmas trees.

'Why don't you take your grandad to pick a tree,' he says to you. 'You pick any one that you like.'

He presses a stripy candy cane into your hand. You struggle to open it but your hands are too cold.

'What do you say, Jess?' I say.

'He's not my grandad,' you say.

You pick one of the biggest trees. I'm not sure it will even fit in the living room. By the time you've chosen, the rain has stopped. The man doesn't take card payments. He says that he'll get one of the guys to follow us in the van with the tree in the back and that we can give the guy the cash when he drops it at the house. I'm starting to feel a little woozy. I ask the man if it will be okay for us to ride in the van with the tree. The man looks pointedly at our soaking wet clothes. It's only around the corner I tell him and he looks down at you and he nods.

I get into the van and it stinks of cigarettes. The driver stands next to the van, smoking before he gets in. He seems to be about seventeen. The smell from the cigarette smoke seems to turn my stomach slightly and I tell the driver that I don't feel well. I might just put my eyes closed for a minute, I tell him, realizing at the same time that that isn't a phrase. The driver looks at me blankly and shrugs. You stand by the door of the van but you can't climb up and the man helps you: lifts you up and puts you on the seat next to me. You smile. You like being swung about in the air like that, I remember. Inside the van, you put your hand on my elbow and you ask me if I'm sick.

'Just a bit sleepy, Jess,' I say. 'Just feeling a little bit tired.'

When we get back to the house, the driver takes the tree out of the back of the transit and hauls it into the house, leaving needles all over the carpet. The tree comes with a stand and the driver brings it into the living room and stands it upright in the bay window. The branches don't unfurl immediately, so that the tree looks kind of smudged, like it has just got out of bed.

'How do you feel about that, Jesse?' I say. 'Not bad, right?'

You take a fistful of Christmas tree in your fist and you let the feeling of it run through your hand. Needles sprinkle the floor at your feet. I pay the man and I give him a tip and he leaves. I take you upstairs and I take your clothes off and towel you down and give you some new clothes to put on. Even your socks are soaking wet. I go into the bedroom and change out of my wet clothes and I dump them into the washing machine. I feel awful. The taste of the cough mixture sits in my larynx and I can't seem to get rid of it no matter how much I swallow. Just sits there. Making me feel nauseous. I go downstairs and I lie down on the sofa. My head is starting to ring. Feels like a migraine. You come into the living room and stare at me. You seem concerned.

'Why don't you just lie down with me here just next to me,' I say. You curl into my flank. You scrunch your eyes closed.

We must both have fallen asleep because that's where Caroline finds us when she gets home at three. When I open my eyes I can see her standing over us, but she swims slightly in my vision. She's wearing a smart suit. She looks a little like Ellen for a moment.

'Well we really *are* having a lazy day,' she says.

'What's this?' she says, pointing at the Christmas tree.

'A Christmas tree?' she says. 'I thought we weren't going to get one this year. Isn't that the kind with all the needles?'

'He wanted to get one,' I say. 'We went to the garden centre. I thought it would be a nice thing.'

'You look awful,' Caroline says. 'You're shivering. I don't think you should have gone out in this cold when you're already feeling poorly.'

She strokes your back and then leans down to smell your head.

'He smells like rain,' she says. 'Was he wearing his raincoat?'

'I am actually feeling a little green around the gills,' I say.

She puts her hand flat against my forehead.

'Jesus Pol,' she says, 'you're burning up. Go up to bed and I'll bring you some soup or whatever.'

She takes her coat off and hangs it on the end pillar of the banister and goes into the kitchen.

I go upstairs and lie down in the dark. But in the dark, in the bedroom, it gets worse. I fall asleep and I start having strange dreams. I dream about Athens. In my dreams I stand in a hotel bedroom. The ceiling of my room is made of polystyrene tiles. It is hot. I press a button next to the light switch to turn the air conditioning on. I brush my teeth and come back into the room and notice then that there is a repetitive dripping sound.

When I wake up from the dream I can see Dr McCaul standing

at the bottom of my bed. He says something about sweating profusely. He looks angry. I try to tell him not to be angry with me but the words don't come out properly.

I dream about rising seas, walls of water, a huge tidal wave heading towards a sunlit beach, and carried aloft atop the wave is a squad of Kourist protesters, their torsos wrapped in Kourist flags like hula skirts. And there on the beach, Nye Bevan twerking.

I dream that your hands are in my hair. That you are sitting on my shoulders like you used to do with your hands in my hair. That we are running full tilt like that. You bouncing on my shoulders.

I can hear you crying. I can hear Caroline shouting, telling you to stay in your own room, that she will be in in a minute. She puts her cool palm on my head and a washing-up bowl that smells like bleach next to my head on the bed. Here lovely, she says, be sick into this.

I dream that I am in a shop where they are selling feta cheese cut from huge slabs. The slabs are stacked on top of one another in a ziggurat. The cheese is bright white, whiter than white.
    'Very hot?' the man behind the counter says, catching my eye, fanning himself with an open palm. 'Very hot. Very, very hot.'
    At the back of the shop there is a large open-fronted masonry oven. Moist stinky heat gasps from the mouth of the masonry oven. A woman is making parcels of pastry with feta inside and is painting them with oil and honey and loading them, on trays, on a peel, into the oven. She holds the peel that she uses to place the trays in the oven in her right hand, and when she has finished loading the oven, she leans on the peel as though it is a staff. I buy one of the honey-covered parcels of feta and the

man behind the counter gives me a paper towel to carry it in and I walk out of the shop. I bite into the parcel. The mixture inside is scalding and rancid and sweet and I feel instantly nauseous. I want to spew the hot white cheese out of my mouth.

'Here,' Caroline is saying, through the darkness. 'The bowl is right here. I'll put a fresh towel on the pillow for you, okay? Don't try to eat anything else.'

In the dream I am climbing the Areopagus. At the summit. As I get closer to the top of the hill, the wind starts to pick up. I'm only wearing shorts and a T-shirt. I'm wearing my bumbag with my passport and money in. The wind whips at my legs. There are bulbous blue veins bulging at the front of my shins and at the back of my calves. I am suddenly ashamed of them. The few long hairs at the side of my head are blown about in the wind. I feel exposed. The man from the garden centre is there. He has a stall and is selling trinkets relating to the temple site. He is selling navy blue baseball caps with an image of the Acropolis, stitched in gold thread, on the front of them. I ask how much they are and unzip my bumbag and he tells me that they are fifteen euros. I can't justify spending that much I tell him. The man shrugs. I give him an apologetic look and I replace the cap back on the rack. From the top of the Areopagus I can see across the city. There are lots of low-rise buildings. The ground is rocky and uneven underfoot. There is sand in the wind, sand in my mouth, making my mouth feel like sandpaper.

Dr McCaul is there. Talking to me in a raised voice, as though I'm deaf. We're monitoring you here, Pol, he is telling me. We don't want to take you into the hospital unless it's completely necessary. You're very feverish right now and you're losing a lot of liquid. It's very important that you stay hydrated. He'll be reachable by phone, he is telling Caroline now. But just speak to the GP if he's still like this tomorrow evening.

'On Christmas Eve?' Caroline is saying. I can hear her sobbing. 'We aren't going to get through to the GP on Christmas Eve.'

Some students are setting up a trestle table with a plastic banner attached to the front. The banner has the emblem of the Kourist movement on it: a red anemone with a black centre. Underneath the emblem there are some words written in Greek. They have a small generator attached to a set of speakers and a cordless microphone. One of them is speaking into the microphone to test the sound, but the sound of the wind distorts the sound of his voice. He moves the microphone away from his face and he spits the little bits of sand that have blown into his mouth on to the ground, the tip of his tongue protruding like a lizard. I sit down on an outcrop of stone. There is a small knot of audience members who are also sitting, cross-legged, on the stony ground. Some have brought fold-up chairs to sit on. They are all in their teens or early twenties. One or two are looking in my direction. I wonder how Cynthia will be able to get up on to the hill in her wheelchair. I cross and uncross my legs. One of my legs is going dead. In the dream I can feel the pins and needles in my calves, in my feet. One of the men is telling me that there is limited space for audience members. He asks me if I am here for the talk or if I am a tourist. But I mishear him.

'I'm not a Kourist,' I say. 'I'm just here out of curiosity.'

The man looks at me with a slightly mocking expression when I say the word Kourist.

'There is limited space,' he says again. 'We would be so grateful if you could sacrifice your space for one of us.'

His voice is heavily accented: not only Greek but also transatlantic, as though he has been taught to speak English by an

American. I feel as though I recognize him from somewhere. I stand up and make a show of collecting my things.

'By the way,' he says, still smirking. 'Nobody uses that term, man.'

I can hear Caroline speaking on the phone to Mac. She's saying something about the sun coming up, something about the temperature going down. Then she is next to me. We're not going to the hospital, she tells me. We're through the worst of it. I've been brave. I'm a fighter. She presses her forehead against my scalp. She calls me a stupid idiot. A Christmas tree, she says. She smiles. I can feel her teardrops against my cheek.

'What about Iceland?' I say.

'Lapland,' she says. 'You're in no condition to worry about that right now.'

'Did you tell your parents?' I ask.

'They had insurance,' Caroline says. 'They gave them some vouchers or something as well. We'll go next year.'

'What about Jess?' I say.

'He's going to have to get used to disappointment at some point, wouldn't you say?' she says.

'You could have gone without me,' I say. She laughs ruefully.

'You don't really believe that, Pol,' she says.

'Is Mac cross with me?' I say.

'Is *Mac* cross with you?' Caroline says. She rolls her eyes.

By the evening of Christmas Eve I am feeling well enough to sit up in bed. I ask Caroline to bring you up to see me but she says it's better not to risk it as you're still feeling a bit coldy. She seems distracted. I ask her if she is okay.

'I'm fine,' she says. 'Just trying to figure out what to do about tomorrow. I was just on the phone to Caoimhe and Jamie.'

'Do you want the curtains open or closed?' she says.

'I'm sorry,' I say. She turns to face me. She looks tired. 'Thank you,' she says.

I realize that I know that voice, the man from the dream. The Greek man with the American accent. His voice is the voice of the Cypriot man who used to sometimes call our home in the middle of the night to talk to my mother about the Independent Scientific Platform. The Independent Scientific Platform people bombarded my mother with literature when we were first referred to the neotenics clinic in 1994. The literature warned my mother not to trust the neotenics doctors. Neotenics was a con and neotenics doctors like Mac were shills for the government. People who subscribed to the Independent Scientific Platform believed that our condition was not a naturally occurring phenomenon at all. They believed that it was the unintended consequence of a government-backed scientific experiment that had gone awry and had been hushed up. It all started when the Soviets tried to develop technologies that would cause newborn babies to grow into adults immediately after they were born. This was supposed to help them to have a bigger army. The experiments were conducted secretly. The pregnant women who were injected with the complex cocktail of hormones were told that they were participating in a pilot scheme for a new medicine designed to cure morning sickness. When the Western powers found out about this technology, they tried it too. It was all part of the Cold War, part of the arms race. Whatever *they* did, we also had to do. But the hormones were too unpredictable and the trials had to be abandoned when only a few He Hakari Nēke children had been born. The Independent Scientific Platform magazine once included an interview with a spokesperson for a Tuskegee survivors' group. The Independent Scientific Platform people pointed out that a preponderance of people who had been born with HHN had been born in Germany, during the height of the Cold War.

One coda of this theory was that HHNs were believed to be adults in the truest sense. The fact that they were adults had to be covered up by the government. The government wanted HHNs to be treated as children because they believed it would prevent their claims from being taken seriously. As such, shills like Dr McCaul were paid to tell HHN parents that their children should be treated as children, no matter how old they appeared to be, physiologically. It was challenging. It was strange to have to talk to people who looked like grown men and women the way that you would talk to a child. But the neotenics experts warned that any sudden change in the parent–child relationship precipitated by a heterochronous shock would lead to serious developmental issues later on.

'Pol has been through enough trauma already,' Dr McCaul told my mother, for example.

I am lying awake in the middle of the night on Christmas Eve. After a while I get out of bed and I go into the next room and begin to pack away all my notebooks into a cardboard box. Soon, Caroline wakes up. She comes into the room and asks what I am doing. I've had a revelation, I tell her. All of this stuff is just blocking me. Like I've built a pillar and tethered myself to it. Caroline picks up a mug that I've accidentally knocked on to the floor and places it carefully on the table.

'So you're going to give up your writing? What are you going to do instead?' she asks.

I tell her that I have been thinking about the contribution I can make to the Kourist movement. Not in an uncritical way but just the fact that I have this nearly unique experience. A Unique Vantage Point. Because of my condition. I am going to write something about it. Maybe submit it to one of their magazines.

'Like a useful idiot you mean?' she says. She picks up the box of notebooks and holds it close to her midriff, as though she hasn't decided what to let me do with it yet.

'Why can't you be excited for me,' I say.

'Tonight of all nights, Pol,' she says. 'This night of all nights: please don't wake Jess.'

When I come down in the morning Caroline already has her coat on and is standing in the hallway.

'I think we might just go over to your mum's after all,' she says. 'He's done his presents but he's not talking to me. Honestly, the past forty-eight have been a bit of a shithole.'

'I want to come with,' I say.

'I don't think you're up to it, Pol,' she says. 'Just go back upstairs and rest. Everybody understands. There's always next year. Let's just try not to think about it too hard.'

'I want to come with,' I say.

When Jamie opens the front door to my mother's house, Caoimhe is standing behind him with a champagne bottle.

'Happy Christmas!' she says, popping the cork, spraying the champagne everywhere.

'Go inside and say hello to your grandma,' Caroline says to you, but you ignore her and go into the toilet and lock the door.

'How are you feeling, Pol?' Jamie says.

'I'm okay,' I say. 'Just feeling a little hoarse.'

'Lucky horse eh?' says Jamie.

They have put a miniature Christmas tree next to her bed, but her head is turned in the opposite direction from it.

'Hello Grandma,' Caroline says when she walks into the room, and Caoimhe smiles tolerantly.

While Jamie cooks the dinner, Caoimhe mixes some powder with water in a sports bottle.

'This is your granny's Christmas dinner,' she says to you. 'Doesn't it look yucky? Aren't we lucky to be having all of this lovely food instead?'

She takes you into the living room and you watch, intrigued, as she positions the nozzle of the bottle in my mother's mouth. Then she tips the bottle upwards and you watch my mother as she nuzzles the protein shake from the bottle. Caoimhe takes a red paper napkin with reindeers all over it out of her pocket and dabs gently at the corner of my mother's mouth.

By the time Caoimhe and Jamie serve the dinner, it's already dark outside. You say that you don't want to sit at the table and you go back into the living room and lie down on the floor. I stand up from the table as if to go after you but Caoimhe tells me to stay sitting, that she'll get you instead.

'Just leave him,' Caroline says. She has a glass of sherry in her hand. 'He's probably exhausted. He'll probably just pass out on the rug.'

Over the meal, I tell Caoimhe that the followers of Bartholomew Playfere were not allowed to celebrate Christmas and that they believed celebrations like Christmas and Easter were Babylonish customs. Jamie nods interestedly.

'I *think* that you *might* have mentioned that *last* Christmas,' Caoimhe says, smiling wickedly at Caroline. 'I *think* you might have mentioned that *every* Christmas *ever*.'

After dinner Caoimhe, Caroline and Jamie begin to clear the plates away. Caroline tells me to go and sit on the sofa while they clear up. It's dark in the living room. Through the front window, I can see into the front windows of other houses across the street. The other houses look warm and uncomplicated, with large Christmas trees on display. I realize suddenly that I don't even know if Caroline and you ever got around to decorating the tree that we bought. I sit down on the sofa. My mother's gaze is fixed on a spot above my head. I notice that Caoimhe has put some framed photos on her bedside table. One of them is of my mother and father on their wedding day.

'We were supposed to be going to Lapland,' I begin to say to my mother. But after that my words dry up. Her jaws are slightly open but her lips are closed, which gives her a haughty expression. She has lost a tooth or two. Behind me, in the dining room, the wreckage of the roast is still laid out on the table. You are sitting at the table alone, picking at the tablecloth with a fork and murmuring inaudibly to yourself. There is a dim chatter of conversation coming from the kitchen. Slowly I stand up and walk towards the table. I pull the plate with the roast turkey towards me and I peel a swatch of flesh from the half-eaten bird. I bring it over to my mother, holding it in the palm of my hand. Then I lift it up to her lips. At first she tries to move her head away, but then she seems to register what it is. She opens her lips and clamps the meat between them. Then she pulls it into her mouth with her tongue and begins to chew.

'That's good,' I whisper, reaching out with my hand to stroke her white hair away from her brow. 'How good is that?'

Dracula

On the first Monday of the new year we have an appointment at the neotenics clinic in Queen Square. There is a battery of tests. The audiologist asks me to repeat the words that I can hear in the headphones that she clamps around my head until I can't hear any more.

'Closet,' I say. 'Angel. Terrific. Trial. Disturb. Caves. Loosen. Reptile . . .'

The audiologist nods. She tells me that my hearing is still quite good for somebody my age. Caroline stands in the corner of the room gnawing at her thumbnail, with one arm folded over the other and one hand held to her mouth.

After the audiologist, I have to go up to see Mac. We wait on two black padded chairs in the marble-tiled corridor. Opposite us, hanging on the wall, is a gigantic portrait of Princess Diana. Caroline brushes the few strands of white hair this way and then that way across my head. She clutches on to my hand. I don't know if she's doing it to show affection or just to stop my hand from shaking.

'Isn't it crazy to think that, had she lived, she would have been like eighty by now?' Caroline says.

'She wouldn't have been eighty,' I say. 'She would have been like fifty.'

'Even still,' Caroline says, 'you get my point.'

They gave me a sticker at the reception desk, with a black-and-white photograph of myself on it. But the resolution is so poor that it just looks like a jam of black pixels. The sticker doesn't adhere to my jumper so I have to keep smoothing it with my hand.

'Just let it fall off,' Caroline says. 'If it falls off, it falls off. That's their problem, not yours.'

In 1994 there was a couple in Northern California whose daughter experienced an acute heterochronous shock (at almost the exact same time as my own) which left her with the mind of a nine-year-old in the body of a twenty-six-year-old. McCaul was actually called in with a team of experts to treat the little girl. He told her parents that they should always remember that the little girl was still a little girl, despite the fact that she looked like a grown woman. She wanted to play in the garden and go on the swings. She wanted to play with her friends. She was frequently arrested, interrogated by the police, for hanging around playgrounds in the hot Northern Californian sun. Understandably, the police took her to be a twenty-six-year-old woman. Raising an HHN child is hard for any family. But in this instance the parents became more and more convinced that their daughter – Leann Davis – was acting in a way which did not conform to their understanding of the condition. They were part of the Independent Scientific Platform. And instead of changing their opinion of the science based on their experiences of their daughter's behaviour, they changed their perception of their daughter's behaviour based on their understanding of the science. They were angry and abusive to her. Then they began to believe that she was acting out as a result of the trauma that she had experienced. They took her to a psychiatrist and to a therapist and to a Native American faith healer. Only when all else had failed did they come to the indomitable conclusion that the might of the government had been brought to bear on their family. The government was poisoning Leann. The Davises took Leann off her stabilizers. Leann got sick. But still she just wanted to behave like a little girl. She would try to climb into their bed at night because she had night terrors, but by now she was nearly six feet tall, taller than either of her parents. The Davises came to believe that the government was somehow putting drugs, was putting poisons, in the food that Leann was eating. These drugs were to blame for Leann's extraordinary behaviour. The Davises created elaborate rituals: paying neighbours to do their shopping for them, or travelling long distances themselves to do basic grocery shopping across state lines. But the government outwitted them at every turn. Wherever they bought their food, the government had always got there first and had always already poisoned the produce. Mrs Davis even did a few days in the county jail for common assault when she shoved a man in a suit – who she believed she had seen tampering with the groceries in her shopping cart – into a pyramid of pineapples, scattering the pineapples everywhere. Finally they began to only eat food which they had grown themselves, but even this didn't help because the government had somehow tampered with the chemical composition of the soil. When they packed their worldly possessions into their Winnebago and headed out into the Californian night at four o'clock in the morning on 4 July 1997 (forgetting to even turn the taps in the upstairs bathroom off, so that when the cops arrived everything was ruined), did they remember that they were scheduled for an emergency home visit from the sheriff's office? Did they know then what would happen when the sheriff's officers arrived and found that the house had been abandoned, that they had taken off? When the sheriff finally arrested the parents and brought Leann Davis in, she was emaciated and shivering. And after three days in protective custody, she died of congestive heart failure.

A nurse comes down the corridor towards us wheeling a vacant wheelchair in front of her. I can tell by her facial expression that she is about to apologize.

'I'm so sorry,' she says as she nears. 'They should have given you this at reception. All patients over seventy have to be in a wheelchair while they are in the hospital. Hospital policy. It's just for insurance purposes.'

Caroline goes to correct her, but before she gets a chance to say anything I thank the nurse and climb into the wheelchair.

McCaul fidgets with his fingers as we enter his office. The new medication hasn't worked. Whether it has made things worse is unclear. How are you feeling, Pol? I'm sorry that you're going through this, Pol. We're working as hard as we can to figure this one out. It's not an exact science. Still, I can see that he is shocked anew by seeing me again. I've lost some weight because of my convalescence from the Christmas tree incident. When it takes it out of you at this stage in life, Mac says, it takes a long time to come back from it. By which I think he means that you never really come back from it. It takes it out of you and then it never gives it back. When I go to shake his hand, his hand barely touches mine, as though he is handling a baby bird.

The issue is the neurological decay. Like anyone in their seventies I am going to continue to be experiencing some noticeable neurological decay. We can do things to help deal with that. But it's going to be difficult to reverse the process since it's already begun to take place. My foot taps, uncontrollably seemingly, on the footrest on the wheelchair.

'It's really unfair,' McCaul says. 'It really is terribly unfair. You always had such a lively mind. Even when you were a child.'

'Where's Jesse?' I suddenly wonder as we're leaving McCaul's office. 'Who's looking after him?'

Caroline runs a hand down my arm, down the sleeve of my jacket. My arm is just lost inside there. I've become so small.

'He's with his friends,' Caroline says. 'Let's not worry about Jesse right now. Let's just worry about you.'

Outside the clinic, the nurse wheels me down the ramp and then waits patiently as I stand up and put my waterproof anorak back on. Insurance reasons, she reminds me, when I tell her that it is kind but unnecessary for her to wait for us. The black anorak glistens in the light rain and the pinkish streetlight. In the middle of the square there is a garden, and in the night-time the leaves are dark green and in the light from the street lamps they glisten. I can make out a venerable old Scots elm and a holm oak among the holly bushes. And in the middle there is a flash of yellow – the yellow leaves of a beech tree – and it creates the optical illusion that only one tree stands in daylight while the rest are in darkness. A man in a high-vis jacket is locking the gate that leads into the garden from the street. In the street, there is a straggle of protesters. Some of the protesters are wearing black polyester capes and plastic fangs in their mouths. One has scraped his black hair back and oiled it down and looks kind of like the Count from Sesame Street. Another of them stops us. He seems frazzled.

'Are you a patient?' he says. 'Are you a doctor? Do you work here, man?'

'No,' I say. Caroline takes my arm and we put our heads down and walk quickly through the crowd towards the bus stop.

There is a Kourist rally happening in Trafalgar Square. The protesters outside the neotenics clinic are a spillover. There is a sex dungeon beneath the Palace of Westminster they say. There are newborn babies wailing in the dungeons down there.

We get off the bus on the high road. I try to step down from the bus at our stop but I do so too gingerly and nearly fall down and Caroline catches me. I can feel a whimper of frustration building in my chest. The driver offers to put the ramp down so that I can walk down more carefully instead of stepping off. The ramp takes ages to come out of the bus. The bus makes an irritating bleeping noise as the ramp is coming down. I look around at the other passengers and try to detect expressions of impatience on their faces. The rain is falling. Kilburn High Road looks grey. The paving stones are all mangled, so that every few yards there is a big puddle in the middle of the pavement. There is a boy on a BMX bike wearing a large grey hoodie with rainwater dripping from the brim of the hood. The bus stop is right outside a shop that used to sell old leather jackets. It's all shuttered up now. I turn around to Caroline and I point to the shop.

'Didn't that shop used to sell old leather jackets?' I say.

'I really couldn't say, Pol,' Caroline says. She is checking her phone. She must be checking to see if your friend's parents have called. 'Let's just get you home now.'

The next day is Caroline's day off so on the way home she suggests that we can stay up late and watch a movie or something after you have gone to bed. She takes one day off per week now. Sometimes Nick drops off our groceries or even once he took our sheets to the laundrette. Caroline brought home a card signed by all the staff wishing me well. The school set up a web page where people could donate money to buy me a gift, but in the end only three people donated and the total was something like twenty pounds.

'If it was more, then I would have said that you should take a photo of yourself with the item that you bought and post it on the page because there's a function for that,' Caroline said. 'But if it's only twenty then I suggest you just pocket the cash.'

Back at the house I collapse into the armchair. My legs are just like two toothpicks. We could get a wheelchair, an electric one for me to zip about in, Caroline had suggested. But McCaul told us that once I start using a wheelchair it will be difficult for me to go back to walking. The muscles just waste away. They just waste away. It feels like an infection, like a virus, turning my body into maggots and then into flies, into moths. I run my forefinger along my forearm and it feels just like the skin of a moth. Makes me almost retch. I turn the TV on. The first three headlines are all about Trump: how he told the crowds at his rallies to beat up hecklers; how he complimented Kim Jong-un for his ruthlessness; how he led in the polls. The fourth item is about the Kourist protests in London. One of the protesters is being interviewed. The neotenics clinic is the centre for research into adrenochrome technology, the protester claims. The doctors who work there are in charge of developing a technology that will stop people from ageing. The technology that they're piloting takes young people's blood and injects it into older people's bodies. Caroline is cooking.

'That's why all the people were dressed up in Dracula costumes probably,' Caroline shouts from the kitchen. 'They probably thought you were a Dracula.'

She laughs.

'Are the Draculas the patients?' I ask. 'Or the doctors.'

She thinks for a moment.

'I think that the patients are Draculas, and the doctors are the Dr Frankensteins,' she says.

The Coup of 18 Brumaire

Sometimes I have dreams that I am driving in a big car a long way: thousands of miles. And then in the dream I wake up and I am at home. When I tell Caroline, she is putting on her bra, looking in the mirror, and she says, well what do you think that means, before walking out of the room without waiting for the answer. Other times Caroline tells me that she feels that she deserves at least one year of peace, one year of tranquility in her life. A sabbatical, kind of. When she says things like that, *I* walk out of the room without answering. How do you think *I* feel, I want to say. Is this what *I* had in mind?

Caoimhe has had a revelation. She invites me over to talk to me about it. In a box at the bottom of the bottom drawer of the armoire in my mother's bedroom, she's found a stack of letters from my father. She could tell that these letters were real because they were in envelopes with German postage stamps on them. She spent a full day transcribing them into Google Translate. Not good, she tells me.

Seems like my father did in fact start writing letters to my mother at some point in the late 1990s. Some of the letters are postmarked from Heidelberg, where his sister lived. But some of the letters were postmarked from Ireland, from Connemara. It was strange. His letters were phrased like apologies when they were really accusations. He had theories about why he had been unable to be a parent, unable to be an artist. Great art comes from youth, he thought, and he had been robbed of his youth by all the bullshit that his parents had put him through and then so soon after getting over that, falling in love with my mother and having children of his own. He had gone to live on his sister's farm in order to try to start again somehow. He just needed some peaceful years, some kind of platform from which he would be able to rebuild his life from scratch.

A year before he left, he had been sacked. This was all new news to Caoimhe and me. A new rule had been introduced at the college where he worked that said that all employees who were not British citizens would have to do an English aptitude test. You had to go down to the office in the centre of Bournemouth where they did the driving theory tests and answer multiple-choice questions. The whole thing would have taken an hour. But he refused. He was outraged and said that it was racism. He spoke better English than most of his English colleagues, he declared to his English colleagues. He asked for the union lawyer to help him, but the union lawyer said that he had no case and that he should just do the test. The college actually let him stay on for a while, tried to let the dust settle, to let sleeping dogs temporarily lie. But every time the issue of his contractual obligation to do the test was broached, my father exploded. And in the end, they found somebody else to do his job and they fired him.

He became seriously depressed. He stayed in bed. The stack of papers stood on the desk in his study, untouched, until one day my mother opened the window in the study and a gust of wind blew them all over the floor. He heard the commotion and came running out of his room. I remember it. He punched the wall. It didn't make a dent in the wall, but he broke a bone in his pinkie and my mother had to strap his ring finger and pinkie together with Sellotape. She told him that he should go to hospital but he refused and gave her some fantastical story about being deported. He forced her to admit that she was naïve.

Thinking about it now, I must have overheard my mother referring to my father's neurotic complaint because I remember one day at school my teacher asking me if my father would be coming to parents' evening and I replied that he wouldn't be because he was sick and when she asked what sort of sickness I told her that he had 'neurosis'. I remember the teacher laughing and saying that she thought that maybe I had misunderstood.

I think I knew that he was sick because I remembered a time when I had the flu and my mother brought me breakfast, lunch and dinner in bed in just the same way that she was bringing my father his meals. Bowls of translucent soup and soda bread on a tray. I remembered, too, my mother stroking my head over and over while I clutched the sick bowl, just as she was stroking my father's bald head – this way and that – when I walked past the ajar door of his bedroom and peeked in.

'I wonder whether,' I say, thinking aloud, 'if he hadn't been sick, whether she would have left him, rather than the other way around.'

In another letter from the same cache, my father seemed to be defending himself against the accusation that he was a liar. In particular, he sought to explain away the fact that he had told my mother that he was three years younger than he actually was when they first met and had maintained the deception for the entire duration of their marriage. How did he manage to keep it up? How, in ten years of marriage, did she never once clap eyes on his passport?

'It was just a different time, I guess,' Caoimhe says.

'I have a few more to translate,' Caoimhe says. 'It's a bit frustrating that we don't have the letters that she sent back. It's a bit like listening to someone having a mobile phone conversation on a bus.'

We are sitting at the table in the kitchen in my mother's house. Caroline is on her way over to pick me up from my mother's house to take me to night school. I've been going for almost a month now, on McCaul's recommendation. The night school is in a terraced house near Holborn which was bought by a lifelong-learning charity. The charity was set up by a Jewish communist, a former member of the 43 Group, a veteran of the Battle of Cable Street. He left his library of left-wing literature to the school when he died. McCaul had to pull some strings to get me in, given that technically it's supposed to be only for old-age pensioners.

'Not that anyone would bat an eyelid,' Caoimhe says. 'No offence.'

'You always had such a lively intellect,' McCaul had said over the phone when he called to give me the good news. 'It really is so terribly unfair.'

'What is *wrong* with this family,' Caoimhe says nihilistically when I tell her about McCaul's assessment of my neurological report. 'What a bunch of mere mortals.'

She asks me to tell her about the night school. What am I

studying? She points at me with her cup of tea as she asks and then takes a glug. I tell her that I'm taking a course in the political context of the French Revolution. She raises her eyebrows.

'The French Revolution?' she says. 'The French *Revolution*? *Hooo*ly macaroni that sounds boring as hell!'

I explain to her that it's because I want to write something about Kourism and that a lot of what the theory is based on comes from the French Revolution, which I don't know anything about and so I need to do my research.

'About Kourism?' Caoimhe says, surprised. 'You're not doing your Bartholomew Wellplayed stuff any more?'

'I'll get back to it,' I tell her. 'I just need a break from it.'

'A break?' Caoimhe says. 'I've got news for you kid: you take many more breaks and you'll have breaked your way through an entire career.'

And she grins evilly.

She wants to know also about the kind of people who study at the night school.

'I know when I did my life-writing class,' she says, 'the most important thing was the other people. The teacher was fine, the subject was interesting, but the other people in the class were just such bellends. That's why I had to drop out.'

'Apart from Jamie,' she says, '*bien sûr*.'

Only one member of the group is under seventy: a thickset Chinese man with halting, slightly Americanized English, who calls himself Kyle because we won't be able to pronounce his real name, he tells us. He's allowed in because he's a refugee, fleeing from some kind of political or religious persecution. The other members of the group are me; a bald retired school inspector called Ray; a haughty-looking man in a tweed jacket with a meringue of perfectly white, perfectly coiffed hair who is

Russian but speaks in a posh English accent and is called Alexei; and an elderly couple who sit next to each other: Colin and Sarah. The teacher is a young Asian lady called Dr Tan. She has a list of books that she recommends we read. She has a whiteboard and a whiteboard pen and she draws a timeline of the eighteenth century on the board, starting with the War of the Spanish Succession and ending with the Coup of 18 Brumaire.

Ray, the old, bald retired teacher, folds his hands across his belly and closes his eyes and allows his neck muscles to slacken and his head to fall backwards at a right angle and his mouth to widen. You can see his fillings.

Eventually, Caroline picks me up from Caoimhe's. She waves at Caoimhe from the front seat of the car. Caoimhe waves back. Caroline has the wheelchair in the back of the car. That means that she must have got the man next door to help her carry it from the house to the car. Caroline never wants me to go next door to ask the man from next door to help. I think I know why. I think it's because she thinks that I hate the human race. How one time I had a conversation with the man next door and his relentless optimism irritated me so much that I told him that not seeing how fucked up the human race is is a sign of madness.

'You were spitting,' Caroline says, her eyes glued to a slow-crosser at the zebra crossing. 'Flecks of spit. In the corner of your mouth. The way you get.'

'Nihilistic cheeriness I call it,' I say.

'That's what *you* call it?' Caroline says. Then, after a silence, she says:

'Well it's preferable in my book to nihilistic poopiness.'

'Besides,' she says, 'I don't think that "human race" is the politically correct nomenclature.'

'I don't think I need the wheelchair today,' I say. 'And you don't need to collect me afterwards.'

When I arrive, Kyle, the Chinese man, isn't there. The teacher, Dr Tan, is trying her best.

'What can we remember from our discussion last week regarding the Rousseau reading?' she says. Nobody says anything. Alexei, the well-groomed Russian man, picks up a piece of A4 lined paper and folds it in half and then slides his fingers along the crease five, ten times. Kyle lumbers into the room and apologizes for his lateness. The elderly couple, Colin and Sarah, switch their attention away from the teacher towards Kyle, who proceeds to take two Tupperware containers and a metal flask out of his rucksack before finding his notebook and tin pencil case in the bottom of the rucksack, and then to put the Tupperware and the flask back in the rucksack. He apologizes to the teacher again.

'What can we remember about the events of the beginning of the eighteenth century?' says Dr Tan.

'I really want to know,' says Alexei, 'when we might be looking to move on to the things about pre-revolutionary Paris. I have to say I'm more interested in that kind of thing. The balls, the wigs, Marie Antoinette . . .'

He tails off and leans back in his seat with a self-satisfied air and then says, half to himself:

'*La Belle Époque.*'

'I think it's important,' the teacher says, 'to embed some of this discussion in the ideological and philosophical underpinnings of the revolution. That's really the only way we can fully understand the events of the late eighteenth century.'

Sarah and Colin are conferring in muttered tones. Dr Tan exchanges a glance with Colin, inviting him to share with the group. Colin turns to the group and says:

'Strange to say, but if you look around London today there are still some vestiges left over from the era that you referred to earlier as the *Belle Époque*, but that said, not nearly as many sites of interest as existed when we were children. Strange to say, but at that time people were not so interested in looking at buildings and things from the past but rather they were very focused on the future, on building these great concrete monstrosities everywhere instead of actually seeing the great riches that we had in our midst. You know that it really is remarkable to me when I think about the buildings that existed still in central London then, that were torn down in the name of "progress". Strange to say, but there were a great many grand buildings which housed the gentlemen's clubs of the *Belle Époque* still in existence into the 1940s and 1950s. Some of them were bombed in the war and some of them were just torn down in the name of "progress". There was the Junior Carlton Club on Pall Mall where I remember watching the smartly dressed men go in and out. No women allowed in those days of course. They tore that down in the 1960s I believe. And then there were the great houses where, as you referred to earlier, there were fabulous balls and the debutantes and so forth. A debutante ball was when the young ladies turned twenty-one and they would throw a grand ball in celebration. That was still going on would you believe when we were younger. I remember debutante balls in Londonderry House, which was on Park Lane I believe, and sometimes there would be pictures about it in the paper the next day. No different I suppose to the film stars and so forth from the modern day. But you would remember that, wouldn't you?'

This was addressed to me.

'No,' I say.

'There are still some nice things in the world,' Sarah says meditatively.

'What we could do,' says Alexei, 'would be to underpin some

of the interesting stuff from the *middle* of the eighteenth century
with some of the stuff from the beginning of the eighteenth
century, instead of underpinning the interesting stuff from the
beginning of the eighteenth century with the more boring stuff
from the end of the seventeenth century?'

He looks around the room, trying to garner assent.

'I think,' I say, 'that maybe we should just let Dr Tan do her
job.'

There is an awkward silence.

'It's actually just plain old Ms Tan,' says the teacher, reddening a little.

I go home. I catch the bus from Holborn to West Hampstead
and as I step on to the bus an old lady – older than me by some
twenty years – puts her hand underneath my elbow to help me
to steady myself.

Walking home, up Mill Lane, in the early winter gloom, I can
see across the city, down into the town. The skyscrapers are unlit
apart from the occasional little red lights, and their blackness
merges together into one gigantic black holly bush.

In 1646, when he was my age, Bartholomew Playfere was mustered as a musketeer in the Parliamentary forces. In 1650 he had
a religious experience which left him sprawling on his back in
the back field of the farm that belonged to his father-in-law.
The sky turned black. Absolute darkness filled the air, so that
he could no longer tell if his eyes were open or closed. In 1653
he published *The End of Nightwork and the Sundering of the
Curtain in Twayn*, in which he described the precise location
of the battle of Armageddon as taking place not in the Holy
Land but in the islands off the coast of Connemara. As the seas
rose, Playfere believed, all of the nations of the world would

converge on these islands, would duke it out in an epic battle, the winners of which would be revealed by providence to be the long-lost tribes of Israel, borne on eagles' wings to a place of greater safety to enjoy the diversions of the walled pleasure gardens of the new Jerusalem, the walls of which would be built against the wall-battering western winds.

All of this was probably just bullshit, just based on a misunderstanding. He had seen a map of the islands which was produced by Eamonn mac Lochlainn, the great early-modern Irish cartographer, and which was later reproduced in part by Hakluyt in his *Divers Traffiques and Nauigations of the English Nation*. The edition of Hakluyt which included these maps is now lost, but Playfere refers to it explicitly in his diaries. On one of the islands in the original document mac Lochlainn inscribed the legend *An meigeadán*. Playfere believed that he had discovered the true site of Armageddon. The word in Irish really means something like chatterbox or babbler or prattler. It has no etymological connection to the Akkadian word *Meggido*. In the locality which mac Lochlainn had been mapping, the word *meigeadan* was possibly used to refer to a brook or a river. Playfere wrote in his journal that he was surprised that nobody else seemed to have noticed the apocalyptic significance of this place name (he assumed that it was the name of a village or townland).

I found old pictures of me, from when I was younger, tucked into the space between the mattress and the bedframe, and I knew, without asking her, that Caroline had been looking at them while masturbating.

I sometimes buy a small bottle of gin and I pour the contents into a larger bottle of apple juice and I go for long walks up to the Heath with it tucked into the pocket of my overcoat.

I walk up Mill Lane and over the top of Hampstead. Past where murdered Gaitskell is buried. Past where the last lonely pirates of Jewish radicalism are falling off the planet, into the sky, their little bookish hovels being hoarded by millionaires and billionaires. And I walk down the other side, past the house where Paul Robeson lived, past the Mixed Pond and down to Highgate Hill and that funny Haussmannian Catholic school and all the way round past the Greek Orthodox tucked-away church to Gospel Oak station, where I get on the train. Finally bereft of booze, finally bereft of ideas.

I'm not sure that I have the energy to be an alcoholic, I tell Caroline when she accuses me.

Budapest

Over the next few weeks, I find myself spending a lot of time online looking for Kourist branch meetings that I might be able to go to. I want to avoid any meeting that there is any chance of Cynthia attending. I check her Facebook page to make sure that she isn't in London. She doesn't seem to update her Facebook page very often any more.

I do it in secret to avoid having another conversation with Caroline about it. She uses my computer sometimes, and once she scrolled through my search history and discovered reams and reams of searches related to Kourism.

'I considered it a little alarming,' she said to me. 'I considered it to be a tad askew.'

Sometimes I find that my search history has been wiped. Sometimes I find my old notepads with my notes about Bartholomew Playfere lying around in the kitchen, the bedroom.

'Where did this come from?' I ask Caroline, holding up a fistful of lined paper crowded with notes.

'Just found a bunch of them somewhere,' Caroline replies. 'I thought that you might need them.'

'You were just getting started,' she says later when I press her on her motives for trying to steer my attentions back towards my historical research. 'I think you have a touch of the ADHDs or something. You were getting somewhere when you were doing that research in the BL.'

'The one thing that McCaul *did* say,' she reminds me, 'is that you shouldn't be upsetting yourself. Shouldn't be getting yourself worked up into a tizzy. You know how you are with self-fulfilling prophecies.'

Whenever she says things like this, I feel like I should read to her from the most upsetting passages in the Playfere notebooks:

'And those that sayd to me why art thou come into Towne to make diuisions were answered not by mine tongue but by the Lord who promiseth such fire as will cuppell his creation. Since the last Days foretold and forewarn'd of by our Saviour, are at hand, wherein iniquity abounds, and the love of many waxes cold; hence Father against Son, and Son against Father, betraying one another, and hating one another; hence the Judgments of Famine and Pestilence; Nation rising up against Nation. So that the whole World seems to be on Fire before its time.'

Finally I find a meeting that I can attend. Some of the meetings are exclusively for what they called 'non-Hoarists'. Some of the English-speaking Kourists use terms like Hoarist and Hoarism to describe the politics of the establishment. As in 'hoary': like the old-fashioned world for geriatric. They think that it is a clever homonym, plus it also works because Hoarist rhymes with Kourist. These are the more radical tendency. Other groups welcome people of all ages. Everyone has a part to play, they believe.

The meeting is being held in an old church hall near Holloway Road. The hall used to be the church hall of St Scholastica's, but at some point in the early 2000s the church sold it to a Pentecostalist congregation. A sign over the door reads: 'Fire on the Mountain Ministries'. The new owners rent the hall out for other functions, meetings, parties.

I stand outside the meeting and I wait until I see at least one older person enter the building. Most of the attendees seem to be in their early twenties. Eventually, one woman in her early fifties with short cropped grey hair and a tapestry coat stops outside the building and checks her phone and then enters. I walk in behind her and she holds the door open for me and then glances at me: a slight double take.

Inside, there is a damp chill. The walls are painted light pink and are slightly grimy and darkened by cigarette smoke except for a small corner of the room where the colour of the paint seems lighter. I guess that there must have been a bar there, which was ripped out of the building when it was converted into a Pentecostalist church. The speaker is already speaking when I come in. There are twenty or thirty people in the audience. The lights are dimmed slightly because the man at the front is projecting a PowerPoint presentation on to the front wall. Nobody turns around when I enter the room and close the door softly behind me. Even after all these years there is still the faintest aroma of stale cigarettes in the building. I take a seat.

The man at the front is young, even by Kourist standards. He looks to be no more than twenty-one or twenty-two. He is fair-skinned and red-headed with a newly done undercut. He is wearing a slightly oversized black North Face coat, which he keeps on throughout the talk.

What reading Adonis Dolofonithikos has given him, he tells the audience, is a template, a model. Coming to an understanding of the millennial conflict between the old and the young allows him to see everything – to read the news, to read history – in a completely new light. Things don't happen randomly. He can see that now. Everything conforms to a very clear pattern. He cycles through a bunch of graphs on the PowerPoint presentation. Violence against young people. Incarceration rates of young people. Convictions for sexual assault and sexual harassment perpetrated by the old against the young. Distribution of home ownership based on age group. Distribution of wealth based on age group. These aren't a random array of statistics, he tells the audience. This is an invisible war being waged by an invisible empire.

He talks about the new Kourist policy in England of buying up advertising space for what they call 'denunciations'. Victims of abuse speak to the camera and talk about the ways that they have been exploited or molested and they name their abusers and the Kourist party foots the bill for any potential libel litigation. Sometimes, flicking channels late at night, I come across these denunciations and I watch them. Sometimes, going through the city, you see these billboards that the Kourists have put up, with pictures of abusers displayed next to lists of their alleged crimes.

The next speaker is a little older and when he begins to speak it is clear that he isn't English. He is the organizer of a sister organization in Hungary. He says that he is not here to incite violence, even if the police seem to think that he is. He is here to give a warning. He unplugs the HDMI cable from the previous speaker's laptop and plugs it into his own and for a moment struggles to find a video file and then to link his laptop with the Bluetooth speaker. The video that he shows has been shot on a phone. It shows a row of houses in an area of Budapest being burnt to the ground. Six or seven fire engines battle the blaze. Over the sound of the video, the speaker explains that the houses belong to a landlord who is known for exploiting the student population. The scene then cuts to a man wearing a suit being dragged out of an office building by ten or eleven young women. They drag the man into the centre of a circle of young protesters. There is a large crowd looking on. The man has some blood coming out of the side of his mouth. The scene changes again to footage of a large protest in the night-time. In the darkness, all that is visible is a procession of flaming torches. They seem to be marching down a grand arterial boulevard in the centre of a city. They are chanting an intimidating martial chant. The final scene shows a group of young people wearing balaclavas sitting in a conservatively decorated living room. On a sofa, next to the young people, sits an elderly woman. She seems bemused and docile and says nothing throughout the duration of the video. One of the young people addresses the camera. This is part of a campaign taking place across Budapest, he explains. The government subsidizes housing for the elderly and it leaves the young with nowhere to live. Until the government addresses this injustice, the young are forced to redistribute this wealth unilaterally, by living in the houses which the government buys for the elderly.

'We are not threatening anyone,' the speaker says in his thick Hungarian accent. 'We want Hoarist governments around the world to see that unless they come to the negotiating table with us they are storing up catastrophe for themselves in the near future. They are fattening themselves for the day of slaughter. This can happen the hard way or it can happen an easy way. But it will happen.'

On the way home I pick up some bagels and things for you. You like bagels. The man behind the counter looks at me strangely when I hand over the cash, or perhaps it's just my imagination.

Caroline wants to know where I've been.

'You have to answer your phone, Pol,' she says. 'You have to let people know where you are.'

I tell her that I've been for a long walk. This is what McCaul recommended that I do, I remind her.

'You're supposed to wear those special shoes, those special trainers if you go out for a walk,' she says.

I go upstairs and lie down on the bed. There is a tiny gap in the corner of the room where the skirting board from one wall doesn't meet the skirting board from the other. In my mind's eye I picture a hoard of inch-high protesters streaming through the gap in the wall, flaming torches aloft, marching through the undergrowth beneath the canopy of the deep shag carpet.

'Maybe you could take a Valium,' Caroline says, sitting next to me with one hand on my leg. It's already dark outside.

'We don't have any,' I say.

'I've got some,' Caroline says.

She goes to the bathroom and opens the cabinet and takes down a little white box. She pops one of the little yellowish pills out of the foil-lined tray and brings it over to me. But I don't want it. I ask her to leave it on the bedside table.

'I know it's not good to be dependent on them,' Caroline says, 'but perhaps it will just help you to reset.'

The Eightieth Anniversary of the
Battle of Cable Street

Caroline calls me in from the garden.

'What are you doing out here?' she says, jogging towards me with a blanket outstretched before her like a matador. She drapes the blanket around my shoulders. 'It's *freezing* out here. It's *dark*. What are you doing out here?'

We go inside and we sit on the couch. I can feel my heart pounding through my shirt, I tell her. It's not a neurotic thing. It physically hurts.

'I know,' she says. 'You told me. We got it checked, remember? Just try not to think about it. You know how you are with self-fulfilling prophecies.'

'It's not that he lisps,' she says scoldingly when I suggest to her that your difficulties are normal for a boy your age. 'It's that he *lies*. He lies to Edith so much that she doesn't feel like helping him any more even. Teachers are just people. People don't like liars.'

Our shared anxiety about your school experience takes over the house like a bad smell. One or both of us tends to be up half the night with anxiety. Sometimes I try to do some writing, or at least try to have some ideas about something I can write about Kourism. My Unique Vantage Point. But Caroline comes home to find me slumped, asleep, over my laptop. Sometimes I refer to conversations that Caroline and I have had and it is only when she tells me that the conversation never happened that I realize that it was a conversation from a dream. The autumn comes. It's the tenth of October. The leaves clog the gutters and Caroline has to go up on a ladder which she borrows from the man next door.

'I don't think that you should be doing that on your own,' the man from next door says. 'You know you're probably supposed to get somebody *in* to do a job like that.'

'It's fine,' Caroline says non-expressively. 'I've done it before.'

You and I sit on the wall at the front and watch as she struggles with the broomstick handle to dig the rotten leaves out of the gutters. The leaves drop on the ground below, like cowpats.

'That stinks,' you say, and you hold your nose with your index finger and thumb. I take my finger and stroke the side of your cheek.

Out of the corner of my eye I can see you gnawing at the side of your hand. That was one of the things on the chart that we had requested from the school as part of our disclosure order. They had to show us all the notes that Edith had been writing about you. The order was supposed to be confidential, but obviously in a small community like the school, word gets out. Edith had been distinctly frosty around Caroline for most of the term.

'Frankly, she can have a catastrophic potholing accident for all I care,' Caroline said.

The next day is the eightieth anniversary of the Battle of Cable Street. It's an especially poignant anniversary because it's probably the last major anniversary that any of the veterans of the battle are likely to be alive for. There is a small knot of nonagenarians standing in front of the commemorative mural waiting to have their photograph taken by a photographer who has come down from the *Advertiser*. The surviving veterans will march at the front of the parade. Different community groups – adjudged to have some common ethos with the original marchers – are allowed to march in the parade. Because the night school was set up by one of the veterans, some staff and students from the night school are allowed to march.

I sit in a plastic folding chair at the side of the road. Caroline has given me a special rug to drape over my legs to make sure that they don't get cold. I have no body fat any more, just skin and bone. The air is steamy with autumnal air and the vapour from hot-dog stands at the side of the street. The air smells like maize and meat. The man next to me is wearing a windbreaker made from synthetic material and it makes audible scratchy sounds whenever he moves. On the other side of the street, the new-build housing is interrupted for a hundred yards by an old Victorian terrace. The Victorian houses are painted white, while all of the other buildings around are dark red, so that the houses actually look like the last teeth in the head of a nearly toothless man. Actually they are. Everything else around that part of the street must have been bombed in the war I suppose.

A young man wearing a camouflage jacket with communist emblems stitched to it walks past, and when he sees me – sitting in my chair, with my white ear hair and my tartan blanket draped across my rotting legs – he makes a respectful face and then makes a slovenly, half-hearted salute. I ignore him and he moves along sheepishly. There are floats and banners commemorating the contributions of the West Indian community and the Bangladeshi community and the Jewish community. All of the people participating seem to be older, middle-aged at least. Here and there a sullen teenager, dragged along by their parents, traipses alongside a float, holding a drooping flag barely aloft. There is a Free Palestine demonstration on the other side of the street which is not part of the official march. The Jewish Museum has lent out some of its historical banners to the East London History Society, and they come next. The members of the East London History Society are carrying banners that were made for the London Jewish Bakers' Union in the 1920s. The banners are richly embroidered in navy and gold and mauve and their slogans are written in English and Yiddish. One banner shows an old shirtless man and a younger moustachioed man wearing a blue shirt. The older man is carrying a long-handled wooden peel like a staff. Behind them, the abyssal opening of a masonry oven. At the feet of the two men there is a sickle and a challah. Underneath the sickle and the challah, in Hebrew and Latin characters, is written the slogan:

8 HOURS A DAY.

FOR THE ABOLITION OF NIGHTWORK.

After the official parade has gone past, the hangers-on and single-issue groups begin their demonstrations. There are the black-bloc people and the Palestinians and then a small group of Kourists. The Kourists have flares and music and loudhailers. After they have passed, the streets are littered with their newspapers. I pick one up and leaf through it. On the front cover is a list of their five pledges.

1. REMOVAL OF STATE BENEFITS FROM ALL OVER-65S WHO OWN PROPERTY.

2. MANDATORY MAXIMUM TARIFFS FOR ALL OVER-65S FOUND GUILTY OF SEXUAL CRIMES AGAINST UNDER-30S.

3. MANDATORY RETIREMENT AGE OF 50 FOR ALL ELECTED
   REPRESENTATIVES.
4. CONFISCATORY WEALTH TAX ON ALL WEALTH OTHER
   THAN HOMES OWNED BY OVER-65S.
5. JOBS, EDUCATION AND HOUSING FOR THE YOUNG.

On the second page my eyes are drawn to a cartoon. It depicts a
fat old man in a suit, a lather of drool around his mouth, arm in
arm with a beautiful young woman with manacles around her
ankles. It's not very funny as cartoons go. The fat old man sort
of looks like Harvey Weinstein: a quadruple chin and a ruffle
of scruff and a big nose.

I shall slip the newspaper under my arm and then, when I get
home, I shall leave it on the kitchen counter, where I know that
Caroline will find it.

I've Been Thinking About Trust Issues

I still look forward to my history class at the night school. Not that we really talk about history much any more. We just talk about our memories. Ms Tan sits back and listens. Sometimes we even eat our sandwiches during the sessions and even Ms Tan has started bringing food now. Last week she brought a plastic-covered bowl with rice and tuna and sliced-up radishes.

'I've been mainly thinking this week, inspired by what Pol was talking about last week, about trust issues,' says Sarah.

'We were saying,' Colin says, 'that our relationship with our parents is sort of like the relationship between a passenger and the pilot of a plane. If you can't trust the pilot then you simply can't relax.'

'That reminds me of a joke,' says Ray. 'When they had that plane crash with the small biplane in Windermere and the mother died and the father died and the plane was just totally destroyed? Totally immolated? And the only thing that survived out of the whole plane crash was that little boy? A little five-year-old boy, they found him floating in the water and they didn't even know how because he couldn't swim? Why don't they in future just make the whole plane out of that boy?'

—

It's Colin's turn to speak.

Colin says that when he was denounced by the Kourists he happened to be drunk in a bar with a group of men who used to work with him on building sites. There was a television on in the bar. When his name and address came up on the screen everybody in the bar pointed and laughed and then people started cheering and applauding. They were applauding and chanting Colin's name so loudly that nobody could even hear what the accuser – who was actually Colin's niece – was saying. Then people started buying him drinks and joking around. Colin stayed out all night. They had a lock-in at the pub with him, and the sun was up already by the time he got outside. He walked home through the silent streets of Enfield and when he got to his house he saw that all of the windows were smashed, all of his possessions were looted and swastikas were daubed all over the exterior walls. Hundreds of toilet rolls had been launched over the house, so that toilet paper covered the entire building. They had had to move in with their son, who was a doctor, while their house was being repaired. Sarah began to cry, and she dabbed at her eyes with a hankie.

'That reminds me of a joke,' says Ray. 'There's a Jewish woman and she's on the beach and the beach is crowded and she's just running down the beach in tears, pointing out at the ocean as she's running, and she's screaming, "Somebody *please* save my son: the doctor."'

It's my turn to speak. I tell them how there are certain aspects of my mother's life – her childhood, the early days of her courtship and marriage to my father – that seem so real to me on account of having been told about them so many times. And how fragments of her personality, the personality that she developed in response to those experiences, seem to have become part of me. I try so hard but I can't explain it. Try to choose sadness over panic, my wife always says. Most of the panic comes from trying not to be sad. But I can't explain it. Can't seem to do it. My mother had rebellious brothers. They never wanted to please her parents. Even when her brother Tom came over to England to do labouring work – when Caoimhe and I were little – it just so happened that he got a job on the new Jubilee line station that they were building underneath the Central Mosque. And when he told his father about the building project, his father told the priest and the priest forbad him to go but he went anyway. After six months of nightwork, digging underground, the job was cancelled and he had to go home with his tail between his legs. Of course, I – looking back – suspect that the whole scenario was constructed so that Tom could play out this sadomaso-chistic relationship with his own father. And then my mother, in response to this dynamic that her parents and her brothers shared, was the one person who wanted to please her parents more than anything in the world. They were aspirational people, autodidacts. Her father had a leather-bound set of Seán O'Casey on a shelf in the living room. So she married an intellectual. She had no ability to accept that her marriage was failing although it was almost immediately. She grew to despise her husband because he reminded her that their marriage was both an impos-sibility and a necessity. And he was not self-assured enough to live with her hatred. So they had children. And it was instilled in us that we too should do the nightwork required to keep the family intact. It didn't seem possible to her that he would leave in the way that he did, and she never really believed that it was possible even years afterwards. Sometimes she would play games in her mind, trying to convince herself that there existed some date in the future – an anniversary, an event in London that would be irresistible for him – upon which he would be forced to visit her. And that gave her the strength to persist for a little while at a time, swinging from branch to branch, lingering, hovering in the air for just a sliver of time before regaining her ability to carry on living. There was always a promised land, in her mind, just beyond the horizon. It was hard for her when I met Caroline, I understand that now. It felt too much as though life was moving on. We had all been playing musical statues for so long. She felt as though I had left the room, broken the rules. She was angry about it. She wanted me, I remember, to wait until the following summer to get married. I knew that she just wanted to delay the wedding for as long as she could. Maybe if we just waited a year or eighteen months then that would give one of us the opportunity to get cold feet, to bail out. That's what was in the back of her mind. I remember when we were little and a bird flew into the kitchen. My mother screamed.

'One time I heard this joke,' Ray says, interrupting me. 'This one is quite short but it's just about a man who goes and lives in the countryside once even though he used to live in the big city. And when he gets to the countryside he is just settling in when the neighbour comes around and says how he's having a gathering or a party that night and would the man like to come along. And so the man asks what kind of party it's going to be and the neighbour says well it's going to be like a usual party with a bit of drinking, a bit of fighting and a bit of fornicating. That sounds great says the man, so what time should I come around. And the neighbour says come around any time you like because it's only the two of us.'

It's Alexei's turn to speak.

He tells us that his grandfather never found true love. He was lovelorn. He had spent his life, from his youth, pining for a long-lost, unrequited love. He had loved a woman who loved another. This was back in the old country. This was before the revolution. His grandfather was a cavalry guard. He had a plume

220

on his helmet, and his horse also had a helmet with a plume. He spied a damsel. He loved the damsel. The damsel loved another. The damsel loved a murderer. Not only was the damsel's beloved a murderer, he was a serial murderer. He was being pursued by the police, but nobody except for Alexei's grandfather knew that he was the culprit. The murderer had a calling card. His calling card was that he left a pink carnation on each of the corpses of his victims. Of course, the damsel didn't know that her lover was the Carnation Killer. But Alexei's grandfather did. And so he wanted the damsel to be happy even more than he wanted to be happy himself or whatever. So Alexei's grandfather hatched a plan. He would monitor the couple every time they went out for a date and then every time they did, he would go to another town and then kill a prostitute in that other town and leave a pink carnation on the corpse. That way, he could know for certain that the lover would never be caught, because he would have an absolutely watertight alibi that he was with Alexei's grandfather's beloved damsel in a totally different town.

'Do you know the one about the short-sighted mohel?' Ray says. 'Well, when he did the circumcisions he got the sack, but they let him keep the tips.'

'Please try to stay awake during the sessions,' says Ms Tan to me when everybody else has left. 'It's really a matter of courtesy.'

When I get back to the house I am about to put my key into the lock when my eye is drawn to an unfamiliar shape. On the wall, next to the door, there is a small neon-green drawing. The drawing is about the size of my hand. It looks as though it's been drawn in green highlighter pen: a rudimentary image of a snake, with evil, green-looking eyes and a protruding tongue.

—

The snake, in Christian iconography, represents evil, duplicity, mendacity: all bad things. It's almost impossible for us to think about snakes without thinking about these things.

But the Assyrians didn't see snakes this way. For the Assyrians, the snake was a symbol of new life, of rebirth, just as rabbits and eggs and chicks have come to be in European culture.

For example: when they excavated a temple at Megiddo, they found images of snakes hammered into the bronze.

The Assyrians believed that snakes were immortal. All of this because a quirk of the evolutionary process gave the snake the ability to shed its skin. The secretion of ecdysteroids (which causes snakes to shed their skins) happens in human beings too. We shed our skin too. We just do it more slowly.

There Will Be Fireworks

In the night, I have a nightmare. Outside in the back garden. A hologram of Adonis, the mythical leader of the Kourist Party, looms over the capital. The hologram is seventy feet tall. The Kourist Party are going to make an intervention to prevent the country from spiralling further into the calamity of Hoarist barbarity and mendacity.

In the dream, Caroline takes you outside into the garden to watch. Helicopters with huge speakers hanging from them chug overhead. Adonis' words ring out through the streets.

'The people of this nation will not stand by and allow themselves to be ruled with the rod of rapine, racketeering and rottenness that is being meted out to them by the Westminster swine,' his voice said. 'Fathers will turn against sons and sons against fathers.'

The voice crackles a little. I stay indoors. I don't want to look at it.

'Stay indoors,' Caroline shouts to me through the kitchen window. I don't want to look at it anyway. The phone rings.

'Pretty incredible technology, huh?' says Caoimhe over the phone.

'I guess,' I say.

'There will be fireworks,' says Caoimhe.

I wake with a start and sit up in bed and listen to the deep, black silence for a moment. Caroline stirs beside me. She reaches out a hand and places it on my forehead.

'You're burning up,' she says. 'What's happened? What's wrong?'

When we get up on Saturday morning and go outside we discover that somebody has covered our house in toilet paper. The whole house is covered in toilet rolls. Fifty, maybe a hundred, toilet rolls.

'What the Funkmaster Flex?' Caroline says when she sees it. 'Why? Why us? Why now?'

They have been launched over the house from the front garden. They seem to be big low-quality toilet rolls, of the kind that you might find in a toilet in a municipal building.

'We can't deal with this right now,' Caroline says. 'We need to get over to your mum's. Will you put Jesse in the car?'

Caoimhe and Jamie have invited us over for brunch.

'You know what this is, don't you?' Caroline said when she read Caoimhe's message. 'When in ten years has Caoimhe *ever* invited us over for a brunch?'

'Maybe it's Jamie,' I said. 'Maybe he's having a positive influence.'

Caroline was facing away from me, applying some blusher in the mirror in the bathroom.

'We be walking into a goddamn ambush, pard'ner,' she said.

—

In the kitchen, Caoimhe is taking pastries out of little ribboned white boxes and putting them on my mother's best china. Jamie is chopping up some leaves and some chunks of mango and forcing them into a food processor.

'Sorry for the noise,' he shouts over the loud whirring sound of the food processor. The noise pierces my skull like a screwdriver.

'I can't eat that stuff,' Jamie shouts again, tilting his head towards the pile of pastries. 'It's not that I don't want to. I just can't. Fucks me up for the rest of the day.'

After eating, Caroline and I go into the living room and sit on the two chairs either side of my mother's hospital bed. Caroline reaches up one hand to stroke my mother's. Jamie and Caoimhe finish washing the dishes and then come into the living room and sit on the couch.

'I think it would be good,' Jamie says, 'if we could just clear the air.'

'This doesn't have to be a bad-tempered conversation,' Caoimhe says.

She tells Caroline and me that she wants to go back to work.

'Go *back* to work?' Caroline says sarcastically.

'I think that's the tone that we are aiming to avoid,' Jamie says.

Caroline holds up her hand apologetically. They want to put my mother in a home. They can sell the house maybe, and raise some money that way. Anything left over Caoimhe and I would share, or anyway that could be figured out later.

'Maybe if there was two of us sharing the responsibility,' Caoimhe says. 'But with Pol's condition, he can't be expected to do all this.'

Jamie nods sagely.

'There was a time,' Caoimhe says, 'when I got a lot out of caring for her. It rekindled something in me for which I will always be grateful. But that time has passed now. I'm not good at this. There's nothing coming back the other way. It's not as though she recognizes us. She's locked up in her own imagination. That's her life now. She should be being looked after by people who are good at this kind of thing.'

'For all of her faults,' Jamie says, 'your mother loved both of you guys. She wouldn't want to feel as though she was ruining your lives. She never wanted to be a burden on you.'

On the drive home, Caroline says nothing.

'You're just going to sit there?' I say. 'Don't you think there's a pretty big elephant in the room?'

Caroline shrugs, keeping her eyes on the road. After a while she says:

'I don't like Jamie.'

In the back seat of the car, you start complaining that you feel carsick. We'll be home in two minutes, Caroline tells you. She points out of the window as we drive by the school.

'See Jess,' she says cheerfully and a little hysterically, 'there's the school. So you know that we're nearly home. Can you hang on that long?'

You tell her that you're going to be sick. With one hand on the steering wheel, Caroline fishes with the other hand underneath her seat and pulls out an Aldi shopping bag and reaches behind her to hand it to you.

'If you need to be sick,' she says, 'be sick in this.'

'What I will say,' Caroline is saying, 'is that it really resonated with me what Caoimhe said about your mother not wanting to be a burden. I know that I wouldn't want to be. To be waited on hand and foot. You can't sacrifice your own life for somebody else's well-being.'

'I think it was Jamie who said that,' I say.

'And quite honestly,' Caroline continues, 'I think that we'll look back at this and think that we should have done it sooner. The whole thing with Caoimhe living there. That's something to do with arrested development or something don't you think? Some way of preventing herself from moving on with her life, growing up, having her own family. Who knows? Maybe Jamie *has* managed to break through to her somehow, to unlock something.'

I can tell by her facial expression that she has something else to say. The corners of her mouth twitch slightly when she is deciding whether or not to say something, almost as though she is about to cry. In the end she says:

'But that's just me.'

When we get back home, Caroline changes into her tracksuit bottoms and sets to work trying to pull the toilet rolls down from the house. It's harder than you might think. A little rain begins to fall and the paper begins to stick to the walls. It starts to turn to gunk, like papier-mâché gunk. Gunk in the gutters. Gunk on the windowsills. Maybe we should just wait for it to rain properly and then the rest of it will gradually wash away. I sit outside on the front garden wall and I talk to her while she is doing it.

'The thing is,' Caroline says, 'toilet roll invites toilet roll. The longer this toilet roll is on the house, the more people will think that the house is toilet-rollable. You've seen the other houses. That house on Mapesbury Road.'

She's out of breath. She has a broom and is trying to reach up to the bonnet roof which covers the bay window at the front of the house in order to wipe away a large white turd of sodden toilet paper. I say nothing. I don't want to engage with that part of the discussion. After a while I say:

'I just feel bad that I can't help.'

Caroline nods.

Afterwards we watch TV in the living room. Caroline's parents are coming next week to give Caroline some help. We offered them the sofa bed in the living room but they said that they'd prefer a hotel. So they booked a room at that Marriott on the intersection of Kilburn High Road and Maida Vale.

Caroline channel-flicks. There is a woman standing in front of a green screen and on the green screen there appears a series of images of a man in his mid-sixties wearing a suit, and with a comb-over. Occasionally the man is pictured standing alongside other people, but the other people's faces are pixelated. He looks cheerful and well-fed. The woman is standing in front of the green screen and is telling a story about the man. The man is a supervisor at a warehouse. The woman was a worker at the warehouse. The man encouraged her to do sexual favours for him and implied that her job would be at risk if she didn't do them.

'You know what this is, don't you?' I ask Caroline. She is listening intently to the story and she shushes me.

'They're called denunciations,' I continue. 'The Kourist Party buys blocks of advertising time late at night and uses it to identify individuals that they consider to be enemies. They're basically daring these guys – these enemies – to sue.'

After a while the woman decided to speak to the HR department and the HR person let it slip that there had been numerous similar allegations. The woman threatened to take her complaint higher but was told that the man had been dismissed. Only later in the year did she discover that he had not been dismissed at all but had simply been moved to a different warehouse in a different part of town. When that happened, she decided to form a chapter of the Kourist Party at her warehouse, but when the bosses found out about that, they fired her.

I wonder aloud if Caroline has seen any of the literature produced by dissident groups within the Kourist movement about what they believe about so-called mixed relationships between older and younger people. The caricatures of lecherous old men that they print in their newspapers. They remind me of the caricatures of lecherous Jews that you might find in anti-Semitic propaganda from Nazi Germany, I muse.

Caroline changes the channel.
'It's too depressing to think about,' she says.

Something Bad Is Happening

The boy doesn't have a sense of reality. That's the upshot of the extensive tests that the educational psychologist has done. This often happens when there is a lot of inconsistency in a child's life. It isn't anybody's fault necessarily. Of course the educational psychologist is aware of the medical issues that I have been having. He rifles through his papers to try and find the name of my condition but eventually gives up. Caroline presses her thumbs together.

'Sometimes,' the psychologist says, 'when people lie, it's an attempt to create closeness. The more extravagant the lie, the more care is expressed in the willingness on the part of the interlocutor to *not* call the lie out. This might be what Jesse is trying to elicit.'

'What does that mean?' Caroline says. The psychologist opens his palms and stretches his fingers. My eyelids feel leathery and scratchy with tiredness. I squeeze them closed and then open them again.

'Lying can create closeness between a child and a caregiver,' the psychologist explains. 'If you tell a lie and the person that you lie to knows that you are lying but doesn't humiliate you for it, then that is a powerful indication that that person cares about your feelings. Such experiences *can* become almost ad*dic*-tive for a child.'

'So he's attention seeking?' I say.

'That might be what we would have called it in days gone by,' the psychologist says cautiously.

'It's understandable that he might be a little attention seeking,' Ellen says, back at the house. She is sitting in the armchair next to the fireplace in the living room and is drinking tea out of the mug that Caroline made for me that summer when she did her pottery course. 'These past couple of years have been very hard for all of us and it's inevitable that that will rub off on a child.' She takes a sip from her mug of tea.

'Nobody is to blame here,' Ted says. He shakes his head and looks at us sternly over his glasses. 'It's *very* important that neither of you blame yourselves for *any* of this.'

Caroline's eyes are wet. She stands up and tinkers mindlessly with the little aluminium Child of Prague on the mantelpiece.

Let's go for a walk, I suggest. Just Mummy, me and you. We walk up to the Heath. Up Arkwright Road and through Hampstead and all the way up to the Vale of Health. The light is cheerful and dim and there is an autumnal chill in the air. You are singing a song from Peppa Pig and eating carrot batons from a little plastic bag. When we get to the Vale, we find the whole area has been blocked off. A swarm of police cars and at least three fire engines are parked in the road on the edge of the Heath. As we get closer we can see that a big house, right next to the water, is on fire. Fire is soaring out of the old bay windows. We can feel the heat on our faces. As we stand there, it dawns on me that this house belongs to that peer, the landlord with the super-injunction; a person who the Kourists have identified as a chief Hoarist, an enemy of the people. I remember standing on this spot, Cynthia pointing out the house to me. I feel a wash of emotion – fear and excitement – surge through me. Caroline is asking one of the firefighters whether they suspect arson. The firefighter says that it's not something that he can go into. He tells Caroline to move away. He has a job to do, he says. The heat from the flames is causing me to sweat. Sweat trickles down my back all the way to my coccyx. I look down at you half expecting you to be upset, to be crying. Instead you seem to be transfixed by the fire. I suppose that it's the first time that you've seen a proper fire.

'If it isn't arson,' Caroline is saying persistently, 'then why would there be so many police?'

'Well there you go,' says the fireman, shrugging. He walks away. I feel you tugging at the bottom of my trousers and I crouch down so that our faces are facing each other.

'What is arson?' you ask.

'Arson is when somebody sets a house on fire on purpose instead of by accident,' Caroline says. She kneels down and begins to do up the poppers on your little sou'wester. And for some reason, you begin to chuckle, and then to laugh out loud. You point up at the burning house and you laugh, long and hard. Caroline notices the firefighters looking askance. She puts her finger in your face:

'No!' she says sharply. 'No!'

But it makes no difference. You continue to laugh and point until eventually we yank you away into the trees behind the Vale.

On the walk home, I tell Caroline about a YouTube video that I watched in which a man is dragged out of his home in a small suburban town on the edge of Budapest by some Kourist radicals. In the video they strip his clothes off and cover his body in hot tar and then they roll him around in a pile of feathers: goose

232

down that they have poured out of a dozen slashed pillows. I've read about the story online also. When the perpetrators were brought to trial, the wife of the man stood as a witness. The wife was thirty years younger than her husband. She had been a receptionist in the estate agent's office which the man owned in the centre of Budapest. The man had left his first wife and two young daughters to be with her, had married her when she got pregnant. The wife was delirious with grief while she was giving her testimony. They told her that she didn't have to testify but she told them that she wanted to. She wanted to face her husband's assailants to tell them that she loved her husband, that she didn't need to be defended from him by them. When the assailants took the stand they expressed no remorse. Sometimes violence is needed in the process of facilitating conscientization, they said. The violence of the act was intended to awaken the wife to her condition of chattelry, and they had faith that at some point it would have that effect.

'Why are you telling me this,' Caroline says, angry tears stinging her eyes.

When we get home, she puts you to bed and then comes downstairs. Do you think maybe there's something in it, she wonders. Perhaps we're raising children in a way that will make them hate us, want to kill us. Can that happen? Can a society do something like that? A culture? She starts to get upset.

Now nothing is alive any more. Everything is death. Microwaved. Dead bodies. Dead planets. Dead skin flaking from my body and peppering the collar of my old Crombie. I'll get you one of those rolly things from the everything-shop, Caroline says, those dandruff removers.

Across the street, in the community centre, the Comunidad de

Deus is having a service. A female vocalist is singing a hymn, backed by a keyboard on the organ setting and a snare drum. The music is sad and slow. It sounds a little bit like 'They Won't Go When I Go' by Stevie Wonder. Every now and again, a male voice shouts the lyrics over the sound of the soloist's voice, to help the congregation sing along.

Amyloid Plaques

Mac is rifling through some papers on his desk when I arrive for my check-up. He asks me to take a seat, this will only take a minute. He has put on weight. He seems stressed. He told me over the phone that the police have been stationed outside the hospital all week in order to disperse picketers and protesters. He bundles a stack of papers into his arms and walks out of the office, closing the door behind him. I look around the office. It's full of papers and notepads and cardboard files filled with notes. It has that papery smell, that oil-heater smell that reminds me so much of my father's office in the house at Bournemouth. I stand up and look at the file nearest to me. I gently lift the first few pages and scan my eyes over the notes. The notes are for a woman who lives in Coggeshall in Essex. She is in her mid-twenties. She has experienced signs of rapid cognitive decline and skin fibrosis. Nonfamilial. Histological sample. Gamma secretase. Amyloid plaques.

McCaul comes back into the room and closes the door behind him.

'First things first,' he says, sitting in the big chair behind his desk. 'How is my tan?'

He has been on a cruise. He spent the money that his mother left him in her will on a ticket for a world cruise. When he let us know that he was doing that – taking a month's leave to go on a world cruise – I remember thinking that it was an odd thing to do, a little out of character, a little unbecoming for an eminent physician. He showed us pictures of the cruise ship. It had a swimming pool right on the deck, he pointed out.

I tell McCaul that I am surprised to see him back so soon. He didn't make it the whole way around the world, he tells me. When the cruise ship got to Cuba, he bailed. He took a flight to Jamaica and then a flight back to Heathrow. He didn't like how the tourists fetishized the nobility of Castroism. Fat, sunburnt poltroons standing in front of some old car or some wizened old guitar virtuoso, sometimes even asking if they could hold the guitar for the purpose of the picture. And the little old Cuban men just helplessly sitting there. It seemed unseemly, he tells me. It didn't look good.

'And that *pool*,' he says. 'The *pool* was just like a tin *bath*.'

I kind of think that it's all some kind of revenge that he's exacting on his dead mother. I remember that when my own mother first got sick, McCaul told me that he empathized. He too had had a difficult relationship with his mother that had remained unresolved due to her cognitive decline. His mother had had dementia for almost ten years. They were never close. She didn't approve of his lifestyle, he thought. He had two brothers, and both of them served in the armed forces. They had served in Northern Ireland at the height of the Troubles. His mother always kept two photographs of his two brothers on the mantelpiece in her house and no picture of him. But both of his brothers had succumbed to alcoholism and depression. One had taken his own life in the early 1990s and the other had suffered a massive coronary. It was left to Dr McCaul to take care of his mother, and he had paid for her to have the best possible care in a home in her native Ayrshire. For the whole period that she was living in the home, he would drive up from London every Friday evening and stay in a hotel nearby and spend the whole weekend with her every week. As the condition advanced, she lost her ability to recognize him. He knew from the way that she related to him that she was confusing him with one of his brothers. She would put her frail hands around his head and pull his head towards hers and kiss him over and over.

'Whither are you headed, my lad?' says Mac when he's completed the check-up.

I tell him that I am going to the night school for my class.

It's not a night school, Caroline would always say. But that's just what I call it in my head.

'Let's just be careful if you're going into Central London,' he says. 'There's some kind of Day of Rage happening today.'

He pulls up the BBC News page on his computer and shows me the headline. The Kourists are planning a day of action, and are planning to picket locations where Hoarists appeared to be benefiting unduly from state-funded goodies. Mac clicks the play button on the embedded video clip. Responding to the accusation that his gangs were planning to intimidate weak and vulnerable elderly people, a Kourist spokesperson said that the aim is not to intimidate service users but rather to highlight for the benefit of the still-somnambulant taxpayers the ways in which their money is being spent, financing the leisure activities of an already ostentatiously cossetted demographic. When the reporter asks the spokesperson about the possibility of two Labour MPs sponsoring a bill which would support cutting benefits for wealthy pensioners, the spokesperson responds by saying that the Kourist movement welcomed these moves whilst recognizing that true victory would come from the streets and not from the ballot box or from the jaded nabobs of Whitehall.

'The way they talk is just so specific isn't it,' Mac says. 'Som*nam*bulant. Where do you get *that* from?'

The streets are noticeably quieter than usual. There are no huge protests, but here and there I notice little knots of protesters blocking the entry to opticians' shops and post offices. Outside a post office on Lamb's Conduit Street I watch a small skirmish unfold. A young man with an old man trying to get one of the protesters in a headlock. Nearby a woman, perhaps the young man's wife, standing next to a parked car with the window rolled down. Her hand is extended through the open window and is pressed against the car horn. The blare from the horn makes my ears hurt.

As I approach the night school I notice three young men standing in front of the building. One of the men is wearing a fluorescent Patagonia fleece. They stop their conversation as I approach the building and stand almost to attention. One of the men has a clipboard tucked under his arm. They seem more nervous than anything. When I'm a few steps away, one of the men tells me that the building is closed. He points to a notice which is pinned to the door of the building. As I walk up to the door to read the notice, the three men part to let me through. The notice has been written in pen by somebody from the school. It says that the building has been closed and all programmes suspended until further notice in order to safeguard the security and well-being of service users. There is no explicit mention of the Kourist protests. At the bottom of the note there is a sincerest apology and a number that you can call if you need to enquire about reclaiming any fees paid. I don't say anything to the protesters. I turn on my heel and walk back in the direction from which I came.

'This quarrel isn't with you, pal,' the man in the Patagonia fleece calls after me as I walk away. 'You realize that, don't you? We have no quarrel whatsoever with you, dude.'

I walk back up to Commercial Road and go into a pub and order a pint. The pub is nearly empty apart from a small group of men wearing work overalls. The men are watching the flat-screen TV. The news is on and the men are laughing. They are laughing at the captions at the bottom of the screen because the captions are all wrong. The newsreader hands over to a vox pop on the streets of London. A reporter is asking people about the possibility of Kourist-style laws being passed in Parliament. He is asking mostly older people. I turn to face the TV and start reading the captions. An elderly lady with white cropped hair is speaking. A younger man, possibly her son, is standing next to her.

'I THINK IT'S WRONG,' the captions say. 'THE GOVERNMENT SHOULD SPANDEX MONEY ON PAYPAL WHO NEED IT AND THE ELDERLY PAPAL NEED IT THE MOST.'

Now the son begins to speak.

'MY GRANT FAVA FOUGHT FOR THIS CRUNCHY IN THE WAR,' the captions say. 'HE'S EARNED THE RIGHT TO HAVE A COM-FORTABLE RETIRE MOAT.'

The elderly woman interrupts.

'IF IT COMES DOWN TO IT YEAH I WILL GO SPAIN,' the captions say. 'THEY TREAT THE OLDER PAYPAL LOVELY OVER THERE SO YEAH I'D GO SPAIN OR ABROAD OR SOMEWHERE LET THE YOUNG PEOPLE GET ON WITH IT OVER HERE.'

Something about the capital letters reminds me of the closing words of *The End of Nightwork*:

—

'SEPARATE, SEPARATE, SEPARATE, SEPARATE, SEPARATE, SEPA-
RATE, SEPARATE. COME OUT OF HER, COME OUT OF HER, COME
OUT OF HER, COME OUT OF HER, COME OUT OF HER, COME OUT
OF HER ARMIES, COME OUT OF HER ARMIES, COME OUT OF HER
ARMIES, COME OUT OF HER ARMIES, LEAST YE BE PARTAKERS
OF HER PLAGUE. FLYE OUT OF HER CITIES, FLYE OUT OF HER
CITIES, FLYE OUT OF HER CITIES, FLYE OUT OF HER CITIES, FLYE
OUT OF HER CITIES, FLYE OUT OF HER CITIES, FLYE OUT OF HER
CITIES . . . TOUCH NOT HER TRADING, TOUCH NOT HER TRAD-
ING, TOUCH NOT HER TRADING, TOUCH NOT HER TRADING,
TOUCH NOT HER TRADING, TOUCH NOT HER TRADING, TOUCH
NOT HER TRADING.'

I step out on to Commercial Road. It's raining. Raindrops dance
on the roof of a stationary bus. Weighed down by the gravity
of centuries of sin and corruption, Playfere and his followers
had just shrugged off the weight. They had decontaminated
themselves when they went into isolation. Unburdened themselves. Playfere even had a pouch of coins, the last of his military
pension, that he hurled into the sea as the boat left the quay at
Beaumaris. As if the weight of those particular coins was too
heavy for him to carry, as though he feared that the weight
might sink the Ark.

There is an awning covering the entrance of a school on the
other side of the road and underneath the awning a little row
of green birds perch and gawk at passers-by. I look down at my
phone and see that there are three missed calls from Caroline.

The unburdening actually went both ways. The harbourmas-
ter at Beaumaris initially impounded the vessel on which
the pilgrims intended to travel and wrote to John Thurloe –
Cromwell's spymaster – expressing his concern that the ship

contained 'many seditionaries' and 'men who put about that it is right to have many wyves'. Thurloe wrote back indicating that the ship should be released in order that such 'plaguy people' be allowed to 'seclude themselves' in Ireland.

'What does it profit our Commonwealth if we keep in such burdensome and tiresome enthusiasts?' Thurloe said.

Try Me

The following evening, I suggest to Caroline that we go for a walk up to Parliament Hill and smoke a joint like we used to do in the olden days.

A few days ago, Edith came over for dinner and when she left we noticed that she had left a little bundle of weed wrapped in tin foil next to her empty glass in the living room. When Caroline tried to give it back to her, Edith told her to keep hold of it. I'm trying to quit, she told Caroline.

'Señor,' says Caroline, raising one eyebrow when I make the suggestion. Ellen and Ted are over for a couple of days and they can keep an eye on you.

'We're going out for a meal,' Caroline tells them.

'Oh goodie I get to look *after* you,' Ellen says to you, reaching over the side of the settee to where you are sitting cross-legged on the floor watching a feature about sunflower farms on *The One Show* and tousling your hair.

When we get to the top of Parliament Hill Caroline asks me why it is called Parliament Hill and I tell her that it is because this was the site of a druidical assembly before even the arrival of the Anglo-Saxons in Britain. It was commemorated as the place where the Druids came together to make decisions. Caroline nods and says nothing.

From the top of the hill we can see down across the whole city. We are five hundred feet higher than the City of London up here. How tall is The Shard, Caroline wants to know and I tell her that it is about a thousand feet. How come it feels like we're looking down on it then, she wants to know. Shouldn't its tip be higher than we are?

'Because things look smaller when they're far away,' I tell her. And she laughs.

'You've still got it, kid,' she says.

'*Everything is perfect from far away*,' she sings softly, under her breath.

She rolls the joint and lights it and then for a few moments we sit there without saying anything, just smoking.

Images float like smoke into my mind. My mother and Caoimhe sitting right next to each other on the couch in the living room, smoking. I could see them through the living-room window before they saw me.

'You're for it,' Caoimhe saying as soon as I walked in the front door. Caoimhe laughing while my mother shouted at me for disappearing.

'It's so funny,' she was always saying. 'Look at you. Look at him. What exactly are you going to protect him from?'

Drinking alcohol, my mother replied. Making immature choices.

'You know you're driving her mad,' Caoimhe once said.

'You know you're driving her criminally insane.'

There are red lights trickling down the side of the BT Tower. Caroline points at them.

'So nice,' she says. 'So pretty.'

Two girls walk up the hill and they sit down on the grass a few yards away from us. They open green-and-silver cans of supermarket gin and tonic and begin to chat in loud voices. One is talking to the other about an interaction that she has had with a man on a dating app and she is complaining that the man has read too many books. Not that he has read too many books, she wants to clarify. Just, you know, those men who want to shoehorn into every interaction some book that they've read or some fact that they know. Caroline passes me the joint. She doesn't even seem to have noticed the girls chatting. *That's* the difference between us, I think. Maybe. The girls have stopped talking in such loud voices. They're whispering to each other now. One of them looks in our direction and then catches my eye and then quickly looks away.

There's something that I want to talk to you about, I say to Caroline. She pulls the cigarette lighter, thoughtlessly, out of her pocket and places it on the bench beside her.

'Try me,' she says.

'I've been thinking,' I say. 'Don't you think that it wouldn't be a bad idea if I took myself away somewhere for a little while?'

She doesn't say anything. She picks up the lighter and slides its thin plastic trigger underneath her thumbnail and works away at her nail with it, digging out the grey gunk and making the nail translucent.

'Where will you go?' Caroline says.

I tell her that I've been thinking of going over to the island.

I'll have the money from the sale of my mother's house hopefully. Hopefully it will give her a break. Give us all a break. If it doesn't work out, if I can't manage on my own, then I can always come back. It's not far. And if it does work out, then maybe she could come over and join me there, maybe for the summer holidays.

'The summer?' Caroline says. 'That's months.'

I don't reply. The girls have collected up their green-and-silver cans of gin and tonic and the coats that they were sitting on and have moved off, walking back down the hill towards Gospel Oak station.

'It's just,' Caroline says, 'what will I do without you?'

In the weeks and months to come I will revisit this sentence in my mind and dice it into pieces and analyze every word. In the moment, I don't ask her to clarify what it means.

Back at the house, Ted and Ellen are sitting at the kitchen table and eating some leftover lasagne with a glass of red wine.

'Listen,' Caroline says before she has even taken her coat off. She tells Ted and Ellen about my plan. About how I need some time away, how recent events have been causing me to get stressed and anxious in a way which is bad for my mental and physical health. It may seem tricky in the short term but maybe it will turn out to be the best thing for everybody in the long term. As Caroline talks, Ellen balls her hands up into little fists and rests them on the table top either side of her plate. Her eyes rest on a spot on the opposite wall just above Ted's shoulder. When Caroline finishes, she says nothing for a while. Then she says:

'I think this is insane. And I think you should take a little bit more time to think about it.'

Caroline shifts her weight on to one foot and folds her arms.

'I wasn't asking for your advice,' she says.

'I seem to remember you taking a vow,' Ellen says, still not looking at Caroline. Caroline laughs hollowly.

'What on earth,' she says, 'are you talking about right now?'

Ellen's voice takes on an eerie, nearly hypnotic calm.

'Your husband is sick,' she says.

'And after all this time you're taking *his* side?' Caroline says. She moves as though to leave the room but then stops at the door.

'Side?' Ellen says. 'What side?'

'Yes,' Caroline replies, shouting. 'Which side? Because it's neither my side, nor Pol's side, nor Jesse's side.'

And she leaves. Ellen sits still. Then she picks up her plate, still with half a slice of lasagne on it, and carries it over to the sink. The piece of lasagne looks cold and oily. She doesn't make eye contact with me.

'I'm going to bed,' she says.

When they both leave, I sit down at the table and pick up Ted's copy of *Private Eye* and pretend to begin to read it. After a while, I look up and Ted meets my gaze and furrows his brow sadly.

'I think,' he says, 'that neither of them expected that Caroline would be the only breadwinner in the house.'

You're Going to Love It

Ted and Ellen left a couple of days later.

'I'm sorry that we can't stay for your birthday, Pol,' Ellen said, giving me a kiss on the cheek.

'I'll call you,' she said to Caroline.

'Please do,' Caroline said, sarcastically.

'You're going to love it,' Caroline said about my birthday present. 'Just make sure you don't have anywhere to be on the eleventh.'

She seems happier since I told her about my plan, more relaxed. Or perhaps it's just my paranoia.

When I come downstairs on the morning of the eleventh, the living room is tidy. The little side table has been moved over to next to the armchair and there is a bowl full of fresh fruit placed on it.

'You bought me a therapy session?' I say to Caroline. And she laughs involuntarily, snorts a little even.

'I gotta tell you, boy,' she says in a voice which I think is supposed to be Bob Hope, 'you still got it. You stiilllllll got it.'

The doorbell rings and Caroline hurries me into the living room and tells me to sit in the chair next to the table with the fruit. Into the room comes Cynthia. She has a new wheelchair, sleek and chrome. Her hair has grown a little and she has straightened it. She has new glasses, better ones: tortoiseshell. Caroline is bringing up the rear, carrying a folded-up easel and a small plastic case. Caroline can hardly suppress her smile.

'Good, right?' she says.

Cynthia doesn't seem remotely surprised by my physical appearance despite the fact that she hasn't seen me for years, since before the attack. She smiles at me.

'Hello Pol,' she says.

There should be a word for this feeling, I think. As though I realize now that I've been waiting for this moment but I realize at the same time that I don't really know why.

'Hey,' I say.

She trundles over to where I am sitting and she gently moves my arms around, placing one arm on the arm of the chair and one hand on my knee. She asks me to let her know if I am uncomfortable at any time. It's not important to stay completely still for the whole session, she says. Try to think of it as like a haircut.

She gets out her paints and her brushes while Caroline sets up the easel. One of the brushes is bigger than the others. Almost big enough to paint walls with. On her knee she has a reporter's notebook and she sketches on it with a pencil for a few minutes. Then she begins to paint.

She doesn't talk much during the process.

'It is awkward,' she says. 'But it's just hard to concentrate whilst chatting.'

When she's finished for the day she gets Caroline to help her to pack away her things and asks if she can leave them in the corner of the living room.

'I'll be back tomorrow,' she says. Caroline asks if she can get her a tea or anything before she leaves but Cynthia says that she is fine and then goes home.

The next day, I'm already posed when she comes into the living room. It makes her laugh.

'You can relax for a few minutes,' she says, 'while we get set up over here.'

As she is setting up, I ask her about her work. She is taking a year off, she tells me. She didn't enjoy her first year at Oxford but she wasn't ruling out going back. She had had some mental health issues. She decided to go back to her painting and she was lucky enough to get three or four commissions for portraits, including from Caroline. Most of her clients are family or friends at this point but she stands behind the quality of her work and she doesn't feel guilty about charging what she considers to be a reasonable price for the cost of her labour. Without thinking too hard, I ask her about her activism. I heard, I think Caroline mentioned to me, that she had moved to Athens last year.

'*Moved* is probably too strong a word,' Cynthia says, laughing, rinsing a tiny paintbrush in a jar of water. 'I stayed with some friends there for a few weeks last Christmas. It was fun.'

I feel as though she doesn't want to address the question. But I try again all the same. Is she still involved with the Kourist movement, I ask. She frowns a little.

'Not really,' she says. 'I think, as I get older, when I look back, that it was all a bit of youthful dalliance. It's normal to become enamoured with all-encompassing political ideologies when we are young I suppose.'

She looks at me for the first time this morning, and she smiles.

'I think as we get older it becomes clear that the main thing in life is to be nice to one another. And to create beautiful things.'

And as she says these words, like a train crash, I feel my heart break. It will never not be broken again, I realize, without exactly knowing why.

After those two sessions she says that she can work on the painting at home. She takes a handful of photographs with her iPhone. She says that probably she will need to do one more sitting if that's okay but it won't be maybe for like a week or two. I tell her that that is fine. But she doesn't come back in the end. She doesn't even come by to drop the painting off. She gives it to Nick, who brings it to school and gives it to Caroline, who brings it home. The painting is wrapped in brown paper and bubble wrap. We unwrap it in the living room.

'What on earth?' Caroline says when she sees the portrait. 'What is this, some kind of religious painting? I don't think I get it.'

She looks annoyed.

The portrait depicts a wizened old man with a bluish bald head and shoulders slumped forward, with his hands huddled together in his lap. The man is sitting in an armchair in a field. On the arm of the armchair there is a stack of books. He has a sombre expression on his face, not unlike the man from that American Gothic painting. In the background of the picture, two priests wearing black cassocks and black birettas seem to be strolling, talking to one another. On the other side of the picture, there are three beehives, and in the space above the man's head, a crowd of bright yellow bees, swarming.

The A5

For a few days after Ted and Ellen went home we didn't talk much about my plans. A week went by before Ellen called. Now that the dust had settled she wanted to have a serious chat with Caroline about the whole situation.

'Firstly,' Caroline said, 'the dust hasn't settled. And secondly there really isn't anything that I need to discuss with you.'

'I see,' Ellen said. 'Well then let's maybe talk another time.' And she rang off.

A few weeks later, Ellen phoned again. We were sitting in the living room together when Caroline's phone rang. Caroline answered the phone.

'Yes?' she said.

Ellen gave Caroline an ultimatum. She felt that Caroline was taking this decision because she felt assured that she would not have to take care of you on her own because she believed that Ellen and Ted would come over at the drop of a hat to help take care of you. Not only was this not practical as far as Ellen and Ted were concerned, it also did not rest easy with Ellen to think that she would be a participant in the carrying out of this ridiculous plan. They wouldn't step in to pick up the slack if I went to live in Ireland.

'Enabler' was the word that she used.

'One minute,' Caroline said. She left the room and closed the door behind her and I heard her jog up the stairs to our bedroom and close that door behind her. I could hear a low hum of heated conversation through the ceiling. I half considered going upstairs and putting my ear to the door but decided not to. After a few minutes I heard the door of the bedroom open and then the sound of a few steps. I opened the door of the living room and put my head round the door and saw Caroline sitting on the stairs. With one hand she held the telephone to her ear while the other hand was glued to her forehead, her elbow resting on her knees. Suddenly she looked just like a teenager, fighting with her parents, banned from going to the high school prom.

'Can we all stop pretending that he's going to Siberia?' she was saying. 'It's four hours door to door! I mean . . .'

She stopped, interrupted by her mother's interjection. Then I heard her raise her voice, trying to talk over her mother.

'What you don't seem to understand,' she said tearfully, 'I'm scared too. I don't know what the right thing to do is either. But we have to make some decisions. We can't go on like this. We have to do something different.'

'Anyway,' she said, her voice raised over the sound of her mother's again, 'it's all settled. All the arrangements have been made. It's going to happen. Goodbye.'

She hung up the phone and then sighed and then smiled at me and then burst into tears. After that, her mother didn't phone again.

We took the portrait to a picture framing shop and paid for it to be put in a fancy gold frame and then we took it home and Caroline hung it on the wall, above the mantelpiece. After that we didn't know what to do. It seemed strange not to look at the picture, so we did. We both sat on the armchairs in the living room and looked up at the portrait of me, not saying anything. After a while Caroline said:

'That's enough of that. Time to get on with the day.'

We alighted on a date, a month in the future, for my trip, and pretty soon the time was whittled away to a week.

'Have you got everything sorted?' Caroline said. 'Jesus hasn't the time flown by?'

'It's all sorted,' I told her.

And now, suddenly, here we are, in the bedroom. Caroline is folding my shirts and putting them in my suitcase.

'It will be good for you to go out there on your own,' Caroline says.

'It's a stressful time,' I say.

'And we can talk about the summer closer to the time,' I say.

'There's a lot of things to sort out,' I say. 'Practical things. I know that you're better at that than me.'

'That's not it,' Caroline says. 'You know that.'

'What then?' I say.

'Nothing,' Caroline says. 'Forget that I said it.'

She goes into the next room and brings back the stack of blue-and-white books, the volumes of Adonis Dolofonithikos. She puts them on the bed next to the suitcase.

'I can just put these in a tote bag,' she says, 'and you can read them on the journey that way, if you want to.'

'It's okay,' I say.

'I can't fit them into the suitcase,' Caroline says.

'I'm not going to take them.'

Caroline straightens up.

'Don't you need them?' she says. 'For your writing project? Your Unique Vantage Point?'

I tell her that I've decided that I don't want to write about my Unique Vantage Point any more. I've been thinking that maybe writing factual stuff is not my strong suit. There's a course that you can do online which teaches you how to write a novel. I think, I tell Caroline, that creative writing might be my forte. It's something I've never tried before. Maybe I'm good at it. In the countryside with the space and the time. Maybe I'll be able to produce something good.

Caroline nods, her lips tightening. I can see that she is angry, but I'm not sure why.

'I hear you,' she says.

There is a bus that leaves from the Kilburn High Road and which goes straight up the A5 to Holyhead and drives on to the ferry.

In the end we arrive late for the bus. The only reason that we manage to catch it is because there is a set of traffic lights next to the bus stop and the light is on red. The driver opens the hold, where the other bags and suitcases are all lined up in a row. Some of the bags are in a section on the left, marked off with tape, with a sign printed on an A4 sheet of paper saying *St Albans* stuck to the ground. Some of the baggage is in a section on the right, with the sign saying *Holyhead*. Caroline loads my suitcase into the hold.

'Well,' she says. 'This is a moment.'

I pretend not to know what she means. I turn and walk towards the entrance to the bus.

'How come you aren't crying?' I turn and ask Caroline, with one foot on the step of the bus. The words seem to come out of my mouth without me even thinking.

'I don't know, Pol,' she says.

I can feel a lump beginning to rise in my throat, but I push it down with sheer tyranny of will. I feel scared, suddenly, as though I am standing on the edge of a cliff.

'Is this a terrible idea?' I say. 'Is this a really bad idea?'

Suddenly her placid expression gives way to an expression of feverish exasperation.

'We can't do this now, Pol,' she says. 'Just try to bear this in mind: all decisions are painful. There are big pains and small pains, but all decisions are painful, all decisions are sacrifices.'

The bus driver shouts something at me but I don't register what it is.

'Pol,' Caroline says, 'just get on the bus, and I'll call you to talk about this when I get home.'

And she turns away and walks down the street towards our home.

But she doesn't call. And when the bus gets on to the ferry and the ferry leaves the harbour and sets sail into the Irish sea, I lose my signal. When we land in Dublin, I check my phone to see if there are any missed calls but there are none. Just a text message.

'Remember,' it says, 'all decisions are always painful for everybody.'

IV

I Know Them Boys

Anthony goes from room to room with a broomstick. I follow him with my own broomstick. When we come to a room which has damp patches on the concrete floor, we poke at the roof with the broomsticks. When we find places where the thatch falls away into the room, Anthony makes a note.

'Don't you think the whole thing will need to be replaced?' I ask.

Anthony shakes his head.

'I know them boys,' he says. 'They'll give you a price for a full job which will be far more than they need to do here. You'll save a grand or more if you do some of it yourself and then just get them in to do a repair job.'

It is warm. We have drunk two beers. My head is humming with an afternoon hangover. We go outside on to the front field and the light blinds me. Anthony has bought some lawn furniture and he has put it out on the front lawn. We sit in our chairs and look out at the lawn.

'The stones,' I say.

'Yes, the stones need doing,' Anthony says. 'We can do that next. After that we can get a dog up here. You'll need a dog for the company and also for a bit of peace of mind.'

The previous tenants kept sheep on the land. The land is hilly and barren. There is a variety of grasses on the land: fescue and timothy grass and oat grass. It is difficult to walk on the land without scratching yourself on a thistle or on knapweed. The grasses come up to my waist in some places, up to my knees in most places. Feels like wading into cold water.

Anthony has parked his four-by-four on the grass just beyond the gate at the foot of the drive and there is a swathe cut through in the places where he has driven.

'It'll be a lot of bother to fix this land,' he says sombrely. He takes a drag on his cigarette and shakes his head.

I wonder aloud if he could do with the rest of the field what he has done to the grass beyond the gate: drive over it with his Jeep and flatten it. He shakes his head again seriously.

'That would do no good at all,' he says.

Sometimes his son, Duncan, comes up to the house with him. Duncan is a young teenager now, and he already has a few head of cattle grazing on a field nearby. He got two for his first communion. He nods sullenly when he sees me. He has an awkward, gawky walk.

Sometimes, in the way that they interact, I can see that Duncan hates Anthony. I want to ask Anthony about it but I can't find the right way to do it since Anthony doesn't seem to mind.

'Teenagers,' Anthony says.

Sometimes I see you and Caroline in the shapes and in the shadows of the high yellow-green grass. The shape of your hair. The shape of your clothes. Walking away from me.

—

Sometimes, once in a blue moon, if we get really drunk together, I tell him about my family at home. I can't blame Caroline, I tell him. I have a condition that makes me very difficult to live with. I find it hard to look after myself and I need care from her. It's to do with my mother, I tell him. It's to do with my father. Plus it isn't really fair to expect her to adapt to rapid changes. Rapid changes aren't good for the mind, aren't good for a child, for child-rearing. She has the best years of her life ahead of her. She deserves the right to enjoy the physical side of life in a way that I can't provide for her. I know that when I tell him all this he judges Caroline, he thinks I'm mad. It's not rocket science. There are women who love men and there are women who don't. I know it and he knows it. I can see that in his eyes. The next morning, the feelings of guilt make for the worst kind of hangover.

Sometimes I talk to you. Walking in the long grass, I imagine that you are walking beside me invisibly. I try to explain things to you, things that I never had the chance to explain to you before. But somehow it becomes muddled. I find myself skipping back and forth, clarifying, modifying. You say nothing, you just listen. I hope that maybe while I sleep my ghost comes out of my body and goes and stands next to your bed. I imagine you waking and peeking and seeing me there. It's a selfish thing to wish for, I suppose. The timeline got fucked up. Otherwise I would have been given the chance properly to explain a bit more to you when you were old enough to understand. After all this I don't feel unburdened at all. I wonder if I have managed to unburden anybody in my entire life.

'I never expected to be such a reliant person,' my mother said at our wedding. 'But I turned out to be one, so I'm so grateful and relieved that Polly has found somebody who is so reliable.'

–

'Who are you talking to out there?' Anthony says, grinning, as though he has caught me in a lie.

George Saunders

This night I go down the mountain. I'm not supposed to go down the mountain. But I do it nonetheless, every now and again. At the bottom of the mountain is the whole village with the pub and the shop and the William-Yeats-Stayed-Here house. Some of the houses are boarded up now. Some people have left. They left without even selling their houses.

'Sell them to who?' Anthony says when I express surprise. 'You take the little money that you have and you try your best somewhere else. Especially if you have children.'

I go into the pub and park myself at the bar and I buy a drink. The barman eyes me. Or maybe he doesn't. Perhaps it's my imagination. The gin and bitter lemon, when it arrives, is tepid. Tepid blue spicy water. At the other end of the bar there is a man with a grey beard. I recognize him from somewhere.

I go out into the dark outside the pub. It's really dark now. There are only four street lights in the village. I light a cigarette. The bearded man comes outside as well and stands with his back against the wall on the other side of the threshold of the pub. I realize then that the man is George Saunders. I look over to him and smile and he smiles back. I ask him if his name is George Saunders and he says that it is. I tell him that my wife bought me a copy of his book and that I had read it and enjoyed it very much. He tells me that he is gratified. He tells me to thank my wife from him and smiles.

We stand together in silence for a few moments. Larks swoop down towards us through the darkness and one perches on the guttering that runs along the single-storey roof of the little pub. The lark issues a short, conversational little call. I think for a moment how much more suited birdsong is to the night-time than it is to the day.

I ask George Saunders what he is doing on the island. He has been running a summer school, he says, at the William-Yeats-Stayed-Here house in the village. He had been invited to run the summer school by the Irish government. And he had been intrigued by the stories which linked the island to the end of the world, so he had decided to do it, to come and have a look around. Only when he arrived on the island had the political situation become squirrelly. He had arrived on the very day that the Kourists had blockaded Heathrow. Before he could make any alternative arrangements, his flight back to London had been cancelled and so he was stranded here. He's seen pictures of planes fluttering around Heathrow. He doesn't understand why it has to be such a big deal: planes. He tells me that he isn't too worried. He will find a flight back to America from Dublin at some point, he says. He asks me if I can lend him a cigarette and I ask if he smokes and he says that no he doesn't usually but he feels as though he could do with one. He has two daughters. He misses them. He never intended to be away from them for so long. For a moment I consider telling him about you but I decide not to broach the subject. He lights his cigarette.

He asks me what I do. I tell him that I am a writer. That I have come to stay in a bothy that my family own on the hill above the village as a writing retreat. He asks what sort of thing I write and I tell him that I am trying to write a science fiction novel. He asks what it is about. I tell him that it is set in the future. In the future, I say, there exists the technology for people to upload their memories, their thoughts, their feelings and ideas on to a kind of cloud platform. When people die, they will continue to live on in the cloud, with their whole personalities stored there in a digital format. This way people can interact with their relatives through an interface which is sort of like WhatsApp. This will work well for a while, but then people will want to actually interact with their deceased relatives rather than just having them communicate through a computer. So new technologies will be developed which will create a kind of hologram version of the person who has died, who can now speak to you and interact with you in exactly the same way that the person did during their lifetime. Now you have people walking around and interacting long after they have died, in hologram form. These new people are better for the environment than fleshly beings: they don't consume food or create methane or take up any space. Years go past. Everyone adapts to this new reality. But at some point, we turn our attention towards people who have, like, debilitating forms of dementia, Alzheimer's. What if – the scientists and technologists propose – we harness the same cloud technology that we used to recreate the personalities of the dead people, and use it to recreate the personalities of the people whose personalities have rotted away as a result of these terrible diseases? So that's what they do. When people are first diagnosed with Alzheimer's they upload their souls into the cloud and then, when they reach a stage in the condition when they can no longer really function or interact with people, the tech guys make a hologram version of them and the hologram person goes off to live happily in the bosom of their family. The problem is that, for some reason, these hologram people don't remember why they are here. Something about the stage at which they uploaded their minds into the cloud means that they tend to not be able to remember the process that they agreed to enter into. They eventually become depressed, racked with existential anxiety. They beg and plead with their families, with the doctors and tech guys, to turn them off, to euthanize them. They can't after all take their own lives because they really only exist in holographic form. The people who control the super-computer now have the power over life and death. Only this raises all sorts of other ethical dilemmas. Are these people not human beings? Parliament debates the issue. There are pro-life campaigns and pro-choice campaigns. The legislators agree that the hologram people should surely not be encouraged to commit suicide, even if they are depressed and anxious. But is it right that they should be denied the choice of whether to live or die? The government decides that the Alzheimer's hologram people will be allowed to be euthanized. But this will only be allowed if they agree to undergo an extensive period of psychoanalytic psychotherapy, which will be funded by the health service. The hero of the book that I'm writing, I tell George Saunders, is one of the therapists who has been given the responsibility of treating the hologram people who are asking to be euthanized. The therapist's major contention is that the hologram people should be introduced to their former bodies. He is writing research papers about it. He is studying the ways in which the hologram people – living, cogent, thoughtful beings – respond when they are introduced to the physical people – with their blank stares, their blank, unknowing faces – that they once were. And he believes that this process, this coming-to-terms, is what will cure the hologram people of their suicidality.

—

Afterwards I go back up the mountain. I decide to take a short-cut through some woods. But soon I get lost. It's cold and dark. This can't go on. At some point I stumble into a little clearing in the woods. Above me the sky is white with stars.

'Variety,' I think to myself spontaneously, 'is the spice of life.'

When I finally arrive back at the bothy Anthony is there. He has come by to help me with my injections like he sometimes does.

'What did you do today?' he says.

'I went down to the pub,' I tell him. 'I got a drink down there.'

I don't tell him about George Saunders.

'*Did* you now?' Anthony says, as though he doesn't believe me.

Sailing

When I first arrived at the house, Anthony wasn't there. I sat on the threshold and lit a cigarette. I had known how to get to the house from the little harbour. I walked all the way. I didn't have much to carry. Even still, I had to stop every hundred yards to catch my breath. I remembered from the last time we were here: the winding road up the hillside, the rusty double gate at the top of the drive. When I finished my cigarette, I left my bag on the doorstep and walked out on to the land behind the house, a barren, undulatory parcel of land like a swelling yellow sea. Before I got close, I could see him, bent over in a ditch, smacking a stray dog. When he straightened up he turned and faced me, a cigarette in his mouth. He squinted to see me better.

I gave him a stack of fifties and told him that there would be more coming.

'How long will that hold me for?' I asked. Anthony paused.

'I'll tell you if I need any more from you,' he said.

He didn't remember me. I could tell, the first time we spoke. He looked too tired to remember much. I was unmoored, in his imagination: an anemochorous bit of fluff that had floated into his skull and would soon float back out again.

'The bothy,' he said, 'has seen better days.'

Soon after I arrived it was Christmas. After he had his dinner with his ex-wife and his son, Anthony drove up to the house, and when he got out of the car I could see through the window that he had half of an uncooked chicken wrapped in greaseproof paper and two half-drunk bottles of whiskey under his arms, and three cans of Smithwick's, held together by the four plastic rings. He carried the three beers with one finger, one index finger hooking the vacant plastic ring like a fishing hook.

There were still a few feathers on the bird, and it took me a little while to prepare it. I didn't really know how to. Anthony sat in front of the fire. When I finally brought it through, he rubbed his red hands together. I cut into the chicken. Beneath the brown, crackling skin I could feel the cold, rubbery resistance of uncooked flesh. The flesh was translucent. I could see it when I nudged the body open, wheedling with the carving knife.

We ate the half-uncooked chicken. Anthony said:
    'Wouldn't it be good for you to have a television up here? For the company?'
    He pointed to the cabinet in the alcove, in the corner of the living room. Anthony had rammed the cabinet into the alcove a week before. It didn't fit properly. The ramming of the cabinet into it had torn bits of plaster away on the walls on either side of the alcove.
    'I don't need a TV,' I said. 'I already have too many things distracting me from my writing.'
    Anthony said nothing.

'One day I'll get married again,' Anthony says sometimes. 'I haven't given it much thought.'

He seems to me, when he says things like that, to be an alien life form among us.

At other times he might say to me something like:

'You'll find someone else. There are plenty of fish in the sea. Plenty of mature ladies looking for the companionship of an older gentleman.'

And I can tell from the slope of his shoulders and from the blank shift of his eyes that not only is this not something he truly believes, but it is actually something rather similar to a joke.

Anthony's dream is to open an aquarium or a sea life centre on the island. He speaks of the fecundity of the sea around the island. There is much idiosyncratic marine life. He shows me a photograph of the photograph of the basking shark that is framed behind the bar in the pub in the village. He has heard about other islands that have sea life centres. He is perturbed that his island is falling behind the other islands.

'We have to modernize,' he says. 'We have to go into the future.'

Has Anthony ever lived anywhere else apart from the island, I want to know. He is tying up the hornbeam hedge at the front of the house with a ball of twine. He snaps the twine with his bare hands. Sometimes he chews it a little first to weaken it. He doesn't turn to face me.

'Once,' he says. 'Westport. Only for a few months, mind.'

Later on he asks whether I have lived anywhere else. And I tell him that I lived in Germany once, that I'd lived in England also.

'Sounds like the Second World War,' Anthony says.

It struck me that Anthony was like Cynthia. He too seemed to move in straight lines. It had something to do with pride. They moved through life with a sense of pride. And I thought about the other people that I knew: which ones moved in circles and which ones moved in lines. I thought that Caoimhe moved in straight lines. And Nick moved in circles but Shirley seemed to move in straight lines. Edith seemed to move in straight lines. Maybe it had something to do with goals. The goal, I think, is not to feel panicked all the time. The goal, I remember Caroline saying, is to be sad rather than panicked. Panic comes when you're trying too hard not to be sad.

We have a radio in the house that we listen to sometimes when we are working on the building or on the land. We pick the old bits of brick out of the mud at the back of the house and every now and again I clutch my back and Anthony tells me to sit down, to take a breather. I fear that I might be getting in the way more than anything. We listen to the classical music station. I prefer listening to classical music that is chosen by somebody else. Sometimes the pirate propaganda stations break through the signal.

'The callow embers of Hoarist tyranny still smoulder on the island of Ireland. The Irish collusionists continue to harbour the enemies of the nation in their republic. The Irish people remain oblivious to the reality that our struggle is identical to theirs. We call on the Irish people to join the struggle and to throw off the manacles of oppression and to refuse to continue to provide succour and comfort to the enemy.'

I always look at Anthony when these announcements come on the radio. He never looks up from his work.

I read to Anthony from the *Irish Notebook*, my father's old copy, with the yellow pages and the biro in the margins. 'A Small Contribution to Occidental Mythology.'

'The old man is eighty-eight,' I read. 'He was born before Rumania, he was four when Dickens died, he is a year older than dynamite.'

When Dickens died. I'm dying here. I know that. There isn't much fanfare. I'm sure that Anthony knows that too. That I'm just sort of dying. That I'm *going to die*. It seems as though my death should correlate somehow with something important that will happen in the world. But now it seems that it won't. It will just happen in a moment when I am encountered by others, who will only exaggerate the significance of the event: in their words, in their mannerisms, for courtesy's sake. In order to avoid any awkwardness.

Most nights Anthony leaves the house after dark. I watch from the window as the pinky-orange tail lamps drift down the hill, through the blackness, like two twin phosphorescent sea beasts drifting down to the bottom of the ocean.

Anthony's other property is a church, which he is also trying to restore. It isn't really a church. It served as a church, briefly, when the island community was at its largest, in the 1920s and 1930s. When the human population of the island began to recede again, the church was abandoned. Long before it was ever a church it had been a friary for Benedictine monks.

Part of the friary had burned down in the nineteenth century. They never rebuilt that part of it. It remained a ruin: four walls surrounding a patch of grass. The chapel, though, still stood, and there were still pews and an altar inside and so the community briefly used it as their church. But after the depopulation of the island, this last bit of the friary succumbed to the elements. Wind blew through the gaps where windows once were and vandals wrote messages in red paint on the interior walls.

Anthony is convinced that it was tourists who had vandalized the chapel. Nobody from the island could have destroyed their own history in that way, he was sure of it.

So This is what You call Deadmocracy.
You Have Been Commandead to Resist
You Have Been Weighdead, You Have Been Measuredead, You Have Been Foundead Wanting.

He found some pamphlet literature as well, scattered on the floor of the chapel. He was worried that there had been a Black Mass in there. He gathered up the pamphlets from the floor of the chapel and took them up to the house and burned them in the grate.

'It was terrible morbid stuff,' he said, pulling his Gaillimh GAA cap down over his brow. 'All about the end of the world and so on.' He looked across the grass at the sun.

He told me that he was sentimentally attached to the chapel because it was the place where his mother had gone to Mass every day when he was a child. It was only then that I realized that the house in which we were standing had been his mother's old house.

We pull the old couch out of the house and on to the front field. While it's there, we might as well sit on it, Anthony says. Periodically he asks me to tell him about the book that I'm writing, but I change the subject. The sun is going down, finally. He is worried, now, about the cows pissing on the sofa. It is a good sofa, he tells me. It would be a shame if a cow pissed on it. He waits for me to say something. The shadows of the high grasses lengthen towards us in the light from the setting sun. The sunset demolishes the houses on the horizon and it demolishes the last grey stalks of grass. He fishes in the pocket of his North Face coat and pulls out a cigarette from one and a lighter from the other. He clicks the lighter twice, three times, then four times, but no flame is forthcoming and he puts the cigarette back in his pocket and hurls the lighter into the grass. He switches the radio on. 'Sailing' by Rod Stewart comes on. He changes it to another station, but it's only static. He picks up the radio and switches it off and then tosses it into the long grass after the lighter.

'We'll have a dog up here soon,' he says, making a promise to himself.